Spy Stuff

Spy Stuff

Matthew J. Metzger

SPY STUFF

JMS Books LLC
10286 Staples Mill Rd. #221
Glen Allen, VA 23060
www.jms-books.com

Printed in the United States of America

ISBN: 9781530638772

For Kay, my greatest ally when it comes to spy stuff.

Chapter 1

"WHY DON'T YOU tell us a bit about yourself, Anton."

Anton wanted to say, "Are you kidding me?"

The entire class stared back blandly. There must have been thirty-five of them, all lounging professionally. A red-haired boy by the window was chewing gum and staring right at him. A girl with long brown curls was texting, the phone just lying on the desk in the open like she didn't give a damn. A couple of Asian boys in the back row were playing paper football.

"Um," Anton said, glancing at the teacher. "I'd rather not."

The class sniggered, the noise rippling like wind through long grass.

The teacher sighed and rapped her knuckles on the desk. "Quiet!" She was short, with black hair in a tight pixie cut, and blue earrings that swung every time she moved. "Well, Anton, you won't have much of a choice soon. None of you will!" she added loudly when the class sniggered again. "This term's PSHE project will hopefully get some of you to buck up your ideas about respecting your fellow classmates—"

"Respect Kalinowski? Not likely, Miss!" a scrawny boy with a face like a rat shouted from the back. The boy by the window with the red hair casually turned around and threw a book at him. "Oi! Polack!"

"Detention, Walsh!" the teacher barked. She jabbed a finger at the redhead. "And not a word, Kalinowski!"

Quiet settled again, but an uneasy sort of one. Anton guessed that Miss Name-He-Couldn't-Remember didn't have awesome classroom control.

"Right, well, for now—class, this is Anton Williams. I want you all to make him feel welcome—and no throwing books at him, Kalinowski!"

"What about paper?"

"No throwing anything!"

Kalinowski pulled a face; Walsh disregarded the order and threw the book back, hitting Kalinowski in the back of the head.

"Walsh!"

"He started it!"

"Kalinowski would start a war if it amused him, I expect you to be grown up enough to ignore him!" she snapped.

Anton shifted on his feet uncertainly, unsure if he was supposed to stay where he was or sit down somewhere. A girl at a nearby table shifted her bag off the spare seat and beckoned. "Come on," she whispered, and he slid into it gratefully. "I'm Emma," she added in a low voice. "Was it Anthony?"

"Anton."

"Oops, sorry," she said, and smiled. She was very pretty: huge, round eyes that were either black or brown, a chubby face with sweet dimples when she smiled, and long, dark brown hair that curled lightly at the ends. "Don't worry about them, they're just bored. It's PSHE first thing Mondays, and it's really dull."

"PSHE?"

She blinked. "What school did you *come* from? Personal, social and health education?"

"Oh," Anton said, and flushed. "Um, it was just called form time. We didn't really call it anything."

"Well, it's *so* crap here," Emma whispered, as the teacher lost her cool and stomped over to Kalinowski to take the book away. "We were doing religions last term, and we totally missed out Hinduism *and* Sikhism, how exclusive is that, it's not like—"

"Ems!" a voice shouted across the room. "Stop boring the new kid to death, give Miss a chance first!"

Emma twisted around in her chair. "Walsh, why don't you take your ignorant opinion, and shove it up your wrinkled, hairy—"

The teacher slammed a book down on a desk deafeningly, and a startled silence shot through the room.

"Quiet," she said in a dangerous tone.

Quiet was granted.

"Now," she continued softly, "we have our PSHE lesson for this period, and if we do not finish the lesson in this period, you will *all* be back here for lunch. And I will continue teaching you in lunchtimes until the PSHE curriculum is complete if you think Monday morning is playtime. Am I clear?"

The chorus of 'yes, Miss' was disgruntled, but grudgingly accepting.

"Brown." Emma straightened. "You will show Williams around and make sure he gets to all of his lessons until he finds his feet." The door opened, a boy with scruffy brown hair lurching into the room, and the teacher sighed loudly through her nose. "Just sit down, Larimer, and don't say a word."

He did. Quiet settled again, albeit a little more tenuously than the first time.

"Now, our project for this term is 'identity.' We will be looking at how people can identify with different labels and groups, such as race, gender, sexuality, and so on, and at the protected characteristics in law."

A groan went up.

"You will be paired up," she continued, "and work together on a project exploring your own identities. At the end of the project, each of you will present your partner—stop smirking, Larimer, for God's sake—back to the class. The idea is that, in theory, you will have more respect for each other, something sorely lacking in this year group, and a better understanding of the differences between individuals."

A hand shot up. The scruffy-haired boy, Larimer, nearly fell out of his seat, he put it up so quickly.

"What, Larimer?"

"Miss," he said, licking his lips. "Er. What if I don't want to... present myself...to my partner?"

The class sniggered. Anton, figuring it was safe, joined in.

"Larimer," the teacher said dryly, "I have it on remarkably good authority that you are quite happy to present yourself to whosoever is amenable to your doing so at any given moment. Now is not the time to get shy about it." The sniggering got louder. "In any case, I am not so stupid as to partner you with Walsh or Kalinowski. You will pair up with the person sat next to you—with the exception of you, Anderson and Crabtree. Crabtree, swap seats with Walsh."

There was a general rummaging and shuffling, and the teacher stalked out from around her desk to lean against it, arms folded and staring at the class. She wasn't quite scowling, but she definitely wasn't smiling.

"Shall we start with the obvious? What's an identity? Can someone give me an example of an identity?"

"Polack!" Walsh shouted. Kalinowski flipped him off without even turning round.

"Walsh, if you don't stop using that disgusting term, I will write to your parents again."

Walsh pulled a face that meant he didn't much care.

"Anyone want to offer an identity that *isn't* an ethnic slur?"

"Poles aren't an ethnicity," Larimer protested.

"Polish," Emma said, rolling her eyes. "Someone can identify as Polish."

"Thank you, Brown. Anyone else?"

"British."

"Scottish."

"Black."

"Gay."

"*You're* gay, Larimer."

"Bugger off, y'fa—"

The teacher cleared her throat loudly. The offending boy shut up quickly. "Yes," she said tartly, "many of those are good examples of identifiers. Any more? Williams?"

Anton flushed. "Er," he said. There was an obvious one. *His* one. But…he fumbled it, knowing to sound uncertain pushed it away from yourself, made it not yours. "Trans…gender?"

"Yes," she said. "That's a good one—though it's important to remember transgender people can identify as just male or female, not just transgender."

"What, like, both at once?"

"Malefemale," Larimer said.

"That's called bigender, idiot," Emma said scathingly.

"What, like bisexual?" Kalinowski asked.

"Yes."

"That would be *amazing*," Walsh chipped in. "That'd be like both sets—you could have a penis *and* a va—"

"*Gender*, you morons, not *sex*," Emma said, and Larimer and Walsh both started sniggering. "Oh, real mature."

"What do you expect, Brown," the teacher said in a tired tone, and rapped her knuckles on the desk. "I want no more crass jokes. This is a sensitive subject. Don't for one minute believe you're all the same. There's thirty-six of you in this class, and you will all have very different experiences—even those of you who share some identity labels."

"I don't want to share no labels with Kalinowski, God knows where he puts 'em," Walsh called out. Kalinowski, once again, casually flipped him off.

"Hopefully," the teacher said loudly, "some of you might grow up over the course of this project. Now. In your pairs, I want you to list as many labels as you can think of, and then divide them into groups, such as nationality or sexuality. I will come around and check your progress—and *no*, Walsh, you may *not* write any foul terms."

Anton chewed on his lip as Emma tore a page out of her notebook and started making a spider diagram. How awkward could this get? Tell Emma his labels, when he'd switched schools to *hide* those labels? Not likely. And have her present his labels in front of this lot? Whose shitty idea *was* this?

"This is a shitty idea," Emma said quietly, and Anton jumped.

"This lot are just going to find it all *so* funny. I really hope there's nobody in our year who's closeted or has a hidden disability or anything, these guys can come off so foul…"

"Are they always like this?"

"Yeah," Emma said. "They're harmless really, they don't *mean* it, but not everyone gets that, you know?"

"I guess," Anton said awkwardly.

"Right, labels!"

"Um, well, you seem to know all the…sex ones," he hedged, feigning ignorance, and Emma rolled her eyes.

"*Gender*," she corrected. "Sex is between your legs, gender's in your head." Anton itched with the urge to tell her he knew that very well, thanks. "I went through a phase," she admitted, starting to scribble sexualities on her spider diagram. "Not a gender phase, a sexuality phase."

"A phase?"

"Uh-huh. Okay, phase is the wrong word, but for a while I was *so* into girls. Like, I thought I was a lesbian for a bit. Maybe I'm more bisexual though, I came back around to guys."

"And…you're okay just…saying that?"

"Everyone knows," she said dismissively.

"Oh."

She blinked, and cocked her head. "Oh," she said. "Did you come from a shitty school where I wouldn't say that?"

"Yeah," Anton said meaningfully, and she winced.

"Well, I don't know about the other years, but this one's okay. They might sound like a bunch of immature pricks, but they're generally okay. How do you spell bisexual anyway, is it an 'i' or a 'y'?"

Anton let himself relax fractionally, spelling it out as Emma scribbled, and cast a wary glance across the room to where the rat-faced Walsh was flicking paper balls at the redheaded Kalinowski, and scruffy Larimer was sniggering into his sleeve. Emma seemed…confident enough. And Kalinowski *had* just laughed at the Polack jokes. Maybe she was right—

"Fuck off, you bender!"

"*Larimer!*"

—or maybe not.

❖

EMMA WAS A good guide. The morning was a mess of confusing classes, faces Anton couldn't remember five minutes later, and constant in-jokes that he didn't get, but Emma stuck to Anton like glue through it all. The class were kept together for the common core subjects, but split up for modern languages—French versus German—and the arts subjects. This school didn't seem to believe in sets, but Anton noted that not everyone in the class had the same maths textbook. It wasn't what he was used to, and Emma and her frantic, constant whispering was the only grounding he had.

Lunch came too soon—after maths and the fastest catch-up in English ever on *Hamlet,* because his old school had used the *Romeo and Juliet*-favouring exam board instead—and Anton's building anxiety about what the hell this new social world demanded of him for lunch was destroyed by Emma tugging on the cuff of his blazer.

"Come on," she said. "You can sit with us for lunch."

"Oh," Anton said. "Thanks." He didn't know who 'us' actually was, but it was better than nobody.

"The canteen here is awful," Emma continued, towing him down a couple of corridors to her locker. Anton didn't have one yet, and waited awkwardly. "You have to buy the food to sit in there, and the food's just dire, so we go to the drama studio in winter—it has benches by the radiators—or the playing fields in the summer."

"My old school canteen was okay."

"Where was that?"

"Lambeth," Anton lied. He hadn't moved, but that was the story he was sticking to. It was easier that way.

"Ew," Emma said pointedly. "Okay, so don't worry, I'll introduce you proper, not that crappy intro Miss Taylor gave you—and just as an FYI, it's totally okay to just punch Jude whenever he gets gobby, he practically expects it."

"We're…going to sit with them?"

"They're totally harmless, don't worry," Emma reassured him, tucking her arm through his as though they'd known each other for years. It was totally unfamiliar—the girls at his old school had avoided him like the plague, and Anton's skin itched with the urge to pull away and ask what she wanted from him—but kind of reassuring, too. Emma was…nice. So far. And she'd been quite crass to Walsh earlier, so he must kind of like her if she went and sat with those boys for lunch, right? Then Anton was towed into the drama studio—a surprisingly small space dotted with clusters of people in blue uniforms—and there they were.

"Guys," Emma announced, tugging him towards the cluster— three boys and a girl, crowded around a radiator on the slightly dusty floor. "This is Anton."

"We know," Larimer said. He was a very gangly boy, far too tall for himself and with hands that were more like spades attached to sticks than functional body parts. He looked like he'd been messily arranged by a pretty drunk God on a Friday afternoon. Even his eyes didn't match—one was pale blue, one was bottle-green.

"Don't be an arse," the girl said. She was petite and ash-blonde, and smiled up at Anton. "Sit down," she added, patting the floor. "I'm Isabel."

"Thanks," Anton mumbled.

"That's Walsh, and that's Larimer—they're like a set of shitty jokers, just ignore them or punch them when they get too stupid," Emma advised. Up close, Walsh's rat-like face was even more angular than Anton had realised, but he offered a toothy grin and a vague 'sup, nutfucker?' that was somewhere between warmly irreverent and just plain weird. "And that's Jude."

Turned out that Kalinowski was Jude. And—

Oh, *crap*.

From three feet away, as opposed to a classroom away with tables between them, Jude Kalinowski was…good-looking. Very good-looking. He was lean and wiry, broad-shouldered but not bulky, with freckles and fair hair spotting his bare arms. He had a wide easy smile that turned itself up to beam at Anton, with stupidly perfect teeth and a dimple in the left cheek that did something a bit funny to Anton's stomach. His hair wasn't just red, it was *red*, a brilliant ginger that seemed to bend the light, springy and soft-looking, and Anton wanted to reach out and touch it.

He realised he was staring gormlessly, just *staring* into bottom-less, deep brown eyes, and swallowed. "Er," he said.

"You talk his ear off already, Emma?" Jude asked genially, and gave Anton another one of those crazy smiles. Anton's heartbeat stuttered. Oh shit. Oh-shit-oh-shit-oh-shit.

He sat down, to hide the sudden attack of the jitters, and let Emma's denial wash over him.

"Word of advice, Anton?" Jude said, leaning forward. He was sitting cross-legged, his knees almost able to touch the floor despite the position, and Anton's brain unhelpfully informed him that it meant Jude could probably get his legs behind his own head. Anton swallowed very hard. "Ignore about…ninety percent of what comes out of Emma's mouth and you'll be fine."

"Hey!" Emma protested, swatting at him. Jude laughed, fending her off. "You're such an arse."

"You love me anyway."

"That's what you think," she retorted. "So, Anton, where're you from?"

Anton focused. He looked away from Jude and those dark, dark eyes and red, red hair, and focused on the story he'd come up with, the story Mum and Aunt Kerry had helped him in crafting, the story the head had accepted and fed to most—if not quite all—of the staff.

"We had to move after my parents split up," he recited faithfully, and began his fake story.

He didn't dare look at Jude again for the entire telling of it, in case his composure came undone, and the story—the story he *needed* for this, the story he *had* to have to let this new life begin—was ruined.

Chapter 2

"OI, WILLIAMS!"

Anton jumped violently, nearly dropping his textbook. It was three thirty, the end of the day, and he'd been all set to get out of there and recover from the insanity of a new school.

Then Jude yelled his name, clapped a hand on his shoulder, and Anton thought his shirt collar would catch fire from how hot his neck suddenly felt.

"Where d'you live, then, new kid?"

"Um," Anton fumbled. "Near the tube station."

"Edgware or Stanmore?"

"Edgware. Glendale Avenue."

"Cool, s'on our route, you can walk with us f'you want."

Larimer was hovering—standing still, he apparently could just about manage not to crash into stuff—and Anton swallowed.

"Yeah, okay," his mouth said before his brain could catch up, and Jude beamed. Anton's stomach twisted.

Jude and Larimer discussed their German lesson until they passed out of the school gates, giving Anton time to settle his flush and his stomach, before Jude turned to him and out of nowhere said, "So, what football team?"

"Sorry?"

"What football team's yours?"

"Oh. Spurs," Anton said without thinking.

"*Sweet*!" Jude cheered, as Larimer groaned and called them both kikes. "Shut it, Larimer, the guy knows where the good shit's at."

"You mean, you both know how to lose."

Jude snorted and slung an arm over Anton's shoulder. Anton tried—and failed—to crush the way his stomach dipped. "Ignore the wanker," Jude said, his breath hot at Anton's ear. The hairs on Anton's arms stood on end. "He's just jealous that *his* team are a pile of shit."

"Better than your lot!"

"Better at bribing refs, maybe."

"Saturday's match—"

"—was bent as fuck!" Jude argued. "That was *never* a red card, he didn't even *touch* him—!"

Anton offered an agreement with Jude—even though privately, he thought it *had* been a bit of a dirty tackle—and tried to keep out of the brewing argument, until Larimer fell off the pavement and nearly got his foot stuck in a drain, and Jude laughed so hard that Anton had to prise himself free before they fell into the road.

"Fuck you both," Larimer swore.

"S'what you get for growing ten inches over Christmas," Jude jeered. "What about you, Anton? You gonna end up a six footer like this wanker, or stay a midget? What are you, five six?"

"About that," Anton said. "My dad's only five four," he lied.

"Unlucky," Jude said.

"You can't talk, your old man's a right fat git."

"Hey, fuck you, I could've been in the cast for a gladiator movie!" Jude bragged, exaggeratedly flexing an arm. Anton hesitantly smiled as Larimer cracked up—naturally, because it was total crap—and shook his head when Jude looked to him. "Traitor."

"New don't mean stupid, Kalinowski," Larimer snorted, and nearly walked into a lamppost.

"Karma!" Jude yelled. "So, Anton," he said, hitching his bag a little higher on his shoulder. "Aside from Spurs, what're you about?"

Anton fidgeted. "Usual," he said eventually. "You know, films and stuff."

"Game of Thrones fan?"

"Uh-huh."

"TV or books?"

"Both," Anton admitted. "I mean, the books are kinda massive, but they're cool, too."

"M'not much of a reader," Jude admitted, shrugging. "Takes too long to get to the story if you're reading it, y'know?"

"Mm," Anton said. He didn't know, he was too fast a reader for that, but it felt weird to disagree with Jude's lazy smile. "I like that fantasy stuff though. And historical stuff. The grimy stuff, not like…church reforms and stuff."

"What, like Rome and Spartacus and shit?"

"Yeah."

"My dad would kick me off the telly if I tried any of that," Jude said, sounding a bit wistful. "If it isn't football or the wrestling, he'll put the racing on. And that's shit until someone crashes."

"The Grand Prix," Larimer said loftily, "is the pinnacle of sporting…amazing…ness."

"Sporting amazingness—yeah, totally. Twat."

"Oi! Dickhead."

Anton tuned out the idle insults as they turned off the main road and into the housing estate. He was only brought back by Jude's elbow in his ribs, and then he jumped away like he'd been shot. Just in case…just in case Jude *felt* something, you know?

"Sorry, mate," Jude said, blinking.

"Um. S'okay. What'd you say?"

"Asked if you'd clocked any of the girls yet."

"Clocked—sorry?"

Larimer laughed. "Who're the fit girls in our class?" he translated, and Anton reddened.

"Not my thing," he blurted out without thinking, and then red became purple as Larimer's face lit up and he cackled.

"No *way!*"

"Lay off, Larimer, even a gayboy'd have more luck than you," Jude retorted casually.

"I—I—"

"Hey, relax, s'cool," Jude said, shrugging. "Long as you don't fancy Will Thorne, that's just fucking sick, man."

Anton laughed weakly, his heart beating a rapid tattoo of relief under his ribs. "Not my type," he said, even though he couldn't be sure he knew which boy Thorne was.

"Hopefully, not anyone's type," Larimer said.

"Tell you what, mind, that Bee Lewis hasn't got a gaydar," Jude continued cheerfully, kicking a pebble into the road.

"What?" Anton said.

"She were staring at you all the way through English," Jude grinned.

"The blonde one," Larimer added helpfully. "Hides behind her hair all the time. Big glasses."

"She's pretty under there, she had to tie it back in food tech last year 'cause Bitch Briscoe did her nut," Jude continued blithely.

"Um. Well. Not my type either," Anton mumbled. His face still felt too warm, but Jude and Larimer just laughed and said something about her not having a decent rack anyway. "Um, can you...my last school, it wasn't...okay."

"What, gays?"

"Yeah."

Jude shrugged. "F'you don't want it known, it won't be known."

"Yeah, what d'you reckon we are, girls?"

Anton forced himself to laugh as they reached the corner of Glendale Avenue, and hesitated. "Thanks. Um," he said. "See you guys tomorrow, I guess."

"You walk in?" Jude asked. "Larimer usually gets the bus, but I walk to school."

"Oh, I, um, my aunt drops me off on her way to work," Anton hedged, and his brain nearly decided to fuck a lift and walk with Jude when Jude just gave him that huge, toothpaste-ad smile and shrugged.

"Okay, man. Laters!"

"Lat—fuck, ow!" Larimer swore, turning and tripping on a

rock. Jude cackled. Anton's stomach fluttered at that noise, too, traitorous thing that it was, and he hurried up the avenue before his brain could do something *really* stupid like invite Jude over or something equally suicidal and retarded.

Anton lived in a reasonably big house on Glendale Avenue with Mum and Aunt Kerry, and Aunt Kerry's two little girls. It had once been Nana Lauder's house, and she'd left it to Aunt Kerry when she'd died. Only since Mum and Dad had split up, Anton and Mum lived there, too.

Aunt Kerry's car wasn't in the driveway, but the front door was on the latch, and Max, one of their massive cats, was sitting on the stairs. He offered Anton an unimpressed look, and proceeded to start washing his arse.

"Charming," Anton said, dropping his keys in the dish on the hall table. "Mum!" he yelled.

"Kitchen, honey!"

He dropped his bag and toed off his shoes before following her voice. Max followed, too, but then Max thought his name was Kitchen, so Anton didn't pretend it was out of any sense of liking them. Molly, their other cat, was sitting in a sun patch on the kitchen windowsill, though, so he picked her up—all five million pounds of her—and perched on one of the island stools to hug her.

"How did it go, then?" Mum asked, up to her elbows in chicken carcass. Anton wrinkled his nose at the funky smell. "Oh, don't pull that face. It'll be good!"

"Is there going to be that garlic and pepper sauce thing again?" Anton asked doubtfully. Molly started to purr loudly, and nuzzled the underside of his jaw hopefully.

"It will be *good*," Mum insisted, which meant it was the garlic and pepper thing. She'd tried it the previous week and Lily, Anton's five-year-old cousin, had thrown a *huge* tantrum at the funny taste.

"Okay," Anton said doubtfully, convinced Lily would convey enough disgust for both of them.

"Don't make me ask again, honey."

"It went okay," Anton said. He swallowed. "Nobody guessed."

Mum's face softened. "Of course they didn't guess," she said gently, and Anton shrugged.

"It's still…I still can see the…my face is too soft."

"Oh, honey, that's because you're looking in the mirror and you're *expecting* to see it. They don't know any different than what you say to them. Of course they won't guess."

There was the crux of it. A new school didn't make Anton nervous, not really. A school was a school, after all. It was the fear that they would work out that he wasn't—yet, *really*—a boy. That under his clothes he wore a binder over his breasts, and his voice was only as low as it was because of the voice exercises. He'd been terrified he'd turn up, and everyone would instantly go, "*Anton*? Who names a girl Anton?"

"What about PE?" He was dreading PE. His new timetable said it was the following day, and he was terrified. What if the teacher insisted he change into his gym kit in the changing rooms with all the other boys? They'd see his binder. They might even be able to guess he had nothing in his boxers. And what if they did swimming in the summer? Or—

"Anton," Mum said firmly. "Don't worry so much, eh? One step at a time."

"But—"

"The headmaster said he'd let your PE teacher know the situation and proper measures would be taken. Now stop worrying. How did your day go? Are your class nice?"

Anton hugged Molly tightly, and pushed it aside. "Yeah," he said. "There's this girl, Emma, she's really nice. I'm not sure about some of the boys yet. But I walked back with Jude and Larimer—"

"Larimer?"

Anton blinked. "Er. I don't actually know his name."

"What do you mean, you don't know his name?"

"Well…everyone calls everyone by their last name, and nobody's said his first one yet," Anton said blankly. He hadn't even noticed. "Well, um, I walked home with him and Jude, anyway."

"Sounds like you're doing just fine."

"Well, I'm behind in English. They're doing *Hamlet*, not *Romeo and Juliet*."

"Oh, please, Anton, like you'll be behind for long," Mum laughed. She arranged the last of the stuffing and put the chicken in the oven. "You'll be fine with English. And it's more important you focus on settling in, if you ask me. Make some friends, join a club or two—"

Anton shrugged awkwardly, and Mum sighed. She started to wash her hands. "I *know*," Anton said at the pointed look she gave him. "I know. I know what Ellen says." Ellen was his psychiatrist, a gender specialist in West London.

"And what does Ellen say?"

"That social transition means living a normal social life in my preferred gender role," Anton recited. "But it's hard."

"Honey, you have already come a long way. Too far for 'hard' to be an excuse," Mum said. She dried off her hands, then came around the worktop to hug him. She was slight, like he was, and if he'd been happy as a girl, Anton figured he'd have been happy to end up looking like Mum. She was pretty, with the same fair hair as him. He had a narrower face, thankfully, but the same brown eyes, too.

Most importantly—and oddly, he supposed, for someone like him—he didn't look too much like Dad.

The divorce had been…bad. Anton still felt a bit guilty, deep down, no matter how many times Mum and Ellen and Aunt Kerry had told him it wasn't his fault. But at the end of the day, if he'd been…cisgender (Ellen hated him saying 'normal') then he'd have just been Natasha, and Mum and Dad would never have started arguing.

But he wasn't. He'd freaked out when his periods had started—he'd only been eleven—and Mum had realised it wasn't a normal level freakout. Dad had been worried then, too, especially as Anton had taken to ripping up any of his sheets or clothes that got blood on them, and had refused point-blank to wear skirts or girly clothes as they felt wrong. He could remember the horror of it, the crying himself to sleep when his periods came, and the inability to pin down exactly why he hated them so much.

When the child psychologist had said it was a perfectly normal part of being a girl, Anton had simply replied, "I'm not a girl, though." And it had clicked. He hadn't known the words—hadn't known transgenderism existed, or that there were others like him—but he'd known the feeling. And finally, he knew at least one sentence that could express it.

Then things had fallen apart. Mum had cried, but then been fine. She'd hugged him and said he was still hers, no matter if he wasn't Natasha anymore. Dad, though...

Dad thought he was mad. Dad thought he was mentally ill and Mum was encouraging his delusions. They'd argued for months before Mum turned around and said she wasn't raising 'our *son*, Chris!' in that environment. She had demanded a divorce, and dragged Dad through the courts when he'd tried to stop her. Dragged up everything, the way Dad had refused to take him to his appointments with the gender specialist, the way Dad would throw out any clothes that were 'too boyish' and would sometimes just shake Anton and repeat his old name—"Natasha, you're *Natasha!*"—at him until Mum would catch him and shout herself hoarse. Everything.

It had been the ugliest divorce *ever*. In some ways, it still wasn't over, thanks to the custody visits. And Dad still had *some* rights, which he tried to hold onto with both hands. He had only signed the paperwork to let Anton change his name after Mum had threatened to apply for full custody and shut Dad out of his life forever. And Dad still—*still*, years after that visit to the child psychologist's office—called him a 'her.' Still said 'she' and 'Natasha.' Still accused Mum of blocking access to 'our daughter.' All the neighbours had to know about Anton by now, the amount of yelling matches they'd had on the doorstep, and Anton hated it. Sometimes, Anton even hated Dad for what he insisted on doing.

Because it *was* hard, and maybe it *was* a little bit crazy, but...

But in the boys' uniform, with a boy's name and being referred to as 'he' and having the prospect, when he turned sixteen, of being sent to the clinic properly and maybe starting medical transition instead of just talking about it all the time...with all that, Anton was happy. He was happy like that.

And was being happy such a crime?

Chapter 3

ON TUESDAY MORNING, Anton got a locker key from Miss Taylor, and spent most of break with Emma trying to find its home.

"They don't exactly write the numbers on them big," she complained, "and they're all out of order."

"What's all out of order?"

Anton jumped at that deep, easy voice—and then his stomach dropped when Jude slid his arms around Emma's waist and hugged her from behind, resting his chin on her shoulder in a very familiar, intimate pose.

Shit.

"The lockers," he said numbly, to force his brain off the despondency. He shouldn't be surprised, really. Jude was good-looking, Emma was pretty…it was natural. And it wasn't like he could have dated Jude anyway, not if he didn't want anyone to find out about him.

"Oh, right," Jude said. "On the up side, it'll be yours until you leave school again. They don't swap them around every year."

Anton nodded, keeping his eyes very definitely away from the sight of Jude hugging Emma like that, and started on the next column of lockers, squinting at the tiny numbers.

"Are you even awake yet?" he heard Emma ask Jude.

"Not really."

"I can tell. You're almost sweet when you're sleepy."

"Mehhh."

Anton swallowed dryly, and finally found it. The key needed a bit of a jiggle to unstick the lock, but it finally popped open. And sitting inside was nothing but air, and an envelope.

"What's that?" he asked.

"I dunno. A treasure map?" Jude suggested. Emma hit him. "Ow!"

"You're an arse," she said loftily. "It's for you," she added to Anton. Sure enough, when he turned it over, his surname was printed on the front in tidy handwriting.

"What is it?"

"Open it and see, moron. Ow!"

"Jude, either be sweet and sleepy, or go be a prick somewhere else."

"But I wanna be a prick *here*," Jude whined, wriggling against her back as though he was trying to hide behind her, even though he was taller than her.

"Tough shit."

Anton ripped the envelope open. Inside was a card. It was just a plain celebratory type card, balloons and stuff on the front, but when he flipped it open *welcome to 10B!!!* was written inside in a blue bubble, surrounded by little scribbled signatures and variances on the central message.

"Oh," he said.

His stomach twisted violently. It looked like the whole class had signed it. And something about it felt funny, like...they were being nice to him even though they knew nothing about him. Some of them had even written his name, so it couldn't have been pre-prepared, and...

"You knew this was my locker, and you let me look?" he asked Emma, who grinned.

"Yeah, well, didn't want to be *too* obvious," she said. "One of the girls pushed it in this morning."

Anton swallowed, scanning the signatures. Jude and Emma

had both signed it. Walsh had called him Welsh Williams. He *thought* Larimer had signed it near the top, unless there was someone called Fatima. And it was...stupidly nice of them. *Stupidly.*

"Thanks," he croaked.

"Welcome," Emma said quietly.

"S'tradition, mate," Jude added. "You're one of us now. We're gonna join you to the hive mind at half term and then you'll start to morph into Walsh."

"Jude!" Emma protested, elbowing him in the gut. Jude grimaced and escaped.

"Uncalled for!"

"Your *face* is uncalled for!" she retorted, then slid her arm through Anton's and hugged his elbow. "You okay?"

"Yeah, just...just surprised. It was really nice of you all, though."

"We don't get new people very often," Emma said. "And anyway, the boys will all accept you if you like football. Jude said you're a Spurs fan?"

"Uh-huh."

"The cardinal sin is being a fan of Manchester United," she confided. "It's not allowed. And rugby you can support England or Wales, nobody else, and especially not Scotland."

"And if you ever say anything nice about France, we'll fob you off on 10A and you'll be their problem."

"And everyone in 10C is a prick."

"No, Ems, a douchebag. A are the pricks."

"Oh wait, yeah, A's the form with that retard Barnes in it..."

Anton fell into step between them, still staring at the card, and let himself be guided to history without paying much attention. He just stared at signatures—most calling him nothing, some calling him Williams, the odd one calling him Anton—and took a deep breath.

He could do this. He could totally fucking do this.

ANTON TOTALLY COULDN'T do this.

Because fourth period was PE. And Anton had always hated

PE. Not for the doing of sports or anything—he liked football, and athletics wasn't too bad—but for the whole…getting changed, wearing shorts and tight tops, everyone staring at everybody else thing. He had a note from his mother, and another one from the head, but…what if the PE teacher didn't give two shits about transgender kids? What if he didn't understand why Anton couldn't change with the other boys? Worst of all, what if he made Anton change with the *girls*?

Finding him was the first step though, so as the class milled into the sports hall, Anton caught Emma's sleeve before she could disappear into the girls' changing rooms.

"I need to speak to the PE teacher," he said.

"Mrs. Salter? Oh, sure, it's that little office at the end of the corridor, see? Just before the gym doors. Knock and wait for her to tell you to come in, she hates people barging in, you get extra laps for that."

Somehow, Anton hadn't imagined the PE teacher would be a woman. He'd always had male PE teachers before, and suddenly his imagination provided him with some enormous female weight-lifting champion type. Brilliant. The *least* sympathetic type of person *ever*, probably.

So he knocked, but his stomach was already in his shoes.

"Come in!"

He cracked the door open and slipped inside.

The office was a messy collection of files, random tennis balls, and trophies in a dusty cabinet by a tiny window. The desk was groaning under the weight of a million bits of paper, and the woman behind it looked up sharply when he shut the door behind him.

Anton blinked, thrown.

"Who're you, then?"

Mrs. Salter was…petite. And pretty. She was probably only Anton's height herself, a slender black woman with very long braided hair swept up in a high ponytail. She was wiry, whipcord muscle showing on her bared arms, and all limbs. She could have been a gymnast or a ballet dancer, and yet there was a sharp, calculating look on her face that made Anton think maybe he hadn't been too far off the mark after all.

"Uh. Anton Williams. Miss."

"Don't know you. What do you want." Her voice was sharp and perfunctory, the words flat and unquestioning. She wasn't asking; she was demanding an answer immediately, and Anton held out the notes from Mum and the head on nervous reflex.

"I'm in your next class, 10B. I'm new."

"So?" She didn't take the notes.

"I…the head's agreed…some different stuff for PE."

Her eyes narrowed, and she took the notes. "Sit."

He slid gingerly into the rickety chair in front of her desk, and fidgeted with the button on his blazer. She scanned the notes with a disinterested expression, then dropped them almost carelessly on the desk.

"Yes," she said. "I remember Mr. Martins mentioning something about you."

Anton felt his face heat up.

"You've been given permission to wear a T-shirt instead of the vest the other students wear."

"Yes. Miss," he added hastily.

"Have you brought one?"

"Yes, Miss."

"In future, it will be black, and it must not be longer than the waistband of your shorts. Boys wear black vests, girls wear light blue ones. If you do not bring a black T-shirt next week, you will be given a detention and a vest from the spare kit box. I will *not* reserve a T-shirt in that box for you, Williams, so if you forget your own, it's on your head."

"Yes, Miss."

"Which changing rooms would you prefer?"

"I can't change with the others," Anton blurted out. "They'll figure me out."

"You can't change in the corridor either," she said bluntly, then pursed her lips and pointed a pen at the closed door. "Next to the gym doors is a staff toilet. It's a single bathroom, no stalls, but it's lockable. I will inform the rest of the staff that it is for your use for changing on Tuesday afternoons until you feel comfortable changing with the other boys."

Somehow, her use of the word 'other' made a rush of relief sweep up Anton's spine.

"Inform me if you join any sports clubs and I will amend that to include those dates. The sooner you can change with the other boys, the better, but you may use that for the time being if you wish."

"T-thanks, Miss."

"Other pupils will notice, though, Williams. You won't be able to keep it quiet forever."

"No, Miss."

Her sharp face softened ever so slightly. "10B is a fairly easy-going group. They're a pack of feral idiots on the playing fields, and I know they're a peril to the more sensitive members of staff, but they're a nice enough bunch underneath the act. I wouldn't imagine you'll have any real problems with them."

"They've…they're nice so far. Miss," Anton told his knees. Mrs. Salter, he was rapidly deciding, was crazy intimidating.

"Understand, Williams, that I will not treat you any differently from any of the other boys. You will work to their standards. You do not have to be *good* at sport, but I demand of all my classes that they try. Laziness is not tolerated in my lessons, nor will I accept any excuses. If you try hard, then I will recognise that, but none of my pupils—whatever their gender identity—are permitted to use excuses and idleness to get out of PE."

"No, Miss."

"However, I also recognise you will have some challenges with PE," she added, more quietly. "The others may find out, Williams. If they do, and if they are in any way abusive about it, then I want you to inform me or another member of staff immediately. Bullying and discrimination is *also* not tolerated in my lessons, whatever the source of it. Do you understand?"

"Yes, Miss. Thanks, Miss," he added quietly. He wasn't stupid; he was going to take support wherever he could get it.

"Anything else?"

"I…I wear a binder, Miss. A looser one for PE 'cause they make it hard to breathe sometimes, but, um, if one of the other kids sees it…" She raised her eyebrows, and Anton took a deep breath before ploughing on. "My aunt always calls it a back support if people see it."

"I see."

"That's…that's what I'll say."

"You may call it whatever you want, Williams. I will not, however, have you playing up a back injury. You may tell the others it is one, but it's not an excuse to slack off."

"No, Miss. I won't."

"Good. Go and get changed—you need to be outside the sports hall in five minutes. Do you have football boots?"

"Trainers, Miss. I own some, though."

"It's football boots until half term. Make sure you bring them in future."

"Yes, Miss."

He'd never been so glad to escape a teacher's office—and yet, as he slipped into the indicated staff toilet and locked the door to change into his looser binder and PE kit—he also felt oddly positive about PE. Which was a first in…

Well, ever.

THE FOOTBALL BOOTS were for, unsurprisingly, football.

Despite the cold, they were sent out onto the playing fields to do laps of the faintly-drawn football pitch, the chill encouraging them to run faster, and nobody noticed Anton's chest at all. His T-shirt, on the other hand…

"This term is football!" Mrs. Salter shouted, her voice loud and carrying in the still winter air. "Today I want to see your abilities so I can start dividing you into appropriate teams later on. For now, pick your own. Anderson, Carter, Lewis, Neale, Patterson, Walsh, and Zimmerman, up front! You will be captains for this lesson, one team each until we run out of people. We'll rotate through the register every lesson after this one. Questions?"

"Miss!"

"Thorne?"

"Why's the new kid got a T-shirt on?"

For a brief second, Anton's lungs seized. Then Jude laughed. "He doesn't want you checking out his sick abs, Thorny."

"Fuck off, ginger!"

"Shut it!" Mrs. Salter barked. Her voice was like a whipcrack, and Anton shivered with the force of it. "Kalinowski, grow up, you're past due. Thorne, is my permission for Williams' attire sufficient for you?"

Thorne was a pale boy with pale hair, pale eyes, and a pale face. He didn't look like he had enough blood to go as pink as he did. "No, Miss."

"*What.*"

"I mean...I mean, yes, Miss—um, *sorry,* Miss," he decided finally.

"Extra lap. Go." Thorne went a violent red, but dutifully turned on his heel and started to jog down the pitch. "Faster, Thorne! Anybody else feel like questioning me?"

Silence.

"Good. Anderson, pick your first player."

Anton hated being picked for teams. His old class had all thought him a total freak, which made him last to get picked in PE no matter how good he was. He wouldn't mind so much for things like hockey, he was awful at hockey, it was fair enough to not want him on a hockey team. But he was good at football, and yet he felt the uncomfortable prickling sensation of flushing with embarrassment as, one by one, the other kids—with skills and friends and classmates who knew how good or otherwise they were—were picked and teams slowly began to form.

It seemed to be very friend-locked. Walsh immediately picked Larimer and then Jude; the same girl who'd picked Emma picked Isabel right after her, and—

"Williams."

Anton jumped as Walsh drawled his name, and blinked. There were still a good...ten kids to go, and...

"Oi, Anton, move," Jude ordered, and Anton fell into the cluster, a little startled. "Lemme guess," Jude said, clapping his shoulder. "Last to get picked at your old school?"

"Uh, yeah."

"You can't be any worse than Walsh," Larimer opined.

"Oi! Twat, you're the one who trips over the ball every game."

"You any good at footie?" Jude asked, as Larimer and Walsh began to argue.

"Yeah."

Jude grinned. "Yeah? What position?"

"Goal."

Jude's face lit up, and Anton's stomach ached. "Yeah? Fucking *sweet*. We're all shit in goal. Walsh is a bitch of a striker, don't get in his fucking way if you're in goal *against* him, and I do a mean defence, but we're only any good with our feet. Catching shit…nah."

"What you gassing about, Kalinowski, you catch great with your face."

"Yeah, and your gob."

"'Scuse me," Jude said genially, still grinning, then casually retreated, seized both Walsh and Larimer by the hair, and knocked their heads together with a sharp clack.

"Kalinowski! Don't ruin what little brains either of your gormless friends have! And Williams, wipe that smirk off your face, don't pander to Kalinowski's delusions that he's funny!"

"No, Miss, sorry, Miss," the other three choroused, and Anton bit his lip to hide the smile. There was a warmth in Anton's stomach that was nothing to do with Jude's smile or his proximity when he slung an arm casually over Anton's shoulders as the captains finished picking. It was something a bit like belonging, something Anton had been chasing for years, and although he didn't quite—yet—dare join in with the teasing, he laughed and didn't try to defend Jude when Larimer retaliated with a battle-cry and rugbytackle into the cold, hard grass, he felt he was *supposed* to be standing there, right there, in this new group.

"Larimer! Leave your overwhelming desire for physical contact with Kalinowski *off* the pitch!"

"Get in goal, then, Williams," Walsh said, clapping Anton on the shoulder and nodding towards two cones set out in the grass. "And let's see how good you really are."

Anton got in goal. And when the kick-about started, Mrs. Salter prowling the edges of each game and making notes on a clipboard, he saved every one.

Chapter 4

"YOU SHOULD COME to football club."

"Shit!"

Anton jumped nearly a foot in the air. Jude, he was beginning to realise, had skipped out on the whole 'make someone aware of your presence before getting within two feet of them' part of etiquette.

And, because he'd missed out on it, he just laughed.

"Dick," Anton groused, and closed his locker door. He'd snuck away at the end of PE to change back into his uniform, but Jude had caught up to him anyway, it seemed.

"Yep. So. You should come to football club."

Anton bit his lip, hefting his bag onto his shoulder. "Uh. I can't," he said feebly, and turned away to head for the gates. He half-expected Jude to drop it, but heavy footsteps followed, and then an arm was slung over his shoulders like they were best friends, not...not guys who'd known each other like two days.

"Why not?" Jude asked, way too close to Anton's ear, and Anton shrugged him off a little awkwardly as they headed outside.

"I just...shouldn't." PE was dangerous enough. Football club...

"You're good, you should!"

"I—"

"And," Jude continued, like Anton hadn't opened his mouth, "you don't actually have to be good. There's a team, too but you have to come to club to get on the team anyway and there's loads of guys who come just to have a kick about. You should come, too. And you probably would get on the team, I reckon you're better than Davies, he's our main goalie at the minute…"

"It's not about not being any good," Anton blurted out.

Jude cocked his head. "S'it about your T-shirt?"

Anton took a shaky breath. "What?"

"Is it about that T-shirt you wear in PE? You got scars or something?"

"Um—"

"'Cause there's no kit rules for football club, just wear football boots, and gloves if you're in goal. You can wear your T-shirt if you want. Nobody'll see your scars."

Anton swallowed. He knew the basics of lying—don't give different people different stories—and yet it still jarred to mumble, "S'my back."

"Eh?"

"It's my back. I have…a back problem," he said.

"Oh," Jude said, and kicked the curb as they crossed the road. "But you played in PE."

"I can *play,* I just have to wear this…brace thing."

"Oh, right, hence the T-shirt?"

"Yeah."

"Don't worry about it," Jude urged. "Mate, if you're worried about the other lads taking the piss, I'll smack 'em in the gob for you. An' they won't anyway. It's just about what team you play for at club, not whether you've got a fucked-up back or whatever."

Anton chewed on his lip. It was tempting. He liked football—it was one of the only lessons he'd liked in PE at his old school, especially as they got to wear shorts instead of the stupid PE skirt—but shirts rode up, guys hugged each other on the pitch, dirty tackles could show things…and changing rooms, what about the changing rooms?

"I don't like people seeing the brace," he said eventually.

"Is that why you disappeared before PE?"

"Yeah."

"Where'd you go?"

"Toilets," Anton mumbled.

"So do that again, if you have to," Jude said, and slung that arm around Anton's shoulders again as they reached the corner of Anton's street. "Look, mate, you're really good, yeah? Don't let some pissing back brace keep you out of goal."

Anton squirmed; Jude tightened his hold until it was a rough sort of…hug-headlock thing, and let go. "I'll think about it," Anton compromised.

"Stop thinking and do. You're like Ems, I reckon, you think too much," Jude said, then that heart-wrenchingly beautiful grin lit up his face like an explosion. "I'll talk you round, Williams, you fucking wait!"

Anton watched him lope away, blinking with the suddenness of the retreat, then yelled after him the most inane question ever. "Where's Larimer?"

"Told him to sod off, needed to talk to you on your lonesome!" Jude yelled back.

Anton grimaced, heat rushing up his neck and face, and told his stomach—as it did a rough lurch sideways—to cut it out already. Jude was going out with Emma. You didn't cuddle your mates in the corridor the way he'd cuddled up to Emma that morning.

Still…it didn't stop the warmth seeping into his blood. Jude wanted Anton to come to football club so much, he'd seen off Larimer and pretty much walked Anton home. Maybe Anton *should* go. Everyone—Mum, Aunt Kerry, Ellen at the clinic—was always saying how he had to start living as normal a life as possible, living properly in his preferred gender. Right? Maybe going to football club, with Jude on his side about the 'back brace' was the way to start?

He let himself into the house, still thinking it over, and absently petted Molly on the stairs before shedding his coat and shoes and heading to the kitchen, following Rose's dulcet warbling. She was only just a year old, chubby, and curly-haired, and waved a mush-covered spoon in his direction genially before continuing her singing.

"Hello, darling," Mum said, ruffling his hair between putting pans away. "How was school?"

"Was okay."

"PE go alright, then?"

"Yeah," Anton said. "It was football. I didn't get picked last either."

"Good," Mum said, and offered him a proper smile. She had her hair all pinned up on the top of her head, out of the way of her housework, and although she looked tired, she also looked happy. Which was nice, because Mum hadn't been looking properly happy for a while. "Did you walk home with...Jules?"

"Jude, yeah," Anton corrected, rummaging in the fridge for a can of Coke before sitting down at the island worktop. Max regarded him with imperious disdain from the other stool. "He, um. He's asked me to go to football club, actually."

"And are you?" Mum asked, looking over her shoulder at him.

Anton frowned at Max. "I don't know," he told the cat seriously. "I mean...if they see my brace then..."

"Then lie about it, it's not like any of them are going to recognise a binder when they see one, darling."

"But—"

"Get Kerry to sew a little NHS label on it or something, there's lots of things you can tell them."

"I told Jude it was a back brace," Anton admitted.

"Well, there you go."

"But—"

"No," Mum said firmly, and abandoned the drying up to slide onto the stool opposite Anton's. Max turned his huge amber eyes on her and seemed to visibly sneer at her harried appearance. "Anton, you can't avoid things you like just because they *might* find out. They're fifteen-year-olds. How many of them are going to know what a binder looks like?"

Anton turned the can around in his hands hypnotically, feeling a flush creeping up his cheeks.

"You need to get back on the horse, sweetheart. And you've always loved football. Go to football club. It's no more risky than

PE will be."

"I don't…I don't want Jude to find out," Anton admitted eventually.

"Jude? Why Jude?"

"He's…he's being really nice," Anton said, his voice so low he could barely feel it in his throat. "He's just being nice to me, even though he doesn't have to, and I…"

He trailed off, but when he looked up, Mum's face had gone soft. "*Oh*," she said meaningfully.

"Shut up," Anton groused.

"Oh, honey, welcome to not every boy being like those silly little idiots at your last school," she teased, and ruffled his hair again before leaning over the counter to kiss the crown of his head.

"Mum!"

"Lay off," she said, and chuckled when Rose caterwauled, presumably for her own kiss. "Oi! Shurrit, noisy. Worse than your mum, you are."

Anton cracked a smile, propping his chin on his hand to watch Mum wrestle Rose out of her highchair and give the squirmy lump a cuddle. Anton didn't mind babies that much, but Rose *was* a squirmy lump. And it was a bit awkward because she looked just like her dad, and Rose's dad was He Who Shall Not Be Named in this household. A bit like Anton's, he supposed.

"How's job-hunting?"

Mum's face turned severe. "Don't you start fussing about me," she said sternly, jabbing a finger at him. Rose wriggled and started blowing bubbles through her lips with wet farting noises. "You focus on settling in at school. And your Jude."

"He's not *my* Jude!"

"Mmm, but he's being *so* nice to you."

"Mum! God, you're embarrassing." She laughed. "Anyway, he has a girlfriend."

"Well, then, daydream," Mum advised. "All the best ones have girlfriends, darling."

"I thought it was 'nice guys finish last.'"

"Then he must not be that nice," Mum countered, and hefted

Rose above her head to pull faces at her. She looked a bit younger with baby Rose, less...less like she'd had a hideous divorce and lost her job to having to move in with her sister and dealing with her daughter becoming her son.

Anton slid down off the stool and wandered around the island to hug her on an impulse.

"Thanks, Mum," he mumbled into her shoulder, awkwardly hugging around Rose, and felt Mum rest her cheek on the top of his head.

"Get yourself sorted, darling," she murmured, "and don't you worry about us, eh?"

APPARENTLY ANTON GAVE up easier than Jude, though. Nothing more was said about football on Wednesday—the focus seemed to be on Walsh, as Larimer had found out by some sneaky means that Walsh had a crush on some girl called Melanie. Anton didn't get the joke, but apparently having a crush on Melanie was ten kinds of embarrassing all at once—until three thirty-three, when Anton was collecting his things from his locker, and a *presence* appeared.

"Hi, Jude."

"See, you're getting used to me already, new kid," Jude said amiably, and banged his back against the locker next to Anton's. "So."

"So?"

"Football club. Tomorrow. You in?"

"I said I'd think about it."

"And you said that *yesterday*. Twenty-four hours I've given you! How much time d'you need?"

Jude's exaggeration was coupled with hyperactive hand movements and a wide, manic sort of grin that made everything from Anton's hips to his shoulders clench painfully tight. For a brief second, he simply stared stupidly, then realised he was doing it and hastily turned away.

"I'll think about it."

"You already said that," Jude insisted, and fell into step with him. "Look, we need guys who can play. And nobody'll make fun of your back, or I'll thump 'em."

Anton fidgeted. "Why d'you care so much?" he asked quietly, and Jude snorted.

"'Cause you're cool," he said. "I like you, man, let's not get mushier than that, yeah?"

Anton laughed, his stomach warm, and clutched 'I like you' to his memory like it was something infinitely valuable.

"Hey, come over," Jude said, bumping Anton's shoulder with his own. "We have a goal in our back garden, come and shoot some with me."

Anton glanced over his shoulder. "Where's Larimer?"

"Gets picked up Wednesdays. Goes to visit his nan. So? Coming over?"

"We'll have to stop at mine so I can change," Anton heard himself saying, and Jude grinned, slinging that arm over his shoulders again in that weird half-hug thing he did.

"Awesome," he said. "Should be pretty quiet, most of the family don't get home until late Wednesdays. So what about your lot?"

They swapped family stories, Anton slowly getting bolder as Jude continued to simply laugh instead of poking fun or acting like any of it was weird. By the time they reached Anton's house, Jude's arm was resting solid over Anton's shoulders like it was meant to be there, and Anton's heart felt like it had swollen to twice its normal size. Even if he couldn't have Jude—which he couldn't—he had *this*. He had a friend, and Anton had been very lonely for a very long time.

"I'll just go and—"

"What the hell is *that*?" Jude yelped.

Anton blinked, and followed his wide-eyed stare. Max stared back. "Um," Anton said. "Our cat?"

"That's not a cat, it's three feet long!"

"He's a *large* cat."

"That," Jude said in a serious tone, "is a monster."

Max showed his fangs and hissed, displeased at the intruder, and Jude retreated against the front door.

"And it's going to eat me."

"He's too lazy to eat you," Anton said. "Um, I'll just go and change."

"I'm staying right here," Jude proclaimed dramatically, still eyeballing the cat.

"Okay. Uh. Don't stroke him. He doesn't like new people."

"Why the hell would I *stroke* it?"

Anton laughed as he stepped around Max—who ignored him in favour of glowering at Jude—and decided at some point he'd have to introduce Jude to Molly. If Jude didn't like cats, Molly would *love* Jude. She climbed all over anybody who didn't like cats.

Anton locked his bedroom door—just in case—and did a record-breaking change, swapping out his usual binder for his slightly looser one that he used for sports, and finding a baggy T-shirt that he knew wasn't likely to ride up too much. He decided on tracksuit bottoms, it being too cold to walk around to Jude's in shorts but unwilling to risk changing again at Jude's and letting Jude see him in just boxers, and rummaged under the bed for his trainers, heart beating a tattoo in his chest. It'd be just them at Jude's, by the sound of it, and Anton could just…enjoy a bit of football without worrying too much. Jude obviously didn't suspect a thing. He'd bought the back brace excuse hook, line and sinker, and Anton liked Jude, but he didn't seem like he was the brightest bulb in the box. He wasn't likely to work it out if he'd bought it so far, so—

So Anton was actually—for just about the first time—looking forward to just going round a guy's house for the hell of it.

He jogged back downstairs, expertly jumping over Max, and followed the voices to find Jude, who'd vanished. Anton found him on the living room floor, sitting cross-legged by the baby playmat tickling a shrieking, squirming Rose on the tummy. Mum was sitting in the armchair, surrounded by the local papers and their jobs pages, and ignoring them in favour of—oh shit—interrogating Jude.

"Anton, there you are," she said, with a smirk. "Jude was just telling me how good you were in PE the other day!"

"Traitor," Anton said. Jude beamed.

"Anton always enjoyed football at his old school," Mum continued blithely.

"Traitor!" Anton repeated.

"Ready?"

"Yeah."

"Okay. I gotta go, Baby," Jude said to Rose, and gave her grasping fingers a tiny high-five. "You work on that singing, okay?"

"Gurgling," Anton corrected.

"Don't listen to that git, it's totally singing, I hear your talent," Jude said very seriously, then lurched upward from the floor with as much grace as Larimer. "Oh shut up," he said when Anton laughed. "For that, I'm gonna aim the ball for your *face*."

"I'll just save it."

"You better."

Jude only lived a couple of streets away. It had started raining, so they ran it, Jude still in his uniform and Anton marginally better sheltered by the jacket he'd thrown on in the hall. Jude's house was very much like Anton's—a disturbingly clean car in the driveway, rose bushes that were a bit *too* well-tended bracketing the front door, but a messy chaos beyond said door.

"Um," Anton said, eyeing the enormous pile of various shoes in various sizes in the hall. "Big family?"

"Me, dad, two stepsisters, and stepmum. It's actually the younger stepsister, she's thirteen, and she's just like a hurricane."

"And you're not?"

"I'm a hurricane *outside*," Jude corrected, leading Anton through the house. It was laid out similarly to Anton's, a large kitchen at the back with a door leading to a fairly large garden. Jude rummaged in a basket of clothes sitting on top of a dryer, and fished out a T-shirt and pair of battered looking Spurs shorts. Anton barely turned his back in time before Jude's trousers hit the floor with a muffled thump. "You're a prude."

"I'm giving you some privacy."

"Mate, I have two sisters and I'm changing in the kitchen, what does that tell you about my privacy? Okay, you can turn around."

Thankfully for Anton's red face, Jude hadn't been mocking him too badly, and he was clothed again when Anton looked. He shoved his feet into a pair of grey trainers by the back door and unlatched it. "Oh yeah, mind out for the—"

A bundle of fur the size of a small cat shot in past Jude's ankles and vanished under the table. Anton blinked and bent to look.

"—rabbit."

"That's a rabbit?"

"Buzz."

"Buzz?"

"He likes to chew through electrical cords," Jude said, scrambling under the table and re-emerging with an armful of an extremely large, extremely fat brown rabbit, which was gnawing persistently on his arm. "Don't let the fat git fool you, he could outrun our old dog."

He hefted the rabbit back into the garden, dropping it into a large run and securing it while Anton gingerly closed the back door. It was a garden that might have been tidy if not for bare patches in the lawn where the rabbit run had been, various shards of plant pots lying around that had been decimated by something-or-other, and a shed at the very bottom spilling old tools and toys out onto the grass.

"It's nice," he said, honestly. It was nicer than Aunt Kerry's flowerbeds.

"Cheers. We can't get the whole team in here, though, we have a kick-about every Sunday down the park—you should come to that, too—"

"I can't on Sundays, I spend Sundays with my dad."

"Shame," Jude said, fetching a ball out from under a rusty bicycle. "That's much more informal than football club, it's just messing about. Emma plays sometimes when she's in the mood, and Larimer used to bring his girlfriend before they split up. If you get a Sunday off, you should come along, f'you don't wanna come to football club."

"I'll think about that, too," Anton said, and Jude laughed, tossing the football at him.

"Tell you what," he said, "you save every shoot, you come to football club. If you don't, I'll shut up about it. Yeah?"

Anton frowned, then shrugged. "Okay. Deal."

"Knew it."

"Knew what?"

"You're the kind of guy who makes deals only when he knows he's gonna win."

"Wha—hey!" Anton protested, batting the ball away as Jude kicked it with violent force towards his head.

"Oh sorry, should I have said go?"

It was fast—Jude had more energy than the Energizer Bunny on speed—and surprisingly brutal, but also nice—to get to jeer at him, to egg him on, to not have to watch his words or worry so much—

But Anton still let a *couple* of shots slide past him into the net. You know, to win the deal—

"For the record, I lied. I never shut up!"

—as much as possible, anyway.

Chapter 5

BECAUSE ANTON'S BRAIN was basically socially suicidal, he texted Jude anyway on Sunday morning. Just a *sorry i can't come out but good luck neways :)* but it was still a text to a boy with an insanely good-looking smile. And who had a habit of turning that smile on Anton.

"You know," Aunt Kerry said conversationally as she washed up the breakfast things, "I'm beginning to be able to tell when you're texting that Jude. And Maggie said you never stopped blushing the whole time he came over on Wednesday…"

"I'm just wishing him luck for football," Anton said. The doorbell chimed at the same time as the phone.

Cheers m8 but tbh its a case of who sucks less on sundays!!! ;)

Anton smiled, locking the phone again—and then the smile slid off his face when he heard Dad's voice at the door. "Is Natasha ready?"

Anton swallowed and squared his shoulders as he heard his mum's voice drop in temperature about a bazillion degrees. His stomach twisted as he shrugged his bag onto his shoulder. Every Sunday. Every single Sunday, Dad would do this, this thing where he just refused to accept—

"—name is Anton, not Natasha."

"For God's sake, Maggie. Is she ready or not?"

"*He* is nearly ready, yes."

Anton inched into the hall. Lily was hovering uncertainly at the foot of the stairs, hand in her mouth, and Anton tapped her on the crown of her head and nodded towards the kitchen. "Go help Mummy with the chores."

She fled without a word, and Anton was jealous of her ability to just run away from Dad. He'd tried, when he was younger, but then Dad had gone back to the family court and blamed Mum for his lack of access and it had all gotten really messy. They were *always* fighting about Anton—they'd been fighting about Anton since he was eleven years old—and Anton wanted it just to fucking stop already.

And he didn't *want* to hate his dad, but—

"Ah, there you are, Tasha. Come on, love."

—he kind of *did.*

"Chris," Mum said sharply.

"Look, Maggie, I've had enough of this—"

"So stop being such a prick about it!"

"I am not playing up to this nonsense! We had a *daughter*, Maggie! A little girl! And *Natasha* is still a girl, no matter how long you let her play dress-up!"

Anton flinched, his hand clenching into a fist around his bag strap. His binder suddenly felt tighter than ever.

"What is your problem, Chris? What do you care if we have a son or a daughter—this makes Anton *happy*, and—"

"It's a mental illness, Maggie! And instead of getting her help, you're indulging her! She won't get better if you indulge her!"

"There's no *getting better* to be had! I want my son not to hate his own body—and he *is* getting better, when people like you don't insist on referring to him by the wrong pronouns!"

"The wrong *what*?"

"Oh for God's sake, you ignorant piece of—"

Anton slid his phone out of his pocket and unlocked it. *Where is this kickabout?*

Jude's reply was instant. *Edgwarebury park. just heading out now. u comin after all??*

Maybe, Anton replied. *R u walking?*
No dads dropping me off. its on his way 2 work. u want a lift?
Ur dad works sundays?
Doctor. U want a lift or not??
please. u remember which house is mine? silver audi outside.
LOL v nice, better be the new plate ;) c u in 5!

Anton locked the phone again and shifted his bag to the other shoulder, pushing past his arguing parents. Mum had that tight, angry expression on that he hated, and Dad—the greying, scowling, fat piece of shit who didn't have a right to lecture anyone about how they lived their life given as how he genuinely enjoyed *golf,* for God's sake...

"Natasha, just hop in the car and we'll get going," Dad called over his shoulder. "Now you listen here, Maggie, I will not go along with this—"

An engine rumbled, and another car peeled around the corner slowly. It was probably one of the shiniest cars Anton had ever seen, a low Merc in blinding white, and he had to shield his eyes against it.

"It's more damaging to him that you keep refusing to respect his decision—"

"Her *decision*? She's fifteen years old and has a mental disorder, Maggie! For God's sake, if she said she felt like a cat, would you buy her a collar and a bell?"

The Merc came to a stop at the end of the driveway and Jude slid the window down, grinning from under a pair of ridiculously huge sunglasses. "That the Audi, then?"

"Yeah. S'my dad's."

"Get in," Jude said, jerking a thumb at the back door. "And my dad's car is nicer than your dad's car."

Anton couldn't find it in himself to laugh, sliding into the back seat gratefully. Jude's father grunted what might have been a hello, or a request to take his shoes off in this stupidly clean car, and Anton dropped Mum a quick text of *going 2 play football with jude. tell dad to piss off :(* before sitting back.

"You okay?"

"Not really."

"Sup?"

"Dad's being a dick and shouting at my mum," Anton said, and shrugged. "So I figured watching your game might be more fun."

"Urgh, sounds it," Jude said. "Sorry, mate. If it helps, bet my mum can scream louder than your mum."

"Jude."

"What?" Jude protested at his father's admonishment. "Totally true. Anyway," he added, twisting around to grin at Anton from the passenger seat. "You gonna play in goal?"

"Not got my kit."

"So?"

"So no, I like not being gross in my jeans, thanks."

"Man, you're such a girl," Jude teased. Thankfully, he'd turned back around in time to miss Anton's flinch. "It's okay, I'll just blame you when we lose."

"Wouldn't that be your crap skills?" Anton dared, and Jude's dad sniggered.

"*No*," Jude said, with the exasperated tone of someone explaining something to Lily for the fifty millionth time. "It's because *you* aren't in goal with *your* skills."

"But if you were any good, they wouldn't get to the goal."

"I'm amazing. It's everyone else that sucks," Jude said loftily.

"Yeah, whatever."

Despite Jude's dismissal of him as being girly for not wanting to get sweaty wearing denim, Anton found himself relaxing. Dad would go ballistic and blame Mum again for Anton taking off, but he was allowed to be himself here. Jude didn't know. Mr. Kalinowski *certainly* didn't know. And the other boys, whoever they were—

"Who's coming?" he asked as the car pulled up in front of one of the many entrances to Edgwarebury Park and they got out.

"Cheers, Dad. Uh," Jude pulled a face, as though thinking hurt. "Larimer and Walsh always do. Isabel doesn't tend to, not her thing. Emma sometimes comes by after her volunteer thing, she does some charity shop or something most Sundays. A couple of guys from Walsh's orchestra—"

"Walsh does music?"

"Secretly," Jude said, "Walsh is a rat-faced *pussy*. Ask him what he thought of *Up* sometime—and then duck, 'cause he'll hit you. And music is his major Achilles' heel."

Anton cracked a smile, not quite able to marry up Walsh to anything remotely sensitive.

"Hey," Jude said, and slung that arm over Anton's shoulders. "You alright, mate?"

"Yeah," Anton said. "It's…usual. Mum and Dad having a go."

"What do they argue about?"

"Dad's…Dad doesn't like the way Mum's bringing me up," Anton hedged. "And they row about it all the time."

"What, your mum a hippie or something?"

"They just don't agree on anything," Anton said. "Like…like I've always liked football and Dad thinks it's a waste of time and I should be doing something like…learning the piano."

"I did piano, it's shit," Jude said amiably. "And Emma does violin, tell you something, that shit is *boring*."

Anton laughed, daring to hook his wrist over Jude's shoulder, giving himself a bit of space without pushing Jude away. "It just gets exhausting."

"Yeah, I know."

"Yeah?"

"Uh-huh. My parents split up when I was ten, that wasn't pretty either," Jude said, then they broke out of the trees onto miles of open grass, and he raised his voice. "Oi! Twats! The dream team are fucking *here*!"

"Piss off, you lazy wanker!"

"I told you, I'm not playing," Anton protested, and then hastily ducked out of the way as Larimer rugby-tackled Jude into the grass.

"You fucking perv! Oi! Walsh, get your whore boyfriend off me, he's fucking raping me!"

Walsh just cackled and joined in, and a girl wearing two jumpers with holes in the top one to show off the second one jumped on the growing pile. Anton retreated, leaving Jude to his fate, and found a couple of familiar faces from their form group to stand with until Jude was released and two loose teams of seven—or rather, one of seven and one of eight and a big row about whether it mattered given that 'Andy's fucking shit anyway, it's not an advantage!'—were formed.

Anton guarded water bottles and bags, and watched the game roughly begin. It was the worst football he'd ever seen, closer to rugby the tackles were so dirty, and every player jeering loudly and crudely enough to pass for the terraces at White Hart Lane. They were joined, about half an hour in, by four or five boys coming from some swimming club or other, and about twenty minutes after that, a holler and a flying tackle of brown hair and browner coat sent Jude to his knees by the jumper-outlined opposition goal.

"Emma, fuck off!"

"Just helping you lose!" she crowed cheerily, before kissing him on the cheek and abandoning him to the other boys' catcalling. He kicked the ball into the back of her head, and Anton laughed despite his low-burning envy as Emma threw a water bottle back before crashing into the bag pile next to him. "I see Jude persuaded you out, then?"

Anton blinked, surprised. "Eh?"

"He was going on about it for ages, he's really keen on you joining the football club."

"Oh, right."

"And you should, you're much better than that lot," Emma continued, hugging her knees.

"So, um, what have you been up to?"

"Oh, I do Sunday mornings at a soup kitchen," Emma said. "I want to go into social work and they like loads of experience *and* a degree so I'm busy trying to persuade Mum that it's a good idea for me to go to uni and not end up working in a stupid shop and doing nothing to help other people—I mean what's the point, right, if you can't help other people…"

Anton tuned her out slightly, watching Jude go sliding in the mud and somehow—by pure dumb luck, Anton guessed—knock the ball between the jumpers. Only then there was an argument about whether they'd swapped ends yet, one team saying they had because they'd been playing for like an hour already, and the other saying they hadn't because there'd been no half-time break.

"Jude's dad is going to kill him for dragging all that mud home," Emma said gleefully.

"Oh?"

"Man's like OCD. Have you seen his car? He cleans it *every day*."

Anton sniggered. "Actually, yeah, I got a lift with Jude earlier…"

"It's freaky, isn't it?" Emma said, and laughed. "I swear he measures the lawn to know the *minute* it's over an inch long."

"And then there's Jude?"

"Yep. Total slob."

Anton hugged his knees, laughing when Walsh attempted to headbutt Larimer for the ball but, due to the height difference and having to jump up to do it, missed entirely and went sprawling in the grass.

"So are you and Jude hanging out later?"

Anton blinked. "Er, I dunno. I'd have thought you would have been."

"Oh God no, I see enough of the berk as it is. He's a nice guy and everything, but he's so *exhausting*," Emma said dramatically.

"But…it's school tomorrow, and you won't really get to go out at all, with all your clubs."

Emma blinked. "Why would I *want* to go out with Jude? I see—"

"Well, he's your boyfriend, isn't he?"

For a moment, the world turned itself upside down and shook Anton off the planet—because Emma burst into a fit of giggles.

"*Jude?* Oh my God, no! No, no, no—oh my God, I'm sorry, I thought he'd told you! Jude's my *brother*, not my boyfriend! He's my stepbrother—his dad's marrying my mum next summer!"

"You—"

"We live together—I see far too much of him as it is. That's why he hunts me down every morning at school, I keep forgetting things, and Mum has to bully him out the door to get him in school on time so she just packs whatever I forgot into his bag."

"You're his *stepsister*," Anton breathed feebly, and a hot rush of blood flooded his face. "But he's so huggy with you—"

"Jude's a leech, he hugs anybody he likes. He'd hug Walsh if

Walsh wouldn't break his arm. He hugs Larimer, too—and you, he likes you…"

The heat got worse, and Emma ducked her head to peer at Anton's face, her brown eyes suddenly wide.

"Oh," she whispered. "Do you like Jude?"

"I—"

"I mean, like…d'you fancy him?"

Anton groaned. "Don't tell him."

"Okay," Emma said immediately, and suddenly put her arm around Anton in a gesture very similar to Jude's, albeit less rough and clumsy. "I mean, he wouldn't be a dick about it if he found out, though, you know that? Jude's lovely about that sort of thing. He didn't bat an eyelash when I started going out with a girl. Larimer even got together for a bit with Jude's ex and he didn't really mind. He won't be a dick about it."

"But he's…he is straight?"

Emma bit her lip. "Well…he's only ever had girlfriends, and he's never said anything to me about fancying boys…and I'm sure Larimer and Walsh would have loudly ripped the piss out of him if they knew he did, so…I think so. I'm really sorry. But you never know!"

"Oh come on, Emma, I think he'd know by now."

"He might not," Emma insisted. "I didn't know until last year I could like girls. And some people are, like, forty before they figure it out. Hey, d'you want me to ask him? Not about *you*, obviously, but just, you know, about liking guys in general? He's really chilled about sex stuff, Jude is, so he might just not have told anyone if it never bothered him."

Anton squeezed her wrist. "No, don't. I don't—I mean, yes, I do like him, but I'm not really looking for a relationship right now." Especially not in a new school where nobody had guessed he was transgender. No way was he looking to risk that. Even if Jude wasn't a prick about it, all it would take was one careless comment, and *boom*, Anton would be outed.

"Alright, then," Emma said quietly, then squeezed her arm in a tight hug. "Our secret, if you want. But I *promise*, Anton, Jude's not going to give you any hassle for it. And I'll punch anybody who does, okay?"

Anton cracked a smile, then they both sniggered when the game was decided, in very unsportsmanlike fashion, by a muddy fight in the centre of the makeshift pitches between the two captains.

"Come on," she said, "let's go kidnap him and the other two idiots and go get snacks or something."

As they clambered out of the bag nest, and Anton found Jude's for him, Emma caught his arm and leaned in close.

"Are you gay, then?"

Anton paused.

"I won't tell anyone!"

And he believed her. Something about the open look on her face, or maybe the way Larimer and Jude had twigged and apparently not told the whole class either...

"Maybe."

"So...look, there's this huge argument amongst the girls, and me and Isabel argue about it all the time, but—d'you reckon Will Thorne's fit or not?"

Anton stared at her, bemused by the sudden girly gossip that he'd always been left out of in his old school for being too boyish, for being too much of a freak, for not being capable of understanding or appreciating just because he cut his hair short and wore boys' clothes on non-uniform days.

Then he thought of Will Thorne's pasty face, and screwed up his nose. Emma started to giggle, tucking her arm through his, and when Jude crashed into both of them, muddy and yelling a war-cry, Anton felt...

Fine.

For the first Sunday morning in years, he felt just fine.

Chapter 6

"OI! WILLIAMS!"

The shout—was horrible. It was loud and demanding, a boy's voice, and on pure instinct, every muscle in Anton's upper body tensed up. His heart doubled its efforts, and for a blind, awful moment, he was right back at his old school—the freak, the dyke, the tranny cow who never shaved her legs—

"Wait up!"

His lungs unlocked, and the rush of cold air was dizzying. He wasn't there. They weren't here. It was just—

"S'up, new kid?"

Jude. Jude, flushed from the cold, a dark beanie jammed down over his ears, and grinning that wide, beautiful smile that knocked the air right back out of Anton's chest, for entirely different reasons.

"Um—"

"You alright?"

"Er—yeah, yeah, sorry, um—"

"Look like you've seen a ghost," Jude said, hitching his bag higher on his shoulder, then clapping a hand down on Anton's.

"You just, um, surprised me."

"Only 'cause you're deaf, I yelled like four times."

"At the top of your lungs."

"Well, whispering weren't gonna get your attention!"

Jude's mock-outrage and exaggeration was kind of funny, and Anton's panic died off as they headed inside, warmth sinking into his skin both from the corridor and from Jude's amiable attention. Even if he couldn't go anywhere with Jude, with hopelessly straight, perpetually friendly Jude, then at least he could have a friend. And in Anton's world, those were valuable things.

So he listened with half an ear to Jude's rambling about some TV show he'd watched the previous evening, as they stopped first at Jude's locker and then at Anton's, and let himself relax. Jude would be—could be, if Anton didn't fuck something up—a really good friend. He was so chilled all the time, it made Anton feel relaxed, too, and—

"The hell?"

There was a gift in his locker.

"What?" Jude said.

"What's that?"

It was wrapped in silver paper, a long, thin box. There was no card, and Anton felt vaguely suspicious as he picked it up and turned it over. No card, no label—and surely the class tradition of welcoming new students didn't extend to gift-wrapping presents and breaking into their lockers to hand them over?

"You got a gift? Cool—open it!"

It meant someone had a key to his locker, and Anton fidgeted uncomfortably, unsure what to do. The silver box wouldn't fit through the air vents. Someone had opened the locker to put it inside, and there was no damage. So—

"Why would someone put a present in my locker?" he asked uncomfortably, and Jude shrugged.

"I dunno. Stalker? Secret admirer?"

"Oh whatever," Anton said, but he felt his face flushing.

"You got a stalker!" Jude said in a gleeful, decided tone. "One week and you've got a stalker. Whatever you're taking, I want some of it."

Anton pulled a face, closing the locker door and falling into step with Jude on the way to their form room. He picked at the silver paper absently, finally slitting the end with the ragged edge of his thumbnail and peering inside.

"It's chocolate," he said, surprised.

"Nice."

"Why would someone leave me chocolate?"

"Trying to chat you up?"

"There's better ways than breaking into my locker," Anton complained, and Jude snorted.

"They all have the same keys."

"What?"

"The lockers. They've all got the same locks. Your key'll open my locker. They're not like secure or nothing."

Brilliant. Great—so no leaving his binder for PE in there with the rest of his kit, then, in case this…chocolate-leaving stalker person found it.

"Dunno what's bothering you," Jude said genially, shouldering open the classroom door. They were hit with a wave of noise, and Jude raised his voice. "Eat it and enjoy. Who wouldn't want free chocolate? Oi, Emma, you forgot your lunch. And where's my morning hug?"

"Piss off," Emma told him grumpily, head bent over a hefty tome.

"Watcha readin'?"

"I said piss off, Jude!"

Jude laughed and dutifully pissed off to talk to Walsh, and Anton slid gingerly into the seat next to Emma. She huffed at him, too, then scowled.

"He's driving me mad."

"Jude?"

"Mm. Constant Snapchats last night. I was trying to study, and he was sending me dick pics."

"They were not!" Jude yelled from across the room.

"They were as good as!"

"I thought you'd like a bit of Ann Summers!"

"Why don't you and your dumb friends go f—"

The form room door swung open, and Miss Taylor's eyebrows were at her hairline. "I wouldn't finish that word if I were you, Brown," she said acidly. "Walsh, off the table, please. Sit down everyone—*in* your chairs, if you can manage it. Stephens, gum belongs in the bin. I'm not stupid, I can see you chewing the cud."

The class settled for registration, the odd thing being thrown now and then. Anton had warily decided that he liked Miss Taylor, but in the same way he liked polar bears: at a distance, with reinforced glass between them and him. She was acidic, which was kind of entertaining when it wasn't being aimed at you, but Anton suspected she was a bit soft underneath.

"Walsh, if you so much as *think* about throwing that pen at Kalinowski, your next school report to your mother will involve the terms 'regret to inform you' and 'passed away.' Do you understand me?"

Way deep down.

"Yes, Miss."

"There's a first. Now—stop giggling, Jackson, it's not that funny—we're going to start discussing diversity strands in our PSHE lessons—don't roll your eyes, Walsh, it doesn't improve your looks—and I've decided to start with the LGBT."

Anton swallowed.

"Given the number of times I've heard this class use the word 'gay' to mean 'stupid', I think you need some rather serious re-education on the matter. So. LGBT. Tell me what it stands for."

Emma's hand predictably shot up; Anton sank a little lower in his seat, and tried to look thoroughly bored. He *wanted* to be bored. He wanted to be able to roll his eyes like Walsh and have none of this be about him in the slightest.

But the fact that everyone else looked bored was putting him on edge. Jude was trying to balance his pen on his upper lip. Larimer was staring out of the window. Walsh was trying to balance *his* pen on Larimer's *head*, and Anton felt hot and uncomfortable. None of them thought LGBT was worth bothering with, and they used gay to mean stupid, and probably said things like dyke and tranny as well, and—

"Why isn't straight in the acronym?" a blond boy in the front asked, and Emma huffed.

"Jesus, Justin, how stupid can you be?" she said tartly.

"Yeah, Justin, that's so bisexual," Jude chimed in idly.

"What the hell, Jude?" Emma fired off, visibly puffing up, and Jude stuck his tongue out at her, the pen falling off his face.

"What? Miss said I can't call him gay."

"I might be bisexual," Larimer said absently. For about half a second, silence fell, then Jude cracked a wide grin.

"Good," he said. "You need all the options you can get."

"Fuck off, you twat!"

"Larimer, detention," Miss Taylor said sharply. "Kalinowski, another word and you'll be joining him. How about instead of calling each other stupid for asking questions, you all shut up and have them answered? Because I can guarantee with you lot that Henderson isn't the only one wondering."

The room subsided again, and Anton felt Emma nudge his elbow. When he shifted, she jammed a note under it. *U OK?* He nodded, and she offered him a thin smile.

"Who knows somebody who is LGBT?"

About a dozen hands went up, including Emma's, and Walsh threw out the comment that, "According to Larimer, all of us," before he got clipped round the ear by the girl next to him.

"I'm just saying," Larimer said in a mild voice, "that that substitute teacher we had last term for physics was kinda fit."

There was another silence, then Jude said, "Mate, I'm all about the rainbow and all that nice stuff, but fancying Mr. Reynolds doesn't make you bisexual, it makes you sick."

The class dissolved into laughter. Miss Taylor threw out another detention for Jude, and intervened before Larimer could chuck a book at him—and yet Anton felt...

Kind of calmed.

There was a difference between laughing at someone and *laughing* at someone, you know? And although the class were sniggering, Larimer's bland declaration wasn't...they weren't jeering at him or anything. And Jude just casually saying he was all about the rainbow 'and all that nice stuff'…

"See?" Emma whispered in his ear under all the chaos. "They piss about, but they don't *mean* it. They're just really careless. They won't mind if they find out you're gay."

Anton nodded, thinking of the casual way Jude and Larimer had agreed to keep quiet when he'd let slip about not liking girls, but—

Well. Being trans wasn't like being gay. He knew that well enough. When the girls at his old school had thought he was a dyke, that was bad enough. But when they found out what he *really* was…

That had been so, so much worse.

WALKING HOME WITH Jude and Larimer was becoming a nice routine, as was the way Jude slung his arm over Anton's shoulders as they reached their turning and said, "Game in the back garden, nancies?"

"Naff off, Kalinowski, I'd cream you if you took me on," Larimer scoffed, and tripped on the lip of a manhole cover.

"Sure you would," Jude sniggered.

"Can't anyway," Larimer said, righting himself. "Babysitting."

"Which ones?"

"Sisters," Larimer said.

"Unlucky! Go on then, fuck off," Jude said genially, then leaned more heavily on the arm still around Anton's shoulders. "What about you?"

"Um—"

"Kick-about in front of our goal again? Seeing as how you keep refusing to come to club and all…"

"I'll have to get changed again," Anton said. "And I have to start catching up on the English work, and—"

"Crib off Emma, that's what I do. C'mon, come and break my stepmum's plant pots with me," Jude said, and made a high whining noise. "*Pleeease?*"

Anton laughed, feeling a little flustered when Jude wheedled like that, but kind of…secretly, weirdly flattered by the attention. By the *focus*. By Jude just…actually wanting him to come over, instead of being polite or something.

"Fine," he said. "But I'm blaming you if I fail English."

"You already speak English, who needs more English?" Jude said flippantly, then his arm fell away. "Er, actually, depending how you feel about me asking this, you may not want to come over after all."

Anton's stomach clenched. Jude's voice had dropped, his words suddenly hesitant and slow, and something shifted uneasily in Anton's chest. Ask what? Had Jude—was Jude suspicious of him? It wasn't like Anton had *deliberately* come out at his old school, but—but Jude *couldn't* have guessed, right? Anton had been careful, and Emma had said Jude was dense, and—

"D'you, um…want to maybe…go…see a film or…something with me sometime?"

Anton's brain shifted without a clutch, and stalled. His jaw sagged, and he could feel himself gaping. Jude, by contrast, clenched his mouth shut, and went from pale-and-freckly to a deep red that rivalled his hair in, like, two seconds flat.

"You…" Anton tried, then had to cough and restart. "Er…are you…asking me out?"

"Er, which answer doesn't get me a smack in the mouth?"

"Um…any answer?"

"Yeah," Jude admitted.

"But…you're not—I mean, I didn't think you were gay." Emma had said he wasn't, she'd out-and-out said it! And Anton had—okay, not *liked* it, because Jude was really fit, and that *smile*, and—

His brain got into gear.

"Um, okay."

"Okay?"

Anton nodded. "Okay, let's see a film. Or something."

"Yeah?"

If Anton were brave enough, he'd have said, "Excuse me, have you seen your face? Yes. I want ownership of that face before someone else wises up and gets dibs on it." But he wasn't, so he just sort of…nodded, and felt himself going a bit pink, too.

"Um, cool," Jude said, then grimaced, rubbing the back of his neck. "Sorry. I've not really...asked a guy out before. And I'm not too good at asking girls out either, so..."

"I just...I didn't...think you were into guys."

"Neither did I," Jude said, then shrugged. "Then...you told Tayles that you didn't want to introduce yourself, and *bam*. I know what having a crush feels like."

Anton felt his face heating up, but confronted with Jude's sudden spell of awkwardness, felt spurred on to say, "I think I crushed on you from that first lunch."

"Your taste in guys is shit, then," Jude said, and grinned. "So, um...okay, how about I go...sort something—Saturday? Are you free Saturday?"

"Yeah."

"Okay. I'll sort something out for Saturday. Um..."

"G'wan then." Anton could feel his stomach starting to rise and bump against his heart. He wanted to—to grin, or hug Jude, or kiss him—could he kiss Jude yet, before any date at all, could he—? "Don't...just, I mean...I'm not really ready to be out at school yet."

"Okay."

"But, um, you can tell Emma. If you want."

"Emma?"

"Yeah...she knows I'm..." Gay? But he wasn't gay, and it dampened Anton's giddy enthusiasm for a moment. "I like guys," he finished lamely.

"How?"

"She caught me staring at you," he confessed, and Jude pulled a face.

"*What?* Lame, she's my stepsister, she's meant to be on *my* side, not yours."

"Yeah, well, that's why you can tell her. 'Cause she keeps secrets. But nobody else. Not yet."

"Okay," Jude said, then that grin flashed into being again. "So, um...see you tomorrow? I'll text you some plans or something."

"Okay."

"Okay!"

Anton wanted to laugh at how utterly, painfully awkward it

was, and the way Jude loped away backwards and nearly walked into a woman with a buggy, and—and—

He couldn't laugh. Because he just wanted to explode, or scream, or just *die,* right there, die as happy as he was ever going to get, because...because...

Jude Kalinowski had asked him on a date.

Someone—*anyone*—had asked him on a date, that was a big enough deal. But it wasn't anyone. It was *Jude.* Friendly, funny, fuckable Jude.

Yeah, Anton was pretty sure he was going to die. And it would be totally worth it.

Chapter 7

JUDE SAID NOTHING about a date on Tuesday. Or Wednesday, or Thursday—he just carried on being *Jude*, and on the one hand Anton appreciated it, appreciated that nobody else seemed to know, and on the other...

On the other, maybe Jude was thinking twice, thinking it was a bad idea after all, had changed his mind—or worse, had been joking, pulling some idiotic prank, or—

He wasn't, though, seeing as how he landed against the locker beside Anton's with a heavy bang on Friday afternoon, and grinned. At close range, the smile was kind of stupid gorgeous, and Anton had to swallow back the urge to blurt out something dumb. "Um, what?" he managed instead, and Jude laughed.

"Friendly. Walking home?"

"In a minute, yeah."

"I got rid of Larimer."

Anton paused, tightening his grip on his locker door. "Oh."

"So thought we could sort out tomorrow."

"Tomorrow."

"You know, going out?"

Anton bit his lip. "You, um…"

"Unless—" and the smile dimmed a fraction, "—you don't want to anymore?"

"No!" Anton blurted out, clamping a hand around Jude's bicep without thinking about it. "No, I—" He went red and removed the hand again. "Sorry, I just…I was kind of half-convinced you'd changed your mind or something."

"Nope," Jude said breezily. He was leaning back against the neighbouring locker, arms folded over his chest, and that inane beam started to creep back into place. "So I checked out the listings at The Vue, there's some pretty good shit up for once."

"Um, yeah, yeah, that sounds, um—"

Jude laughed, and Anton rolled his eyes.

"Shut up," he groused. "I'm…still trying to believe it."

"Well, hurry up, I don't want to have to persuade you into the cinema tomorrow," Jude said cheerfully. Anton closed his locker, and Jude peeled himself off the metal to fall into step with him. "There's a café thing nearby that's okay, too, Emma recommends it—"

"You told Emma?"

"That we're going to see a film, yeah. Not that it's a date."

Anton started chewing on the edge of his thumbnail as they passed out of the corridor and into the cold air. It was threatening to rain, the sky dark and heavy. "You can tell Emma, if you want," he repeated.

Jude simply shrugged. "Secret for a bit doesn't bother me," he said. "How secret is secret, anyway?"

"Um, secret?"

"Like, can I hold your hand?"

"What, right now?"

"Yeah."

Anton blinked, and actually found himself glancing down at his hand like it would have to grant its own permission. They were near school, but…but it was quite late, and everyone cleared off super fast on Fridays, and none of the other boys were around. The street was quite quiet, really.

"Um," he said, and flexed his fingers. "Okay."

Jude's hand closed like a trap, and it was like an electric shock went up Anton's arm.

Which was stupid, actually, because it was January, totally freezing, and they were both wearing gloves. But it was like being electrocuted all the same. Jude's grip was firm, and his fingers slotted between Anton's like they were supposed to be there and they'd held hands a million times before. And then he just kept *talking*, saying how they could either go and see a genuinely good film, or a crap one so they could ignore it and just neck all the way through, and how was Jude able to walk and talk at the same time when Anton's brain was just melting into a puddle of goo between his ears just because he was holding hands with a crush?

But that was it, really, wasn't it? Because Anton was weird, Anton was a freak, and nobody had ever even liked him before, never mind wanted to hold his hand and walk down the street doing so. Nobody had ever wanted to be anything to do with Anton before, until Jude turned up with his freckle collection and his big, stupid, *genuine* smile.

Something twisted up, hot and powerful, in the middle of Anton's chest and—just for a minute, because he wasn't stupid and he'd only known Jude a few weeks after all—he out-and-out loved Jude. Just for a split second, but it was there. By not being the freak he'd been at his old school, by being able to check Natasha at the door and just be Anton and nobody else, he'd caught someone's attention in a good way, for once. Just by being able to do that one thing. And Jude was so…so *Jude,* so amiable and easy-going, that he wasn't even put off by Anton's weird little sceptical quirks. He even seemed to *like* them.

The hot thing bubbled over, leaking out of Anton's heart and into his blood and stomach. He felt twitchy, but in a weirdly positive way, like he had way too much energy and nothing to do with it. Experimentally, he tightened his grip on Jude's hand as they turned the corner, and when Jude simply kept talking and squeezed back, the energy bounced out. It had to go somewhere, and Anton had to say something, so—

He stopped against the high hedge of a neighbour's house,

tugged Jude by the caught hand, and kissed him.

Just…leaned right up, and kissed him.

For a split second, Jude didn't move—and then let go of Anton's hand and cupped his face, almost crowding into him, Jude's mouth opening up and just stealing Anton's breath like Jude was supposed to have it all along. He tasted of spearmint and oranges, and the aftershave smell he had in the mornings had worn off in favour of something lighter and fresher, like mown grass and citrus smudged and blurred into one scent. Anton wound his fingers into Jude's sleeves, crushing the coat fabric noisily between his knuckles, and tried to do that thing called breathing, tried to peel himself away from just drowning in Jude, just totally sinking into him, and…

When Jude finally did break away, Anton didn't want to let go. They were all tangled up, his hands in Jude's coat, and Jude's fingers in his hair. Jude beamed, his forehead knocking lightly against Anton's, and his eyes were closed. "S'cold," he said.

"Yeah," Anton breathed. A cloud of vapour rose between them, and he pressed his mouth to the corner of Jude's. "I should probably go." Jude made a high whining noise, and Anton laughed shakily. "I should. Mum'll be wondering soon." Jude whined again. "I *should.*"

"I don't see you pulling away."

Anton clenched his fingers, then slid one to the exposed nape of Jude's neck and kissed him again. That citrus smell-taste-hybrid was definitely oranges, but he'd not had any as far as Anton knew, unless he'd been eating them in his German class while Anton had French? Was it his shampoo or something?

"Oranges," he whispered, and Jude chuckled, deep and low.

"Emma attacked me this morning with some body spray thing."

"It's nice."

"It's for girls." Anton's stomach tightened a little unpleasantly, but the contact—and Jude's quiet, content murmuring—was too nice to get upset.

"It's nice," he repeated instead, and Jude's smile nudged his cheek—then disappeared. Anton sighed as Jude pulled away properly, and stuck his hands in his coat pockets to avoid the urge to reach for Jude all over again. "See you tomorrow," he said firmly, and Jude laughed.

"Yeah. Tomorrow. If we even make it to The Vue."

Anton watched him amble away, tracing his own lips with the tips of his fingers, and thought he'd never wanted to go to a cinema more in his life.

"FUCK," JUDE SAID.

It had been a bit grim overhead when they'd met at the end of Anton's drive at two, and Jude had filched extra cash off his dad—apparently as a reward for his new date not being with someone called Natalie, whatever story was behind that—and suggested they go to one of the big cinemas in central London and then do the cheesy tourist thing or something after.

Only it was totally chucking it down in central London. As evidenced by the water running down the steps into Leicester Square station.

"We'll drown," Anton said, but he had no particular inclination to move. Jude's arm was slung over his shoulders, and Anton had hold of the wrist—just in case Jude touched his chest and felt something, you know?—which dragged it down heavily. It was kind of like a sideways hug. And all of Jude's arm-over-shoulder flops were a bit too close for just friends, but this was *definitely* too close. And Anton had no intention of disturbing it.

"I'm shit at swimming."

"Really?"

"Well, I probably am in jeans and boots and a full coat, yeah."

"Good point," Anton mused, then rolled his head back on Jude's arm. "We could just not go."

"Two hours of groping in the dark, come on…"

Anton twisted under Jude's arm and kissed his lower lip, tugging it out lightly between his teeth. Jude followed him, and then Anton was between him and the wall, tucked into the corner, as close as 'out of the way' as possible given their proximity to the exit. Jude was heavy and hard—well, not *that* kind of hard…probably—and it was kind of smothering but way nice at the same time. Anton could just…wrap his arms around Jude's neck and taste, just relax into it and savour it and let Jude worry about the passers-by.

And Jude, Anton found, kissed the way he kept pursuing about football club: with intent. It was open and gentle, but it was sharply focused, too, like he was trying to map Anton out, like he was committing Anton to memory, like—

Jude's thigh suddenly slid between Anton's knees, and the hand that had been resting on his waist started to drop. Anton was suddenly pinned between a weird, primal urge to push forward against that leg, and the urge to shove Jude away. What if he felt—what if he—?

He twitched as Jude's hand reached his outer thigh, just where it met his hip. When Jude's thumb ghosted inwards, towards the middle button hidden in the denim, as if trying to feel…*something*, Anton seized Jude's wrist to drag it abruptly north again to his waist. For a split second, Anton broke the kiss, heart in his throat, and waited for—something. Some kind of response.

All he got was Jude's fingers curling into the fabric of his coat, and another kiss nipped against the corner of his mouth. Anton exhaled shakily, and nudged his nose against Jude's, that hot coil from the previous afternoon beginning to boil over again in the centre of his chest.

"We're in a tube station," he breathed, a half-excuse and a half-challenge. Jude's smile twisted against his cheek.

"How to make several hundred shoppers jealous at once," he quipped, and pressed a little further into Anton. Anton squeezed his legs lightly around Jude's thigh, and got a muted grumble for it. "You can't bitch we're in public and then grind on me, that's rude."

"Can do whatever I want," Anton retorted breathlessly, then pushed Jude away and smiled. "Okay, we should, um…cinema. You know. Groping in the dark. A bit."

Jude laughed and pulled away properly, dragging Anton towards the flooded stairs by the hand. "If you let me," he teased as they sloshed up them, and Anton squeezed his fingers as the cold air rushed over them, and the fetid stink of the tube station let go.

"No hand job in the back row, then?"

"You're supposed to be *charming* on a first date."

"Trust me, my skills in bed would charm you," Jude said, grinning widely, and Anton huffed.

"I'm not that easy."

"Must be why you're classy, not like the rest of us," Jude retorted, then tugged Anton in to throw an arm over his shoulders again. "I'll get the tickets, you get the snacks. Deal?"

Anton hunched his shoulders to use Jude's arm as a scarf against the rain. "Deal," he said.

"And let's go on the back row, seeing as how you complain about public tube stations."

Anton squeezed Jude's wrist. "I'm not shagging in a cinema."

"I said groping, not shagging. Slag."

"You're the one *doing* the groping."

"You weren't complaining—mostly."

"I wasn't *complaining*, exactly…" In fact, had Anton been cisgender, he'd have probably towed Jude into the toilets or something. It had felt amazing; *Jude* felt amazing, even over the coat, and part of Anton unashamedly wanted to get his hands into Jude's clothes and actually touch him for real.

And the other part of him died of fright at the very idea, because of course if he did it, Jude would want to do it, too. And when he did…

Anton kept quiet all the way into the cinema, up the stairs, and into the right screen, armed with popcorn and an absurdly large bucket of Diet Pepsi to split. It was only when the advert reel started that Jude leaned over, and touched Anton's ear with his lips.

"We don't have to get handsy if you don't want."

Anton bit his lip. "I do a bit," he whispered. "Just, you know. A *bit*. Not…proper intense yet."

"S'fine," Jude said. "You did it earlier—just push me if I'm getting a bit too full on, I won't get pissy."

He draped an arm around the back of Anton's seat, and Anton settled into it, letting Jude idly play with his hair and listening to him mock the overly-loud adverts. By the time the film actually started, the hand had dropped to Anton's waist and that wayward thumb was tucked safely into his belt. The only thing Jude would be able to feel from there, Anton figured, was his hipbone and the waistband of his boxers, neither of which were giveaways. And anyway, Jude's hand was very warm—nearly hot—and tempting Anton to…well, grope back a bit.

When the first big inspirational speech started up—the boring bit of any film, in Anton's opinion—he gave in, and dropped a hand to squeeze Jude's thigh. He got kissed for it, missed half the speech, and lost the thread of the film entirely after that point.

And Anton didn't care. His hand remained tucked between Jude's legs, dangerously high, and yet Jude's thumb, still tucked into his belt, never so much as twitched.

Chapter 8

"OKAY, I'LL BITE," Mum said, sliding into the seat opposite Anton at the kitchen island. "What's up?"

"Huh? Nothing."

"It's Sunday morning, and you're cheerful."

"I'm allowed to be happy," Anton groused, still texting furiously.

"Except on Sunday mornings, when it's nothing but your miserable face because you have to put up with your dad for a few hours," Mum said. She squinted at him. "Who are you texting?"

"Jude."

"And what does Jude say?"

Want to come over? larimer n walsh both skipping out like losers so i cba to go to footie. come entertain me ;) xxx

"Nothing," Anton said instead.

Mum huffed. "Fine," she said. "Keep your secrets. Now can I go and run a long bath and pretend I'm still nineteen and haven't even *met* your father yet, or are you skipping out on his visit again?"

Anton flicked his gaze up to her guiltily, and a sad smile washed over Mum's face.

"Don't give me that look," she said softly, and ruffled his hair.

"You're the only good thing I ever got out of your father, and you more than make up for it."

"*Mum,*" Anton whined, because it was obligatory really, and he couldn't let her get away with that kind of a comment or she'd start doing it all over the place.

"Give over," she said, and shook her head. "So, where are you off to?"

"Jude's."

"Fair enough," Mum said, and rolled her eyes. "I can't wait until you're sixteen, you know. Then I can have a long bath whenever on a Sunday I bloody well feel like it."

"Me, too," Anton mumbled, still texting. Jude was getting up, and kept sending him Snapchats. Not totally clothed ones either, and Anton was sort of hoping for a dick pic, but also hoping *not* for a dick pic in front of his mum. "Then I can tell Dad to fu— erm, sod off, and he can't do anything about it anymore."

"Only until the summer, eh?"

"Yeah. Then I can just cut him out and forget about him."

"Good," Mum said earnestly, and Anton glanced up at her from the phone again. "Go on, get yourself gone. You only get upset when you and your dad argue."

"He makes me feel like a *freak,*" Anton confessed, and Mum rolled her eyes.

"Well, you're not. You're my son, and obviously you managed to find the few good genes your father actually has," she said loftily, then smirked. It was the wicked one, the one she used to pull when they were mocking Granddad's grumblings about 'the yoof of today.' "At least you didn't take after his old witch of a mother!"

"*Mum!*"

"Oh, give over, she's as bad as he is," Mum said, then started gathering the breakfast plates. "Go on, go out, and…do whatever it is you and your new friends do."

"You make me sound like I'm ten," Anton complained, but ducked out of the kitchen semi-gratefully anyway. He did feel a bit guilty about ditching and leaving Mum to handle Dad in one of his tempers, but it was just so shitty and exhausting. Even Ellen said his dad was a bad thing, and Ellen liked to play devil's advocate with just about everyone.

He took his football kit in case the back garden was up for a game instead of the park, throwing a sports bag over his shoulder, and rummaged through pockets of discarded jeans until he found a screwed up five pound note. He made his way out as noisily as possible to let Mum know he'd gone, and wandered around the corner onto Purcell Avenue.

And…paused on the drive. Dr. Kalinowski's car was gleaming in the wintry sun, suspiciously shiny, and there was a pink bike propped up against the door that Anton assumed belonged to Emma. Suddenly, it was a bit intimidating. He'd not really come round of his own accord before—Jude had always brought him—and the prospect of someone else answering the door was a bit…

So he perched on the wall and texted Jude. *Outside.*

U what?

I'm outside.

We have a doorbell! RING IT.

Come let me in!

…

Did you just text ellipses?

Did i text what now?

Anton gave up, and waited. It was cold, but not quite as bitter as it had been recently, and his coat was long enough to protect his jeans from the wall anyway. He didn't have to wait long, either—after maybe another five minutes, he heard the rattle of keys in the door. He slid off the wall, but wasn't quite prepared for—

"You *do* know how doorbells work, right?"

"Um."

"Get in here, it's cold," Jude whined.

"Well," Anton tried. "You…*are* in…um…"

"A towel?" Jude offered, and rolled his eyes. "Doorbells, towels—you fall out of bed this morning?"

Anton shut the door behind him, and glanced down the hall. Empty. So he dared, quickly stepping in and kissing Jude quickly, like a secret. And for once, it felt like a *nice* secret.

"It's just you, me and Dad," Jude said, "and Dad's—"

Something crashed upstairs, and a deep voice shouted, "Jesus fucking Christ! Fuck!"

"—trying to put IKEA furniture together," Jude finished.

"What's he trying to build, a space station?"

"A crib."

"A crib?"

"Yeah, Emma's mum is pregnant. Which is disgusting."

"Why?" Anton asked, toeing off his shoes and hesitating before hooking his coat over one he recognised on the hooks as being Emma's Monday jacket.

"It's proof my dad had sex."

"*You're* proof your dad had sex."

"Er, no. I was left on the doorstep in a box, thank you very much."

Anton trailed behind him on the stairs, because the towel was kind of short and there was a drop of water on the inside of Jude's knee that Anton wanted to touch. He restrained himself, though, and lingered on the landing when Jude disappeared into his bedroom.

"You can come in, you know!" Jude called.

"Not until you put clothes on!"

"Prude!"

"Parader!"

"I'm a what?"

"You're parading! You're naked under that towel."

"You're naked under your clothes," Jude retorted, and reappeared in the doorway wearing a long pair of dark boxers and a white T-shirt. His hair looked like he'd caught fire as he rubbed it roughly dry. "This good enough for you?"

"Close enough," Anton said, deigning to enter the room. He braced himself when Jude closed the door…but then nothing happened. Jude simply wandered back to his wardrobe and started rummaging for jeans, leaving Anton to poke around.

There was…surprisingly little to poke. The room was much smaller than Anton had imagined from the size of the bits of the house he'd already seen. It was smaller than his own bedroom. It was more like the spare room at Granddad's, and Granddad lived in a council flat in Haringey.

But it was actually cosy. The carpet was dark blue and really thick and fluffy through Anton's socks. The curtains were black, with purple galaxies and bright white stars. A Spurs scarf was hanging in the window, bright against the wintry sunlight outside, and the bedsheets were—Anton thought, seeing as how Jude hadn't made the bed again after getting up—designed to look like a grass football pitch. There were two bedside tables, one at the foot of the bed and one at the side, and a bookshelf crushed into the space between bed and door. A desk had been put in front of the bookshelf, with the books spilling over onto it, and a laptop was cycling slowly through a YouTube playlist of music videos. There were little piles of clothes and books and bags all over the floor, and what was either a pile of paper for recycling or some kind of art project taking up the carpet in front of the wardrobe, but…it was nice.

The room was cluttered, but Anton kind of liked it.

"It's nice," he said, perching on the end of the bed and unashamedly staring as Jude wriggled into a pair of jeans.

"What?"

"Your room."

"Oh," Jude said. "Thanks? Sorry, I've only been up, like…half an hour. Hug?"

Anton blinked, then pushed himself up off the bed and walked into the arms-out, fingers-wriggling pose that Jude struck. The hug was tight and warm, and could have been merely friendly or familial if not for the way Jude burrowed his face into Anton's neck and squeezed for just a little too long. Anton's stomach burned warm, the pleasant sensation of being wanted seeping into his blood.

"I'll say hello proper after I've had breakfast and done my teeth," Jude mumbled against his skin, then kissed Anton's ear anyway and pulled away. "Want anything? I try and drink all of Emma's pineapple juice every morning, drives her nuts. Help me."

Anton laughed, called him an idiot, and followed. He didn't help with the whole Emma-enragement, but he trailed Jude around for his morning routine, listened to Jude slowly wake up and start talking nineteen-to-the-dozen like always, and felt…wanted. In a very simple, nice sort of way. Jude liked having him around. Jude carried on with his normal stuff in Anton's presence, he didn't change it, but he seemed to enjoy the company. They could have been just friends, aside from that first hug, and Anton had missed simply having friends as much as he'd felt lonely for never having the prospect of a boyfriend.

Still, he wasn't about to argue when the first thing Jude did after brushing his teeth was turn from the sink and kiss him.

"Mm, spearmint, yummy," Anton said mockingly, and Jude pulled a face as they wandered back to his room and flopped out on the bed together.

"Better than morning breath and last night's fish and chips, trust me," he said. "Hey, d'you wanna stay for lunch? Emma's mum does a roast when she gets back from church and it's really good."

Anton paused. "She…she goes to church?"

Thankfully, Jude seemed to figure it out without Anton needing to make something up. "Yeah but she's not like one of those mad Christian types who hate queers or whatever. Emma went through a questioning thing and told us all she might be into girls over dinner and her mum was just like 'well, okay then.' She's alright."

"What about your dad?"

"Dad spends every day just grateful I don't take after Mum," Jude said cheerily. "He's not going to mind you. So, you want to stay?"

"Um, maybe. I kind of skipped out on Dad's visit so Mum might want me home for our own roast." He opened his mouth again to return the offer, then decided better of it. Dad kept calling him Natasha in front of Lily, and Sundays Lily was most likely to forget and revert to Tasha. And he didn't think he could explain *that* to Jude convincingly.

"So now I've got you into the lair…"

Anton was jolted out of his thoughts as Jude's voice took a flirtier tone, and laughed, shoving his shoulder. Jude sat up, still beaming from ear to ear, then settled with his back against the wall and windowsill, and patted his thigh. "What?"

"Legs!" Jude said, and wiggled his fingers. "I do a good foot massage."

Anton bit his lip. Yeah. And his feet would fit right into Jude's hand, easy. "Um, I don't really like having my feet touched," he tried.

Jude shrugged. "Okay, calf massage?"

Anton hesitated, then slid his legs across into Jude's lap. He flopped back against the pillows to do it, and found himself staring up at a poster of the Milky Way Jude had somehow stuck to the ceiling.

"Now I'm in the lair," Anton asked quietly, "what're you going to do with me?"

Jude's fingers dug right into Anton's left calf, and he groaned as a knot he hadn't realised was there popped. "Well," Jude said conversationally, "making you moan like that seems like a good shout."

Anton smiled at the poster, then propped his head on his hands to watch Jude. He seemed to be actually concentrating for once, frowning over Anton's knee, and the kneading sensation was...actually way nicer than Anton had been expecting. Maybe he really did give a mean foot massage.

"And after this," Jude said, "and when Dad's given up on the crib and gone to buy a ready-built one later, I could always try making you moan proper?"

Anton's stomach tightened, and his throat clenched. "Um," he said, and felt heat beginning to creep up his neck. "I, um—" He wanted to. He wasn't ashamed of that—he *wanted* to, he wanted to be able to just...just get his clothes off without thinking twice about it, he wanted to find out what Jude felt like, if Jude would like hickeys the way Anton fantasised about them, what it would be like to make out with Jude, have sex with Jude—

But he couldn't. He *couldn't*. If Jude found out, if Jude so much as touched him over his clothes...

"Or not."

Anton gritted his teeth. "I just—not yet. Not no, just...not yet. I'm not—"

"Ready," Jude finished, and squeezed Anton's knee. "Okay."

Anton fidgeted with his T-shirt. "I'm not experienced like you," he half-lied. It was true, but it wasn't the reason.

"Well, we're kind of in the same boat."

"How?"

"I've never had a boyfriend before," Jude said, and Anton felt suddenly sick. He dropped his gaze, picking at the dark fabric of his shirt. "I don't really know what I'm doing either. Or what I'm supposed to be now."

Anton unglued his throat. "What d'you mean, what you're supposed to be?" he croaked.

"Never fancied boys before," Jude said. "And, you know, still don't. Not like I'm eyeing up Walsh between classes or nothing. It's just you. And I don't know what that means, if that means—"

Anton had a sudden mad urge to say *it means I'm a girl!* but crushed it ruthlessly.

"—I'm bisexual, or just Anton-sexual, or what. I'm figuring it out as much as you are."

That niggling worry started to boil up again, churning anxiously in his stomach the more that Jude talked. He couldn't lie forever. He had to tell Jude, and sooner rather than later, but…how? How did you tell your new boyfriend that he wasn't as bisexual as maybe he thought he was? That you weren't what he thought you were, what he expected you to be…

What he wanted?

ON MONDAY MORNING, there was a gift in his locker again. It was nothing fancy—a book voucher, in a glittery blue envelope and no explanatory note—but Jude teased him anyway, saying it was probably Bee again, and Anton stuffed it into the bottom of his bag, too wound up to really take the joke. Great. He'd turned Jude bisexual, only Jude wasn't *properly* bisexual because Anton wasn't a *proper* boy, right, and now he was turning Bee lesbian only she didn't even know it. He felt sick. He should have known better than to think he could go out with Jude at all, should have just lied and said he wasn't interested.

So yeah, Anton wasn't above admitting he was in a bit of a mood on Monday morning. He didn't want to be there. He didn't want to work on this stupid labels project, with Emma or with anybody else, and he didn't want another lecture from Miss Taylor about how nobody should judge anybody else. Everyone judged. *Everyone.* And it was never going to stop, and he'd never be exactly who and what he wanted to be, and that was the end of it.

His mood wasn't helped by the general messing around. *He* was in a mood, but everyone else seemed to be buzzing—even Emma was joining in a little bit, swapping texts with Isabel across the room—and Miss Taylor was going from her usual acerbic-but-amused attitude to proper pissed. Walsh got kicked out halfway through the session, then Jude and Larimer got split up from their pair and Jude swapped with Emma. Which only meant Jude had to come and sit next to Anton, and Anton instantly felt torn between a thrill that he got to openly spend more time with Jude in the classroom, and a chill that he had to work with Jude on *this* project.

"Don't worry," Jude whispered once Miss Taylor had turned away to shout at one of the girls for putting on her makeup in the middle of the lecture, "I'm an easy project, I don't have any labels."

Anton felt faintly queasy. "Well, I guess I'll find out," he mumbled.

"Do you have a ton?"

"Er—"

"I don't have to do research, right?"

"You're the one presenting," Anton said weakly, and Jude sniggered.

"If you don't tell me, I'll just make something up," he said.

Anton opened his mouth to—to tell him that there *was* something, that they had to talk, that he needed to speak to Jude in private as soon as possible, that it was okay if Jude was weirded out but *please* could he not tell anyone, that—

And in the exact same instant, his courage failed.

"Make it up," he mumbled, his throat burning. "Sure."

Chapter 9

MUM WASN'T HOME when Anton let himself in, and the house smelled of spaghetti bolognese *à la* Aunt Kerry—with a load of red wine in the sauce, basically—so Anton threw his keys into the bowl, dumped his shoes on the mat, and followed his nose.

"Afternoon, honey!"

Aunt Kerry was Mum's younger sister—much younger. She was twenty-five, with the same sandy fair hair as Anton, and had a habit of singing and calling everybody 'honey' or 'sugarlump.' Despite Mum being *technically* older, Anton rather thought of Aunt Kerry being the old one. Twenty-five-year-olds, he was reasonably sure, weren't Rod Stewart fans. His *grandma* was a Rod Stewart fan, for Christ's sake.

Still, what Aunt Kerry lacked in a taste in music, she made up for in wine-soaked spaghetti bolognese, so Anton rummaged a can of Sprite out of the fridge and took up residence on one of the bar stools at the kitchen island.

"How was school?"

Anton shrugged, twisting the can around in his hands. He'd have to tell Jude. Soon. Really soon, because Jude was getting a bit handsy now, and had been saying he might be bisexual and had to figure that bit out, and…and how was Jude going to react when he found out he wasn't the least bit inclined towards boys after all? How was he going to respond if he'd been all ready to deal with having sex with another guy, and actually what he was going to get was—

"Anton!"

Anton jumped. "What?"

Aunt Kerry rolled her eyes, and turned the burner down on the hob. "Alright," she said, "what's up?"

"Nothing."

"I've asked you how your day went three times, honey. What's the matter?"

Anton bit his lip. "I…I have to…um…"

"Anton?"

Anton took a deep breath, and decided to spill it. "We're doing this project about labels and identity at school, and Jude's been paired up with me."

"Okay…"

"I mean, the *idea* of the project is that we present our partner back to the class with their labels."

"Well, that can't possibly go wrong," Aunt Kerry said dryly.

"And it's *Jude* now, which makes it worse—"

"Why is Jude worse?"

Anton paused, chewed on his lip, then exhaled heavily. Okay. Why not? Aunt Kerry would understand. "So, you know I went out on Saturday with Jude?"

"Your mum said something about the flicks, yes."

"The *flicks*? Really? You're not Nana!"

"Get to the point, Anton!"

"Well, I, um…I went with Jude."

"You said."

"No, I mean…*with* Jude. On a date, like."

"On a *date*?" Aunt Kerry squeaked, then suddenly cackled. "A date! On Saturday! Oh, honey, your mum is going to kill you! Why didn't you *say* anything? With Jude? Jude's that ginger one, isn't he? The one your mum liked when he came over, said you'd made a nice friend round the corner?"

Anton felt his face heating up. "Um, yes. That's Jude."

"So you went on a date, huh? How'd it go?"

Heat went supernova, and Anton buried his face in his hands. "Urgh, Aunt Kerry!"

"Tell me!"

"It went fine, okay!"

"Weren't you with him Sunday, too? Your dad was throwing his usual hissy fit that you'd skipped out—were you with this new *boyfriend?*"

"He's not—I mean—it's just—it was only Saturday," Anton blurted out, "so he's not, you know, it was one date and it went well, and okay we kissed on Sunday and stuff, but…but it's not—he's not my boyfriend yet. Not really." Except that he was, and Anton wanted him to be.

"And why not?"

"Because I have to tell him about…about Natasha."

Silence.

After a minute, Aunt Kerry turned the burner even lower, and pulled up a stool opposite Anton's. "Alright," she said quietly. "So he doesn't know?"

"No," Anton whispered.

"But you want to keep dating him?"

"Yes."

"And he—right now—seems like he wants to date you?"

"He asked me," Anton croaked. "He asked me first, and I thought he was straight, and he said maybe he's not then, and he said maybe he's bisexual but he doesn't really know anymore because of me, and I—he—we kissed a bit, and I have to tell him, but I can't."

"Of course you can," Aunt Kerry said softly. "You told your mum and dad before you even knew what it all really *meant,* honey. Of course you can tell this Jude now you understand."

"But I *can't,*" Anton insisted, and heard—to his horror—his voice crack in the middle of it. "How am I supposed to tell him that, that he's dating a girl when he thinks—"

"But you're not a girl, are you," Aunt Kerry interrupted, still in her coaxing voice. "All you're telling Jude is that you're not physically what he might expect. You don't have to go any more into detail than that if you don't want to."

Anton shook his head, swallowing against a vicious lump in his throat. "I really like Jude," he said hoarsely, "and if he—if he can't—what if he totally changes his mind about me once he finds out?"

"Then he will go the same way as your idiot father and be chopped out of your life," Aunt Kerry said firmly. "You don't need those kinds of people around, Anton. And if Jude does change his mind because you're transgender, and *especially* if he does it without giving you the time to explain yourself and the situation properly to him, then he's a waste of space and you're better off without."

"But he—"

"Does he like girls?"

"Yeah."

"But not boys, not until you?"

Anton shook his head.

"Then he doesn't have much to complain about, honey, as long as you're honest with him," Aunt Kerry said. "Until you medically transition, you won't have anything he's not seen before, sweetie. You're no different to any other new boyfriend, you know. He doesn't know what you like, or what you look like without your clothes on, and he'd have to learn those things about you as you went along anyway. If he's not mature enough to see that maybe it's a bit different, but it doesn't make a relationship a bad idea or something impossible, then he's a complete idiot."

"Oh come on, Auntie, nobody wants to date trans people," Anton mumbled.

"Now you're just being ridiculous."

"But they don't!"

"And how do you know? The media? The internet? Come off it, Anton, of course there's people who want to date trans people. Plenty of trans people are married, have kids, lead perfectly normal lives. Plenty of trans teenagers date. You included, apparently! And they're not dating other trans people, at least not all of them."

Anton cracked a very faint smile, and dug the heel of his palm against his left eye. "How am I supposed to tell him, though?" he whispered.

"Well, when do you want to do it?"

"I don't know. I said—it'll have to be soon, he's getting suspicious and I'm—you know, it's like I'm leading him on a bit, I want to do stuff but I can't, and—"

"Which is nothing even close to the definition of leading him on, honey…"

"—it's only a matter of time before he starts asking questions. So I have to do it soon. And before…you know. Before he manages to figure it out on his own or something."

That would be a disaster, Anton reckoned. He needed to tell Jude properly, like. Lay it out and talk about it, and…rational. All calm and stuff. Not Jude getting too handsy and feeling that something was missing. Or putting his hand up Anton's shirt and feeling his chest. Not like that. He'd freak out, and then Anton would freak out, and it would all go wrong, and any tiny, tiny chance that Jude would be okay with it would just be thrown out of the window. He'd think Anton had been lying to him or something.

"Mmm," Aunt Kerry hummed. "I think you need to tell him before he gets really edgy, honey. Or before he gets the wrong idea and you upset him—he'll want to think you do want to be with him, you know. And if you shy away, he'll form the wrong impression, and then he *will* have grounds to be upset with you when you let him in on it all. So I think the sooner the better, really."

Anton blew upwards into his hair. "Or I could dump him?"

Aunt Kerry chuckled. "Or not. You can't avoid relationships forever because this is hard."

"I *could*."

"No, honey, you couldn't. And you shouldn't. Yes, you will always have to have more awkward conversations with your partners than other people, but that's no reason to hide from the prospect. You don't have some kind of horrendous contagious disease, you know. You have the right to lead a normal life, and that includes relationships."

"What if it's not worth it?" Anton whispered.

And that right there was his overwhelming fear. That he would never find someone willing to look past it, and he'd get stuck in this constant cycle of telling people and getting dumped, telling people and getting dumped, and always hoping the next one would be different. And he was terrified that Jude was just the beginning of that cycle.

"Some relationships won't be," Aunt Kerry admitted quietly, "but most are worth the bad bits because you get so many good things out of them, too. Look at Maggie and your dad. She doesn't regret that relationship for a moment, because she got you. And no matter how much of an idiot your father turned out to be, your mum wouldn't have had you without him. Natasha *or* Anton."

Anton swallowed hard, and ground the heel of his hand against his eye. He'd told Ellen once that he'd lucked out and failed hard at the same time. His dad royally fucking *sucked,* but Mum and Aunt Kerry were like the jackpot.

"Hey," Aunt Kerry said softly. "Don't be so scared of this. Jude is just one boy. From what you've said, he's a very *nice* boy at that. Even if this is something he doesn't feel he can cope with, it doesn't sound like he's going to tell the world, or try driving you out of the school. One awkward conversation, and then you can get on with it and be happy."

"Or he might dump me."

"And if he's the type to do that, then he's the type you don't want to be dating anyway," she reiterated. "Why don't you invite him over tomorrow?"

"*Tomorrow?*"

"The sooner the better," she repeated. "Do it here, honey. That way your mum and I aren't far away if it goes a bit wrong, or if you need a bit of help explaining anything, and we can throw him out if he acts like an idiot. And it's also nice and private, nobody else will hear a thing. Invite him over after school tomorrow, sit him down in the living room or the kitchen, and tell him the whole story, eh?"

Anton bit his lip. "But Mum's got that job interview tomorrow."

"I'll be here."

"She'll cancel if she knows what I'm going to do."

"Then we won't tell her until it's over."

"She'll go mental."

"My idea, not yours," Aunt Kerry said cheerfully, waving a hand carelessly in the air. She ducked her head to peer at Anton's face, and smiled. "Do it tomorrow, honey. Get it all out of the way."

"*How?*" Anton implored.

"Sit him down, tell him you want him to know something before things get too serious, and he can ask all the questions he wants after you've finished talking, and tell him you're transgender."

"You make it sound easy," Anton complained. The urge to cry had worn off, but he felt jagged and raw. He vaguely wanted Molly and some bad TV.

"It is easy. Horrible, awkward and embarrassing, but the words are easy," Aunt Kerry said. "I can always run off some leaflets from your support forums if you want. And there's a support group your mum was really into when you first came out, for friends and family of transgender people. You could give them to Jude, in case he wants to talk to somebody impartial. And I'm sure Ellen would be willing to meet with him if you asked her to. You're not on your own."

"M'not sure Jude would be up for that," Anton mumbled.

"It's worth asking, though," Aunt Kerry said gently, and reached across the worktop to squeeze his shoulder. "Get it over with, honey. And it'll be okay."

"Promise?"

It was a childish question, one Anton was way too old to ask, and he wouldn't believe any answer she gave, but it slipped out around the cracked edges of his fear anyway, seeking comfort.

"Promise," she said.

Chapter 10

ANTON DECIDED THAT Aunt Kerry was right—he had to get it over with.

The problem with 'getting it over with', though, was that his body didn't agree with his brain, and every time he opened his mouth to tell Jude that they needed to talk about something privately, his guts would shrivel up into a tight ball of fear and pain, and he'd just close it again without saying a word. And it was awful, because everyone knew something was up—even Walsh was giving him funny looks—but Anton couldn't just force himself to *do* it. And if he couldn't even get up the courage to tell Jude they had to talk, how was he ever going to get up the courage to tell Jude…tell Jude…

Jude took it out of his hands before PE, though, cornering Anton the moment he walked out of the bathroom near Mrs. Salter's office. "What's up?" he said, and not the usual amiable greeting, but a flat, factual tone that sounded more like Anton's *mum* than Anton's boyfriend. Pitch aside.

"Um—"

"You're twitchy and quiet and kind of avoiding me," Jude said, and frowned. "I said I was sorry about yesterday."

"It's not about yesterday…"

"Then what'd I do?"

"You didn't do anything," Anton said earnestly. "It's—" *Tell him.* "It's just—" *Tell him.*

Jude's frown twisted a little in a way that Anton couldn't put his finger on. "Are you having second thoughts about going out with me?"

"What? No!" Sort of. "No, I—I just…"

Jude's mouth tightened, and Anton just blurted it out.

"You might not want to date *me* after."

"After what?"

"After—we need to talk."

"After…we talk?"

"Yeah," Anton said miserably, and folded his arms over his chest, hunching his shoulders. He felt vaguely sick. "I need to tell you something, and when I do, you probably won't want to date me anymore anyway."

"Oh-kay," Jude said slowly. The look on his face was heading back towards confused, rather than the awful upset expression that had punched Anton in the heart. "So…what, you have another boyfriend who's a total psycho and is gonna kill me?"

That surprised a bitter laugh out of Anton. Fuck, Jude just had no *idea*…"No," he mumbled.

"HIV?"

"What? No!"

"I'd take HIV over a psycho boyfriend, man, you're from South London. He's some gang member south of the river, right?"

"Yeah, sure, I'm dating a nutter from Lambeth," Anton said, a little too throatily for his liking. "I don't have another boyfriend."

"Girlfriend?"

"No."

"You're secretly a hardcore religious nut and we can't even make out properly until we're married?"

Closer, Anton thought sourly, for the practical side of things. But—"No."

"You're a Nickelback fan."

"Er, no…"

Jude shrugged. "Okay, well, those are the scariest, worst things I can think of. So I wouldn't bet on it."

"Yeah, well, I would." God, Anton's gender hadn't even crossed his mind. He was going to totally freak out. He was going to hit the roof, and tell everyone, and…

"Hey." Jude's voice dropped, and Anton felt his gaze almost pulled by that suddenly open, earnest face. "Give me a little credit, yeah? If you want to not go out with me anymore—"

"I *do*, it's just—"

"—then that's okay, but I'm not gonna lie, Anton, I really like you. Like, *really* like you, crush at first sight shit, yeah? You're really cool, you're fun, you're fit, your shirt rode up a bit in PE last week and I got this weird urge to lick you—if there's something you need to tell me, then just tell me, and let me decide if whatever it is is something I'm okay with or not, yeah? Don't decide for me."

Anton took a deep breath and nodded. "I'll try," he said. "But it's…fucking scary, and I wouldn't blame you if it's too much to deal with."

"Okay," Jude replied, still in that oh-so-reasonable tone that made Anton's heart hurt. "Hey, don't look so scared. I'm a pushover, you'll be able to talk me round to just about anything. Unless you're into murdering kittens, then I'm out."

Anton snorted and mustered up a weak smile. "We have cats, why would I be a kitten killer?"

"*Secretly*, obviously," Jude groused, and lifted his arms in that oddly childish gesture. "Want a hug?"

Anton glanced down the still-empty corridor, and swallowed. Then he decided to screw it, and stepped into it. Jude's grip was firm and warm, and smelled of a PE kit that had been buried in the bottom of a bag too long. It was perfect, and Anton clutched hard before letting go.

"Come over after school?" he blurted out, and Jude blinked. "I can't…I can't tell you here, I'll get upset. And if…if it goes wrong, you know…"

"You wanna be in your safe space."

Anton was taken back by the Ellen-esque phrase, and he jumped. "What—?"

Jude shrugged. "I'm not totally thick. It's not my thing to tell, but someone you and I both know used to have some pretty serious issues with panic attacks, okay?"

Anton shelved the information, and nodded. "Yeah. I wanna be…at home. And so Aunt Kerry can chuck you out if you go mental and try whaling on me or something."

"You won't need your aunt to save you, I can't fight to—"

Mrs. Salter's office door banged, and Anton jumped back, startled. He was thrown an acerbic look, and then her gaze narrowed sharply on Jude. "Kalinowski," she said, drawing out his surname like it was a dirty word. "It's bad enough you feel the need to pester your classmates on the field. If you could see to leaving them alone off the field as well, that would be wonderful."

"I wasn't pestering, I was—"

"Kalinowski, you are *always* pestering," she corrected sharply. "Gym, both of you."

She shooed them ahead of her to the gym, where the rest of the class were milling around aimlessly. Anton fell in with Emma, as Jude was promptly attacked by Walsh, and Mrs. Salter's derisive snort could be heard echoing off the ceiling.

"Seeing as how the health and safety executive has decided that making you play football in today's rain is unhealthy rather than amusing, *and* seeing as how this group has as much energy and diplomacy as a pack of rabid hyena pups, today we're going to split you in half and play dodgeball." She promptly had to raise her voice over the cheer. "You may as well get some fun and exercise out of it, but if we could refrain from breaking each other's' glasses, noses, and fingers, that would be wonderful. And I don't care who's stolen whose boyfriend this week, but I want no revenge played out in my lesson. Save it for some other teacher. And girls, I want you to participate properly this week. Throwing something at a man's face is an excellent way to get his attention *or* tell him he's got no chance, so I expect you to crack on."

Anton suddenly didn't like the look in Emma's eye.

"I want you to decide amongst yourselves how to split the class in half, and put the tennis net across to mark out the boundary line. Neale, Patterson, you two come with me to get the balls from the store cupboard. *Now,* Neale, if you don't mind."

Chatter broke out the minute that Mrs. Salter swept out of the gym. "Girls versus boys!" Isabel voted loudly, which led to a fair amount of jeering from both sides. On instinct, Anton felt a hot flush of anxiety, as though his brain had forgotten that nobody here knew.

"You try and kill me enough at home, you have to start here, too?" Jude complained at his stepsister, who merely sneered at him and offered to let him join the girls' team if he was going to be a pansy.

The general consensus seemed to be that letting the girls destroy—or poorly attempt to destroy, from the other side—the boys was a reasonably good idea.

"There's more girls anyway," Walsh said, grinning. "That evens it up."

"You're first to die," Emma promised, with a bit too much feeling.

"Fuck that."

Everything paused as Will Thorne—who rarely seemed to talk, Anton had noticed—suddenly spoke up.

"Fuck what?"

"Girls versus boys," Will said, jutting his chin out and staring directly at Jude. "I'm not being on the same team as Jude."

For a split second, the gym was completely silent. The atmosphere dropped. It seemed suddenly hotter and closer, and all eyes had turned on Will and Jude—the former looking angry, and the latter perplexed.

"You what?" Jude said.

The look on Will's pale face was awful, and horribly familiar: lip curled, teeth showing on one side, and *disgust* written into the lines it made. Anton knew that face. He'd seen it hundreds of times at his old school, and a chill settled over him before Will even said it.

"He's gone gay for that new kid."

Anton's world lurched as several heads turned his way. The chill dissolved. He felt heat creeping up his neck, and shifted uneasily, shoulders slowly rising as though he could defend himself from the stares. Emma's fingers were suddenly in the crook of his elbow, squeezing tightly.

"Yeah," Jude said, equally loudly, "so what's that got to do with my mad skills in throwing things at people, huh?"

Anton's chest felt tight in a way that was nothing to do with the binder. Jude's easy but aggressive admission had made more people stare at Anton, looking him up and down, staring, calculating, *wondering...*

"Don't really fancy a pouf behind me in dodgeball, thanks."

"Go fuck yourself, Thorney, 'cause no fucker else will," Jude returned dismissively. "Fancying Anton's normal. Fancying *you*, now that'd be sick."

"Fuck off, Kalinowski!"

"When's the last time you had a girlfriend anyway, Thorney?" Jude taunted. "Pretty obsessed with gay blokes for a straight guy, aren't you?"

Will clenched his fists. "So it's true then, you've turned for the new fa—"

"Finish that word, and I'll fucking kill you."

Jude's voice was cold and dangerous, his accent so thick that 'fucking' almost became 'farkin.' Will's lip twisted up further, and Anton shrank back. Emma's hand came up to the small of his back and she scoffed. "Don't be such a twat, Thorney."

"Stay out of this, you dyke bitch."

Jude flared. "What'd you fucking call my sister?"

"I called her a dyke bitch—you deaf as well as a bender!"

"Come over 'ere and fucking say it again and we'll get who gets a good fucking!"

"You threatening me?"

"No, I'm fucking promising!"

The noise was explosive. They were getting closer, too, Jude's stance straightening and squaring off, and Will beginning to shift from foot to foot as he advanced. Anton backed up further with Emma—but Walsh was closing in, that rat-like face tight and dark-eyed, his stance even more tense and aggressive than Jude's. Anton could almost smell the danger. A ring was forming around the boys, and—very slowly—Larimer started to clap.

"Fucking lamp him, Walshy," he said in that deep droning voice.

"Face it, *Polski*," Will sneered, his face inches from Jude's. Anton's heart was beating too hard in his throat. The room stilled. "You've gone fucking bent, ain't you?"

Jude moved like lightning. A shriek went up from a couple of the girls—but rather than punch Will, as Anton had expected, he grabbed Will's head in both hands and *kissed* him.

Kissed him.

Full on the mouth, one hundred percent smacker, *kissed* him. The girls shrieked again, and a couple of the boys jeered, and then Jude pushed Will away so hard that he was flung backwards on the gym floor, and Jude spat on his shoes.

"There," he said. "That get all the sexual tension out? Next time you fancy a macking, Thorney, you might want to try asking like a nice bloke, yeah? I don't give out freebies often, *sweetheart*."

Will spat on the floor, snarled—and launched.

Chaos.

The ring that had formed scattered. The girls shrieked, one of them bolting out of the door. Will's fist smashed into Jude's eye as Walsh uttered a noise not unlike a war-cry and bodily tackled Will. Between Will's fist and the force of Walsh hitting the pair of them, Jude was smashed to the floor, and his shoulder seized by Larimer, who bodily dragged him out of the scrum. Both Will and Walsh were roaring at each other, the fight on the floor nothing like the Sunday scuffles that Anton had seen Walsh in before. He was red-faced and bellowing, literally frothing at the mouth, and there was blood streaked all down Jude's face, his eyes looking in two different directions, and—

"*ENOUGH!*"

Mrs. Salter's scream was ear-piercing, better than any whistle, then she hauled Walsh off Will by the scruff of his neck.

"That! Is! Enough!" she bellowed in Walsh's ear. "Quiet! *Quiet*! All of you!"

Slowly, quiet fell. Two of the girls were crying. There was a great bloody flower smeared in the floor where Jude had hit it, and Will's nose was bleeding, too, broken in at least two places.

"What happened?" Mrs. Salter's voice was flat; there was no inflection on the question.

"That fu—"

"Quiet!" she barked. "Bee. Tell me what happened."

Bee went white under her hair, but swallowed and mumbled, "W-Will s-said that Jude is d-dating Anton, and c-called Jude a b-bender, and then he called Emma a d-dyke, so J-Jude hit him and t-then Walsh hit W-Will." Once the stammering explanation was done, she ducked her head, and hid firmly behind her hair again.

Mrs. Salter exhaled gustily through her nose.

"Thorne. Walsh. Kalinowski. *All* of you will stay behind at the end, and we will be going to see the headmaster. Thorne, that kind of language is disgusting and I won't have you airing your mindless prejudices in my class in such a vile manner. Kalinowski, Walsh—I won't have anyone using violence to settle matters either. Even a slanging match I don't disagree with, but resorting to physical violence to get your point across is beneath both of you."

"Yes, Miss," Jude croaked, then pulled a face. "Er, Miss. I think I need to see the nurse."

"How hard did he hit y—"

Jude's answer, before she'd even finished the question, was to lean forward and throw up all over Larimer's trainers.

"Right," Mrs. Salter said, and pursed her lips. "Neale. Go and fetch the nurse, please. And Larimer? Get him sat down before your shoes take another round."

Chapter 11

JUDE WASN'T WAITING outside when Anton left to go to school the next morning.

The nurse had sent him to hospital with a concussion, and although Emma had texted to say he was home before Mum had even called Anton for dinner, Jude had been pretty quiet. So…yeah, Anton was nervous. Jude had practically confirmed they were dating, by the whole not denying it route, and at his old school, that was a death sentence. Being queer *and* going out with someone in the same school? Build the gallows and order in the rope.

He was clinging, though, to Jude's popularity. The others hadn't joined in with Will. Okay, they hadn't much defended Jude or Anton either, but it wasn't like his old school. And Walsh had totally flipped his shit when Will had hit Jude. So maybe Jude being *Jude* would keep Anton out of trouble a little bit?

Presuming, of course, that Jude was—

"Alright, Anton, hear you're a queen!"

Anton flinched, and the classroom door clicked shut behind him. Emma, perched on Jude's empty desk, smacked Larimer, who'd spoken, with her textbook and huffed. "Ignore him," she said, and beamed. "*But*. Was Will on the money? Have you and Jude been going out?"

Anton bit his lip. "Where *is* Jude?"

"He had a mean look this morning," she said, and rolled her eyes. "He was in a right grump all evening. Andy—"

"Who?"

"Dr. Kalinowski. Jude's sperm donor," Larimer supplied, and got slapped again. "Ow!"

"Andy just about blew his lid, he *hates* fighting, and then they rowed this morning about Jude coming in, so I'm not sure if he's meant to be here or not," Emma said, and held out her hands as though inviting Anton for a hug. He steered clear. "*Are* you?"

"Is Jude okay?" he insisted.

"He is in. Him and Walsh are rigging Will's locker," Larimer said helpfully. He was lounging back in his chair, grinning a sort of stoned-looking grin, and Anton swallowed. Slowly, he inched to perch on Walsh's abandoned table.

"So you and Jude are dating?" Emma pressed.

"Um, yeah," Anton mumbled, feeling his face starting to heat up.

"That's good!" Emma insisted, and squeezed his arm. "What're you embarrassed for?"

"I'd be embarrassed if I fancied Kalinowski, too," Larimer said genially, and ducked her hand. "Jesus, leave me alone!"

"Then stop being a dick!" she shouted, then turned that big smile on Anton again. The switch was kind of scary. "I mean, he was all scatty at home so I figured *something* was up, and he had this weird conversation with me the other night about maybe being bisexual—" Anton's stomach tightened unpleasantly. "—but I kind of ignored him, you know how weird he is sometimes. But this is good! When did it start? You asked him, right, I mean—"

"No."

It slipped out before Anton could stop it, and he flushed red when Larimer started laughing. "You what?" he crowed. "You mean *Jude* asked *you* out? Oi! Jude, twatface, c'mere!"

The classroom door clicked, and Anton turned to—

Well, to tell Jude to ignore him, but the sight of Jude's face stopped Anton dead. "Oh my God," he said.

"Beauty, ain't it?" Walsh grinned toothily.

Jude's left eye was swollen nearly shut, the skin black as ink and puffy, mottling to an ugly brown and yellow at the top of the eye socket and trailing all the way down to his jaw. Larimer started laughing, but Anton's heart was hammering in his chest at the sight of it. A coil of anger started forming low in his stomach, and he found himself clenching his fists and saying, "Where's Thorne?"

Jude raised his eyebrows. "Probably getting yelled at by the head, I dunno."

"What have you done to his locker?" Emma admonished.

"Don't know *what* you're talking about."

"So," Larimer said, recovering himself a bit, "what's this shit about you asking Anton out?"

Jude blinked. "Er. I asked Anton out. What's so complicated about that?"

"So Thorney was right, you've gone bender for him?"

"Yeah, but Thorney was being a cunt about it," Jude said genially, shoving Emma off his desk and flopping into the chair. "Anton's fit, I liked, I asked him out. Do we have to go over the birds and the bees again, Laz?"

Emma laughed, relocating herself to Walsh's desk with Anton. Walsh eyed the pair of them, then shrugged and dragged his chair around it to join Larimer.

"Since when did you like guys, then?" Larimer asked.

"Since Anton, apparently."

That hot, horrible feeling was bubbling up in Anton's stomach again, and he shifted uncomfortably on the desk.

"So what, you're into dick now?"

"You *think* with your dick."

"Oh, like you don't."

"Not all the time, no."

"But are you?"

"I dunno, maybe."

"What d'you mean, you dunno? You must be into dick if you're into guys. Have you not—?"

The feeling bubbled over, and Anton lurched off the desk. His eyes blurred as he bolted for the door, skirting around Miss Taylor as she came in, and he shot down the corridor for the toilets. Girls', boys', *any* toilets, just somewhere quiet and hidden, without Larimer asking if Jude was into cock now, because shit, Jude didn't *know* yet and Anton had to tell him, had to tell him *soon,* and now that everybody knew it was going to be totally impossible and awful if Jude couldn't do this, couldn't be with a trans person, and—

"Anton!"

He stopped outside the toilets, and turned on his heel, hesitant. Emma caught up and towed him into the girls' without pause, and didn't say a word until she'd stuffed a wodge of tissue into his hand and squeezed him tightly in a warm, perfume-scented hug.

"It's okay," she then told him quietly, and Anton took a deep, shaky breath. "What's wrong?"

"It's just…" he began, then shook his head. "I can't. Just the way Larimer was talking about it…"

"Ignore them," Emma said firmly. "Larimer and Jude—and Walsh, a bit, kind of—they're just not very easily offended. They won't get it until you tell them that they shouldn't say certain things. But they won't be dicks about it if you *do* tell them it's not cool."

"It's—it's not that, exactly…" It was that Jude was going to totally wig when he found out he'd been getting used to the idea of being bisexual maybe, and admitting to his mates that he was maybe into cock, and then finding out it was a total lie.

But he couldn't tell Emma that, because…because okay, he was ninety-nine percent sure that Emma wouldn't be nasty about it, but she might start treating him like a girl, or dropping hints, or worse, decide that Jude had a right to know before Anton was ready to tell him, and tell him *for* Anton.

So he said, "I can't tell you."

Emma tilted her head before hugging him again. "Whatever it is," she said, "if you tell the boys to knock it off, they will. Especially Jude, you must know he's a total softie if you've been dating him."

Anton cracked a faint smile. Yeah, Jude would knock off the talking about dick. Until he found out Anton didn't even have one.

"How long?" Emma whispered conspiratorially, and Anton chuckled wetly, starting to mop up his face.

"Like a week, not long at all," he said. "One date, on Saturday."

"We-ell, I suppose I can forgive you both for not telling me," she said loftily, and he was graced with another hug. "You okay?"

"Yeah," Anton mumbled. "Just…shit, at my last school, we'd both be dead for this."

"Not everyone's an arsehole," Emma said, then paused. "Well, apart from Thorney."

Anton snorted, and lobbed the tissue into one of the toilets. "That was mild. At my last school, there'd have been knives involved."

"Seriously, you've gone up in the world," Emma said, and squeezed his elbow. "Come on. Ready to face them? Jude'll be sorry, and he'll have hit Larimer for you. And Tayles will have started, so we can just sneak back in and not have to deal with it until break if you really want?"

Anton nodded, and on impulse, reached out to squeeze her hand. "Thank you," he said. "Even though I can't tell you."

Emma shrugged. "Hey, secrets are okay. Just as long as, you know, you know that you *can* tell me if you want."

"Yeah. If I want."

Which he didn't.

Ever.

JUDE LEFT HIM alone a bit for the rest of the day, apart from lunchtime when he simply squeezed Anton's hand in front of all the others and offered a small smile. But he didn't say much, and Anton was grateful for the space. He'd overreacted, and the fear of telling Jude was getting too big. If he kept quiet any longer, Jude was going to find out some other way, or—like Mum and Aunt Kerry had said—get the wrong idea. And Anton didn't want things to go any more wrong than they already had.

So he swallowed as much of his fear as possible, and sought Jude out at the end of school, cornering him at the lockers and saying, "Come over?"

Jude paused. "You okay?"

"Yeah."

"I'm sorry about this morning."

"It's okay."

"Honestly, I don't actually know what upset you, so…"

"Um, I'll explain that, too. I did say we needed to talk."

Jude nodded carefully, and held out his hand. Anton slid his fingers between Jude's and squeezed.

"I meant what I said yesterday," Jude said quietly. "I may be new to this boys' thing, but I know when I like someone, and I *really* like you."

Anton took a deep breath, and nodded. "I'll try and remember that. You better, too."

Jude coughed out a laugh. "You *did* say you weren't any of the things I came up with. Are you secretly an Arsenal fan?"

"Fuck off," Anton said, letting himself be towed by the hand towards the doors.

"See? Piece of cake."

"How's your face?" Anton said, diverting the topic slightly, and Jude shrugged.

"It's okay. Might not be up for any major make out sessions, but it's not as bad as it looks."

"I'm surprised you're even in today."

"My dad's a doctor, I'd have to have my whole head chopped off before I was ill enough to stay at home. This one time, when I was about nine…"

Anton slowly relaxed as Jude started to brighten up and just…talk. Jude chattering, Anton was starting to realise, was a sign that everything was alright. And Anton desperately wanted it to be, so he simply clung on to Jude's hand—even though it was raining outside, and really too cold to not be wearing gloves—and let the noise wash over him all the way home.

Which meant, when he let them into the house and the smell of Aunt Kerry's drunk spag bol invaded their clothes, Anton was…actually in kind of a good mood. Maybe he *could* do this. Maybe Jude *would* listen, even if in the end he still decided dating a trans guy wasn't for him? There was a *chance*, right?

So when Lily appeared in the doorway, took one look at Jude, and screamed, Anton laughed.

"What the hell!" Jude yelped as she tore back into the kitchen. "She's—"

"Mummy, Anton's friend's on fire in the hall!"

"—kinda weird."

"No shi—er, hell?"

"Just ignore her," Anton advised, hanging up their coats. A nervous swoop made itself known when Jude grinned and kissed his ear, but he laughed it off and pushed Jude in the direction of the kitchen. "Go get us drinks or something."

"It's your house," Jude said, but wandered off obediently. Anton took a moment to simply breathe before following him.

Lily had firmly decided—despite having seen Jude before and not having really clocked his hair—that Jude was on fire, and Anton had to wrestle a cup of water away from her before it ended up on Jude's head.

"Nooo, give it back!" she wailed, stretching up to grab his belt as he put the cup in the sink and rummaged in the fridge for Cokes.

"Yeah, Anton, give it back. I might start melting the worktop," Jude said, sliding onto one of the stools at the kitchen island. Aunt Kerry, busy with dinner, simply chuckled at the both of them.

"You're being mean!" Lily yelled, stamping her foot, then turned on Jude, skidding across the tiles to grab at his trousers. "You need a fireman!"

"It's always that colour," Jude said in a serious voice, but he was wearing an ear-splitting grin, and Anton's heart clenched hard at the sheer beauty of him, despite the battered face.

"No, it's on fire!"

"No it's not," Jude said. "It's ginger."

"That's not ginger, ginger biscuits are ginger!"

"They're brown."

"If they're brown," Lily said seriously, "then why are they called ginger biscuits, huh?"

"Because they have ginger *in* them."

"Which makes them ginger and that's not ginger and you're on *fire!*"

"Lily, leave Jude alone," Aunt Kerry interjected.

"Jew?"

Jude dropped his head onto the counter with a muffled cackle into both hands, and Anton couldn't help but laugh at the sight of him. "Oh God," he said. "Come on, let's go into the living room, and—"

"Noooo, you can't, he'll put the living room on fire!"

"Lily, seriously, stop it with the fire, he's not on fire."

"Jew!" she screeched, and Jude did a full body twitch like he was trying not to curl in on himself. "*Jew!*"

"Jude!" Anton corrected.

"*Jude*," she echoed scornfully, throwing Anton a fabulously dirty look for a kid who wasn't even six yet. "Jude!"

"What?" Jude managed, coughing and rubbing at his eyes, still grinning.

"Tell Tasha to stop it!"

Anton *froze.* Like a bucket of ice water being dumped on his head, every muscle seized up, and the Coke in the cans started rattling in his shaking hands. "Lily! Stop it!" Aunt Kerry barked, but Jude—oh God, Jude, totally oblivious Jude—

"Okay," he said. "Who's Tasha?"

Lily blinked, then flung her arm out, and pointed right at Anton. "Anton's Tasha," she said, like it was so obvious.

"Lily, that's eno—"

"Anton was Natasha only then she became Anton and Mummy says I have to say he but I forget sometimes," Lily continued in a loud, inescapable voice. It bounced off the walls and tiles, and one of the cans slipped through Anton's hands and burst open on the floor. Coke was flung everywhere in long, fizzy bursts, soaking his socks and trousers, and through Lily's indignant shriek and Aunt Kerry's yell, all he could see was—was—

Jude.

The wide-eyed, confused stare that Jude was giving him. And the single word, *that* word, the word Anton *hated.*

"Natasha?"

Anton opened his mouth, found nothing coming up to save him, and did the only thing possible.

He bolted.

Chapter 12

"ANTON?"

Anton pushed his face further into the pillow, and tried to block out the voice.

"Anton, it's just me, honey. Jude's gone home."

At least…at least there was that. At least—

"Do you want me to call your mum, honey?"

"No," he croaked wetly. He'd not ruin her job interview for anything, so he unstuck his face from the pillow and told Aunt Kerry she could come in. When she did, she shut the door behind her and perched on the bed beside his hip.

"I've popped Lily next door so Mrs. Lindhurst can keep an eye on her," she said softly, and rubbed a hand up the middle of Anton's back. "Hey. It's alright."

"It's *not.*"

"I think it might be, honey. I know that's not how you planned to tell him, but—"

"He'll tell the whole school! You saw his face! He's—"

"Shocked, I'll grant you," Aunt Kerry interrupted, and kissed the back of Anton's head. He buried his face in the pillow again, torn between wanting the hug, and angry at being seen to cry. He wanted her there, but he didn't, too. "He was very surprised, honey, but I didn't just kick him out. I told him a—"

"You told him *more?*"

"I explained," Aunt Kerry said firmly, her hand scratching softly at his hair. "I told him that you're transgender, your birth name was Natasha, and it still gets Lily confused because she's very young, and you would prefer to come out at school in your own time. That's all, honey."

Anton twisted his face to the side, and swallowed back a fresh wave of tears. "Did you tell him to go," he croaked. If she hadn't, and Jude had just decided to leave on his own, then...then what did that mean? That he was disgusted, or freaked out, or—

"Mm, yes, I didn't think you'd want him to see you this upset."

Anton twisted onto his side, scrubbing his hands at his face. When Aunt Kerry produced a couple of tissues from her pocket, he took them wordlessly.

"I can ring Maggie if you want," Aunt Kerry offered again, and he shook his. "Or Ellen? Her clinic won't have closed, you know."

"No," Anton mumbled, his voice hoarse. "I just...I meant to tell him today. I wanted to tell him today, and then Lily went and said that, and his *face*..."

"I think *his* face was somewhat set off by *your* face, honey," Aunt Kerry said soothingly. "You looked like you'd seen a ghost, and I don't think your Jude knows what to think right now."

"S'not my Jude anymore."

"You don't know that."

"Who'd want a fucking tranny boyf—"

"*Stop it!*" Aunt Kerry's voice was suddenly firm. "You stop that right now, young man. Plenty of trans people have boyfriends and girlfriends, and you know it. So you stop that nonsense right there, and think for a minute."

"I—"

"I told Jude to go home, but I'll tell you this, honey, he didn't particularly want to. He said he'd text you later, see if you were alright. I don't think he's going to be sitting at home right now putting the entire thing on Myspace."

"*Myspace?*"

"Whatever," Aunt Kerry waved a hand briefly, before returning it to that soothing, scratching motion at Anton's scalp. "I think Lily's just pipped you to the post a little, honey. She's started the conversation for you, that's all. He was going to be shocked either way, wasn't he?"

"Not like this," Anton whispered. "I didn't want him to find out like this."

"Would you prefer he found out after feeling you up once too often?"

"Kerry!"

"Oh give over, I might not know your Myspace from your Facebook, but you don't get two children and an ex-husband by being a prude, Anton," she said genially, and bent low to hug him from above, like a warm shield. He'd mostly grown out of such hugs, but just this once, Anton let it slide. "Be brave, honey. It might be the most awkward conversation of your life, but you already did that with me and your mum. And Chris. And your nice, goofy-looking boyfriend isn't going to be as bad as Chris, is he?"

"I don't know," Anton admitted weakly. The problem was, Dad had taught him that logic didn't apply. Jude was so chilled out about being bisexual, or gay people, or whatever…but so was Dad. Dad's best mate was gay. His sister—Anton's late Aunt Jo—had been a lesbian. Dad was fine with gay people, just like Jude, only…

Only Dad was so anti-transgender people it wasn't funny anymore, and it had just taught Anton that you couldn't guess.

"What if Jude tells everyone?"

"We'll cross that bridge if we come to it," Aunt Kerry said softly. "But I don't think he will. I think you need some ice cream and some comfort TV, and just forget about this afternoon for a little while, alright? You're too upset to make any decisions about what to do with Jude right now—and anyway, now the topic's been brought up, he may start the conversation himself. Now come on. Ice cream and bad telly, just like court days, hm?"

Anton wanted to say no. He wanted to stay in bed, but he knew if he did, Aunt Kerry would call Mum anyway, and that would ruin Mum's job interview. And Lily would probably get upset, too, because she was loud and annoying but she wasn't mean on *purpose*, she was just a little kid being a little kid, and she'd work out Anton was upset because of her. So—

"Okay," he croaked, sitting up and scrubbing the tears off his face. "Is there any raspberry ripple?"

BY THE TIME the front door popped open, and Mum shouted, "I'm home!," Anton was sitting on the sofa, buried in the big fleece throw that served as the family comfort blanket, with baby Rose in his lap and watching The Simpsons. Lily, who wasn't allowed to watch it after she'd called Anton's dad an ass one weekend, was loudly helping Aunt Kerry cook spaghetti in the kitchen.

"Hello, darling," Mum said, leaning over the sofa to hug him from behind. "Hello to you, too, petal!" she added brightly when Rose cooed.

"Did it go well?"

"I think so," she said, coming around to drop into the seat next to Anton and kick off her heels. "Not brilliantly, but not terribly either. I think I have a good chance. What's this, eh?" She brushed a thumb under Anton's eye. "You're all bloodshot, darling."

"Yeah, well…"

"What happened?"

Anton swallowed. "I—I invited Jude over to tell him about…about me, you know, about…Natasha…"

Mum's face stiffened. "Oh."

"It's not like that," Anton said, hugging Rose until she squeaked and hit him with her stuffed bunny. "We were in the kitchen getting a drink and Lily kept on at him saying his hair was on fire and when I told her to cut it out, she—she told Jude to make 'Tasha' stop it, and…I just…he asked her who Tasha was, and then she pointed at me and—she told him, Mum, she just came right out with it, and the *look* he gave me—"

Rose yowled angrily, smacking him with the rabbit again, and Mum crooned, taking Rose and then dragging Anton sideways into the new hug, too, resting her cheek on his hair. "Oh, darling," she murmured. "It's alright."

"It's not," Anton croaked. "I just—I just bolted, and Aunt Kerry had to tell him to go home, and he's not texted me or anything, and—"

"Alright, slow down," Mum said gently, smoothing down his hair. "Now, did he say anything?"

"I didn't give him the chance," Anton admitted.

"Then you don't know what he thinks, do you?"

"You didn't see the way he *looked* at me."

"Probably with a lot of shock, darling, I don't think from what you've told me that Jude had much of a clue, did he?"

"I—well, no…"

"Did Kerry explain about you before sending him home?"

"Yeah."

"Alright. I think Jude's probably very shocked and unsure of what to do or what's going to happen—"

"He hasn't texted me or anything."

"—and maybe even what he feels—"

"He's been telling the others he might be bisexual, he even admitted to the other boys he—you know, he must be into boys if he likes me, and—"

"Honestly, darling, I think there's some truth in that. If Jude genuinely believed you were biologically male and it didn't stop him being attracted to you, then I think he must have at least the potential to be sexually attracted to boys. But that's for Jude to think about, not you. It's not really your business what his sexuality is, is it? Leave him to work that one out."

"But now he's found out it's a lie!"

"All he's found out is that he's in the same *practical* position, sexually speaking, as he was before he knew he could like boys. That's it. He's got a better idea of what's under your clothes, darling, but right now, I think Jude is probably having to process quite a lot. Don't get too upset too early, eh? He seems like a very nice boy, and even if he decides he can't handle dating a transgender person, I don't think he's going to be sounding off at school about it, is he?"

"I don't know."

Truthfully, Anton hoped Mum was right. Jude *was* easy-going, even that fight with Will showed he *could* be pushed but only really when it came to other people. He'd lost his temper when Will had insulted Emma, not when Will had insulted Jude himself. But it would still hurt, if Lily's outburst had ruined everything. Anton *wanted* Jude, wanted him more than anything, wanted to find out what sex with Jude would be like and whether or not Jude was any good at presents next Christmas and go to White Hart Lane with him. And Anton wanted to be normal and be allowed boyfriends and dating and all the rest of it, not—not be consigned to the dustbin because what he had in his boxers wasn't what Jude had been expecting.

"Don't jump the gun, eh, sweetheart?" Mum said softly. "Maybe Jude needs a bit of space to get his head around it, maybe he thinks giving *you* some space is what's needed right now. Even if he decides he can't handle it, I don't think he'll be giving you any t—"

"I don't want him to decide he can't handle it," Anton whispered.

"Well," Mum said. "That's for you to duke it out with him, isn't it? If Jude thought he was straight before you came along, and didn't have a problem with falling for you under the impression you've always been male, then I don't think he's going to have a lot of ground to avoid you based on attraction, is he?"

Anton knew better than to try applying logic to people—after all, Dad didn't follow any logic—but he shrugged and tucked himself further into the hug.

"Don't get too ahead of yourself," Mum advised softly, and kissed the top of his head. "Why don't you text him? Just say you're sorry for the way it was blurted out, you meant to tell him yourself, and you're happy to discuss it properly in private tomorrow. Something like that. Open the conversation up again, and maybe you can get an idea of what he's thinking and feeling?"

Anton swallowed. His phone was on the coffee table, resolutely silent, and after Mum squeezed him tight once more then got up to take Rose into the kitchen and get her ready for dinner, Anton leaned forward and picked up the silent mobile.

And hesitated.

He didn't quite know how to put Mum's suggestion. He didn't want to presume that Jude was okay with it, or would be ready to discuss it tomorrow, or—

In the end, he went with his gut.

Sorry.

He left off the kiss, fearing it would be too presumptuous. He left off any further explanation, in case he got Jude's feelings on the matter wrong. And he left off a promise to talk about it, because…

Because, God, what if Jude didn't want to?

Chapter 13

"PLEASE, MUM."

It was a last-ditch attempt, and Anton knew it was futile even as the words left his mouth. Mum's face twisted, but she sighed and reached out to hug him anyway, stroking her fingers lightly through his hair.

"You have to go, sweetheart."

"He's—he'll—Mum, he *knows*."

"He would have found out anyway, honey. You were going to tell him—and even if you weren't, you wouldn't have been able to go out with him very long before he worked it out."

"But—not like *that*."

"I know," Mum said soothingly, and stepped back to squeeze his shoulders. "But Kerry talked to him, and we both think he's a nice enough boy. I don't think he's going to go telling all your friends."

It wasn't that. It weirdly, bizarrely, wasn't that at all—although that was *there*, of course, in the background. It was...it was that Jude was going to look at him differently. Whatever had been starting up would be snuffed out, and Anton didn't think he could go back to staring at that incredible smile while Jude dumped him, and found someone else—probably a girl, but worse if it was another boy, in a way—and moved on.

"*Please.*"

"I'm sorry, honey, but you've *got* to go to school."

She pushed him gently towards the door, and it was like walking through mud. Hip-deep mud. It was drizzling lightly outside, grim and grey and warmer than usual, but Anton only felt cold as he stepped out onto the step and pulled the front door shut behind him. For a long minute, he simply stood there, hand glued to the door handle, before finally peeling himself away and shuffling down the drive. He didn't want to do this. *He really, really didn't want to do this.*

He pushed at the cold metal of the gate—and with a flurry of movement, the hedge shifted as someone brushed the corner of it, the gate stopped dead.

Anton's heart stopped.

"Hey," Jude said.

Fuck. Jude. Jude-Jude-Jude. He was just…just *standing* there, a little frown between his eyebrows, his hair catching the drizzle in bright little spots amongst the brilliant red, and Anton felt his own face shiver and twitch at the edges of his mouth.

"I—"

Jude bit his lip and let go of the gate. Then Anton's heart restarted when Jude simply held out his arms in the universal 'hug me' gesture. For a long moment, Anton simply stared at him, his mind churning over…over whatever this meant, whatever Jude was trying to *say*…

Then he stepped forward and into the offering, sliding his own hands carefully around Jude's ribs and back. Jude's arms closed like a trap, the embrace heavy and warm despite the crumple of their damp coats between them, separated by the icy gate, and the distinctly chilly feel of his hair brushing against Anton's ear and temple. His hold was tight, secure like…like he wasn't…

"I'm not mad."

Jude's voice was very quiet, and Anton swallowed convulsively.

"I—I didn't…I didn't mean for you to find out like that," he croaked.

"But you *did* mean to tell me?"

"Yes," Anton whispered, digging his fingers into Jude's back. Suddenly, it seemed vital that Jude understand that. "I was going to tell you that afternoon, actually. That was…that was the thing we needed to talk about."

"Okay," Jude said simply, and pulled away. Anton immediately felt cold again, and kept a tight grip on Jude's upper arms. "Then I'm not mad," Jude repeated. His eyes seemed to be searching Anton's face, flicking slightly from left to right and back again, and he exhaled a cloud of white vapour into the chilly air. "I think maybe we still need to actually talk about it, though."

Anton bit his lip, and nodded. "D'you…d'you want to…to come over later?"

"I meant now, really," Jude said, and tilted his head. "I mean, we're not going to miss much at school today, and this is kind of…you know, it's a bit more important than what Queen Lizzy said to piss off the King of Spain so much in fifteen-hundred-and-whatever."

Anton managed to crack a watery smile, and opened the gate. Jude slung a heavy arm around his neck, dragging him in to press a rough kiss into his hair that hovered somewhere between oddly familial affection and the casual touching that Anton was coming to associate with Jude regardless.

"C'mon," Jude said. "Have you got an Oyster card? There's this cafe near Baker Street tube station, we can go there. It'll be warmer and dryer than out here, and nobody'll catch us if we fuck off into the city proper."

"Okay," Anton mumbled. He folded his arms over his chest, hunching his shoulders. "I haven't got a card though. Or much money."

"S'okay, I have an emergency twenty in the bottom of my bag."

For a split second, it was all so nauseatingly *normal.* They were talking about ditching school for the day, and emergency twenties. Like they just didn't feel like it, instead of because Lily had…she'd said…

"Natasha."

"What?" Jude said.

"Natasha," Anton repeated quietly as they fell into step, heading for Edgware tube station. "That was my name. Natasha Jane Williams."

"Okay?"

"I changed it just before Christmas. Anton John Williams."

"Why Anton?"

Anton blinked. It wasn't a question he'd been expecting, and it gave him a momentary pause. "Um. Because I liked Natasha sounding kind of Russian. So I wanted a sort of Russian-esque name, you know?"

"Makes you sound like a spy," Jude said. "I was named by a family joke."

"Eh?"

"My nana—Nana O'Brien—she was a raging Catholic and used to complain my mum and dad were going to be raising Jewish babies if they kept having them in a Jewish area, and we ought to move back to Dublin, where my mum's from. We lived round the corner from a synagogue then, I think that's where Nana O'Brien got the idea. Anyway, they expected me to be a girl so had a girly name all ready, and when I popped out with a penis, they figured calling me Jude would piss Nana O'Brien off."

Anton smiled, his voice a little hoarse when he croaked, "Yeah?"

"Uh-huh."

"So you're…Polish-Irish?"

"Nah. English-Irish. My granddad's Polish—war refugee. Me an' Dad are just Londoners. I can't speak Polish or nothing. We went to Poznan—that's where Granddad was from—when I was like…eight? Nine? But Granddad could barely remember any of it and decided he liked his bungalow in Essex better after all."

Anton laughed weakly, the image of a cranky old man with greying ginger hair complaining Poznan wasn't like Basildon popping into his head.

"So what about you?" Jude asked quietly.

Anton bit his lip.

"Start with the easy stuff, if it helps?" Jude prompted.

"Um. My…my mum's from Lambeth. Dad's from Watford. He…he, um, him and my mum split up when I was about eleven. After…after I…"

His tongue tripped on the word, the 'c' stuttering, and Jude's knuckles brushed his lightly.

"After I came out," Anton finished in a rush.

"Sucks," Jude said quietly.

"I…I…"

"Only child?" Jude interrupted.

"Oh. Erm. Yes. Just me."

"Were you a proper tomboy, then?"

Anton smiled faintly. "Not really. I mean, when I was little, I didn't understand what made me different from the boys, so I didn't mind. I wasn't…you know, I wasn't *bothered* by wearing girly clothes. I got to play football with the boys on my road anyway, I just…you know, I just tucked my dress into my knickers."

Jude snickered, rummaging in his coat pockets as they reached the tube station. Anton didn't stop, the ability to talk about it without exactly talking about it starting to unbottle his anxiety a little bit.

"I never liked having long hair, but Mum and Dad let me cut it short, they didn't like brushing it either, so I never…I didn't know, I wasn't one of those kids who says the minute they can talk that they're a boy or a girl or whatever…but I always played with the other boys, I didn't like other girls, but there's loads of girls like that…"

"My cousin Pippa is still like that," Jude supplied as he punched instructions into the ticket machine. "But I don't think she's a girl either, I think she's Satan."

"She…she can't be that bad?"

"She's Satan in a school skirt," Jude said firmly. "She's *evil*. When I was seven, she collected all my Lego and put it in a fire to melt it all together, because I got more ice cream than she did at Aunt Ruth's wedding."

"Really?"

"Yep. Told you. Satan, not a girl."

Anton smiled, then bit the bullet. "Neither was I."

Jude frowned slightly, handing over the ticket and producing his own Oyster card from his bag. "What d'you mean?"

"I mean…" Anton said, following him through the ticket barriers. Somehow, the rush of commuters was as anonymous as being all on their own, and although he lowered his voice slightly, he kept talking. "I'm...I'm *physically* a girl. I was...*born* a girl. But I was never a girl. Not really, not in my head. And when I hit puberty..."

Jude grimaced. "Oh, ew, I think I see where this is going."

"Where?"

"Well, I know what'd freak me out most if I were a girl."

Anton swallowed. "What?"

"Periods."

"Yeah," Anton admitted in a whisper.

"*Ouch*, man."

"Yeah. It was...it was horrible. I felt disgusting. I was *eleven* when they started, it was so awful, none of the other girls at my primary school had one yet, and I felt so vile whenever it happened. I'd destroy my clothes and my bedsheets if they got anything on them, and I'd cry whenever the next month rolled around, and it was just...it felt so *wrong*, it was the most awful thing ever, and I was so fucking *wrong* and—"

"Whoa, whoa, whoa, okay, hey, hang on..."

Jude's voice was close again, and his arms heavy around Anton's neck and shoulders. Anton clung in the midst of the waves of commuters surging around them, and inhaled deeply. The smell of overheated tube station, sweat, and Jude's aftershave surrounded him and calmed him, the old feelings of violent disgust ebbing away again.

"Mum and Dad took me to a psychiatrist," he whispered in Jude's ear, like the secret it was, "and she said it was a normal part of being a girl and I just said, 'I'm not a girl, though.' And it all clicked, right then."

Jude's hand rubbed up and down Anton's back, heavy and solid. "It's okay. You're okay."

Anton squirmed his arms around Jude in return, and squeezed tightly. "M'getting there," he mumbled.

"Yeah, y'are," Jude agreed quietly. "And look, don't freak yourself out telling me, yeah? I'm not going to run away screaming, or tell the whole school."

"You might," Anton mumbled. "Run away screaming, I mean," he added when Jude stiffened. "I mean...I'm not what you thought I was."

"No, you're not. But that's why we're gonna go to this cafe I know about, and we're gonna talk about it proper, 'cause I don't know the first thing about transgenderality—"

"Transgenderism."

"See?"

Anton managed a shaky smile against Jude's shoulder.

"Here's what we're gonna do," Jude said quietly. "We're gonna go give ourselves diabetes with the biggest, best hot chocolates you have ever *seen,* trust me on this, and then we're gonna talk through what this means for us."

Anton swallowed, and pulled back. "Us?" he echoed.

"Yeah," Jude said, and offered his hand. "You an' me. 'Cause right now, I don't know what this means for the physical stuff, and there's obviously things you're going to need to explain to me, but I figure the way you looked at me when your little Lily spouted off, you are a shitty, *shitty* actor."

Anton blinked. "I—what?"

"If you were a good liar or a good actor, you'd have blown that off somehow. Like you were in a play and she's got confused. She's like in infants' school, man, you could have rolled your eyes and called her daft, and I would be none the wiser. But you didn't. You just totally wigged, so you, mate, you're a shit actor. Which means there is no way you've been lying to me all this time about *you,* you know? The guy who's fucking mental in goal, and is gonna come to a Spurs game with me sometime, and is a bigger English nerd than our Emma. You can't have been duping me the whole time about that, and I like that, so I still like you. So let's just talk about it, get me on the same page as you, and then we'll see where we go. Yeah?"

Anton bit his lip so hard it bled. Jude pulled a face.

"Ew, grim, don't do that."

"I—sorry. I just...why are you so...nice?"

Jude shrugged. "Eh. I dunno. Nice guys finish last?"

He offered his hand again, and Anton slid their fingers together, squeezing tightly. A businessman scoffed and ducked around them at the last second, muttering something that sounded distinctly like 'fucking queer kids.'

"Piss off, granddad!" Jude called after him, and tugged Anton towards the southbound platform. "C'mon. It stinks down here, and there's sugar with our names on it."

THE CAFE WAS full of university students, and Jude shooed Anton to a corner before returning with cups overflowing with chocolate-sprinkled cream. Anton clasped his in both hands as Jude settled, their jackets hiding their uniforms. Nobody seemed to care about them anyway, and Anton was grateful for being so ignored just then.

"So," Jude said, using a teaspoon to push his cream into the drink and sink it. "I take it you're still, uh…physically…?"

"Yes," Anton mumbled.

"So if you were to get naked…"

"I'd look like a girl."

He said it in a whisper, and Jude tilted his head. "Okay," he said quietly. "What's…the long term goal, then? I mean, can you make someone more like a guy?"

"Not until you're legal." Anton longed for that day. "You can get hormones—testosterone—and that would make me…you know, boyish. I'd get facial hair and more body hair, and my voice would drop and everything."

"You gonna do that?"

"Yes."

"Okay," Jude said. "And, uh…I'm guessing your back brace…?"

"Isn't," Anton whispered. "It's…it's a binder. So you can't see my breasts."

"You have them?"

"Yes. I'm going to have them removed when I'm older, though."

"Shame."

Anton blinked, then scowled. "I *hate* them."

"Whoa, sorry, didn't think," Jude said, holding up both hands in a placating gesture. "I'm a mostly straight guy, loss of boob is always a bit of a shame to me. Ignore me."

Anton subsided, fractionally mollified.

"Look, I can't pretend to understand this, Anton. I'm a guy. I've always been a guy. Always thought with my dick, too, I was offering daisies and dandelions to girls in my class before I was six years old. My first proper girlfriend, I was eleven. She dumped me when I stopped doing basketball because I wasn't interesting enough anymore," Jude added, rolling his eyes. "I don't get it. I really don't. But I also don't have a *problem* with it, in theory."

"In theory?" Anton whispered.

"Yeah, in theory. If I'm right, and you're too shitty an actor to be faking who you are, then I don't have a problem with it. In all honesty, it actually takes a little pressure off me."

"How do you mean?"

"Well, you're the first boy I ever liked. And I mean *ever*. I didn't know I was capable of crushing on a guy, so I'll admit, I was really nervous about the whole sex thing with you. Wasn't sure my interest would actually extend to playing with another guy's dick, you know?"

That startled a bit of a laugh from Anton's throat, and he ducked his head over the drink to smile stupidly for a split second, his anxiety cracking down the middle and easing.

"I won't *know*, one hundred percent, if I'm actually good with this until I try it out, but I have no…I don't know, moral objection? If being a guy is what you want, then whatever. You're not hurting anybody."

Anton swallowed. "If people found out, you'd be the guy with a tranny boyfriend."

"I'm ginger, my mum's Irish, and I have a Polish last name, trust me, I can take a few hits," Jude said severely, then grinned. "Anyway, it just means I'm like the one guy in London who has a boyfriend with nice legs. Actual guys, you know, biological guys? They don't have nice legs. Like ever."

"We'll agree to disagree," Anton said loftily, and Jude smirked briefly.

"In all seriousness…I mean, I can't make any promises, and I'm not stupid enough to try. If we go ahead and stay trying this relationship deal, then—"

"You want to?" Anton breathed.

"Yeah, I want to."

Anton's throat was suddenly too tight. "Even though I'm…"

"You're what? Lady-parted? Not a problem, trust me on that. I'm not gay, even if you are."

Anton smiled faintly. "Well, I'm not gay either."

"You like girls?"

"Um, no, just boys, but—"

"Then you're gay. You're a guy who likes guys. Gay," Jude said firmly, and Anton suddenly wanted to kiss him with a fierce rush of adoration. "You're still a guy, Anton. I'm looking at you right now, I'm seeing a boy. Literally the only thing I was a little suspicious about was what I thought was the closest shave *ever,* like, it was like kissing a girl for smoothness. But then, you know, my brother didn't even get wisps until he was sixteen, I just figured you weren't done with the joys of going crazy yet."

"Thank you," Anton breathed, his voice cracking slightly.

"Long-term…I don't know. I honestly don't. Maybe the more guy-like you get and the less…andro…andro…what's that word for like…not female or male?"

"Androgynous?"

"That. That word I can't say."

"Your last name is Kalinowski, how can you not say androgynous?"

"Because Kalinowski and androgynous are pronounced totally differently. Duh." Jude rolled his eyes. "Anyway, maybe when you have a deep voice and more leg hair than I have, maybe my brain will be like 'mate, you aren't gay, bail.' I don't know. I can't promise anything about the long-term. But right now? Right this minute, I still really like you. I'm still attracted to you, and until I stop being attracted to you, I'd still like to go out with you and mess around with you. Even if it's not going to be like any of the other fooling around I've ever done. Might as well try, yeah?"

"Even though I'm…different?"

"Hey, I might drop my pants and you think it's the weirdest dick in the world and no way do you want that anywhere near you. Might girl you up."

Anton laughed shakily and shook his head. "Probably not."

"Probs not, no. So…what do you say? All we have to do is just do the sharing thing, talk about stuff. So let's try this dating thing anyway?"

"You can't tell anyone. Everyone would have to think you've gone gay for me."

"Big fucking deal. Like I said, I can take a few hits. And if you want me to keep it a secret, then…okay. It's your secret. I can't say I totally agree with it—"

"It got me driven out of my last school because I was a total freak," Anton hissed vehemently. "One girl threatened to knife me if I went in the girls' toilets anymore, but the boys would threaten to rape me and said I just hadn't worked out what a vagina was for if I went in the boys' instead. You don't tell *anyone*."

Jude levelled him with a flat stare. "That was there, and you were on your own. This is here, and you're not. *But*. It's your secret. I won't say a word if you don't want me to."

"I don't. It has to stay quiet."

"Okay."

"If you don't—if you want to go, then…"

"I don't. I'd like to have another date, actually. I'd like to kiss you. I'd like to fool around with you and find out what you feel like."

Anton's heart seemed to squeeze in on itself, and he swallowed dryly. "You…you still want to?"

The squeeze released, and then his heart was beating too fast in his chest. His own pulse was deafening him—because Jude didn't want to ditch him for this. He was even admitting that it might not work, even disagreeing without treating the issue like a dirty fact or something to be ashamed of, but he wanted to try anyway.

"Yeah," Jude said quietly. "I still want to. If you do?"

"Yeah," Anton whispered, and smiled. "Actually, right now I just sort of want to kiss you."

Jude beamed that ridiculously good-looking smile, and tilted his head again. "So…just get up, walk around the table, plant one."

Anton felt his own smile wobble at the edges, everything a little too raw—but he did it. He got up and cupped Jude's face in both hands, still slightly too cool from the journey, and kissed Jude firmly on the mouth, trying—

He didn't know if you could show thanks, appreciation, apology, admiration, and flat-out adoration in a kiss. He didn't know if you could, and he certainly didn't know how. But he wound his fingers into Jude's hair, and felt a heavy hand on the back of his neck, and he was conveying *something* that Jude could understand, by the pleased little noise he made and the gentle curl of his fingers at the hair at the nape of Anton's neck, so...

Anton didn't know if you *could* convey those things in a kiss, but he tried anyway.

Chapter 14

THINGS WERE...normal, after that.

They'd stayed out the rest of the day, just sort of meandering around Central London, and then the next day at school, Jude was just...*Jude*. He didn't mention it at all, even in private, like he was giving Anton space...and yet he kind of wasn't either, because he kept doing that arm-over-shoulders hug thing and giving Anton rather obvious glances in their shared classes.

Anton loved it.

Mum and Ellen would say he was supposed to talk about it more, but...he liked the *not* talking about it, too. He liked that Jude had kind of...not shrugged and ignored it, exactly, but he didn't seem to feel this urge to ask a million questions and probe into the way Anton felt. Anton knew how he felt. He didn't need Jude to psychoanalyse him, too, because people always did that, they'd have opinions on something they didn't have the first clue about, but Jude...

Jude didn't.

Things just...carried on, like nothing had ever happened, and Anton's anxiety that Jude would see him different, touch him different, was blown out of the water on the Sunday kick-about when

Anton opted to make a save by kicking the striker in the shins, and Jude whooped, beaming, and kissed him in front of the entire park.

Just like everything was fine.

THERE WAS ANOTHER gift in his locker on Monday morning.

Anton stared blankly at it for a long minute, until Emma twigged he wasn't listening to her plans for a fundraising event, and complained. So he took it out of the locker and showed her.

"Aw, that's sweet!" she enthused, taking the tiny box and turning it over. It was wrapped in blue paper this time, with little white snowflakes. "I didn't know Jude could do sweet."

"They're not from Jude," Anton said awkwardly, taking the little box back. If it was Bee, he was going to have to say something—especially now Jude knew about him, and hadn't run a mile. He was proper taken now, not in that weird sort-of-maybe-until-he-figures-it-out-and-dumps-me territory.

"What, you have an admirer?" Emma asked as Anton carefully unwrapped the box. It was the smallest one so far, and when he opened it, there was a keyring inside, two tiny red football boots on a silver chain. They were painted in perfect detail, and even had tiny shoelaces and studs. "Oh, that's neat," Emma said.

"Yeah, but...I'm going out with Jude now. I shouldn't be taking gifts."

"Well, d'you know who's sending them?"

"No," Anton said honestly. He didn't, he only had the other boys' teasing to go on. Bee had never said two words to him.

"Then take it, you can give them back when whoever it is comes forward if you feel weird about it," Emma said pragmatically. She gave a little squeak then, and Anton turned from the locker to see that Jude had appeared, face now buried in Emma's shoulder and wound around her back like a trap.

"Morning, sleepyhead," Emma crooned, petting Jude's vivid hair, and Anton swallowed, mouth suddenly dry.

"This isn't morning, this is Monday, and it's immoral," Jude grumbled, then unstuck his face from her blazer. "And you left your lunch on the side, I've got it."

"Fuck," she said conversationally. "Thanks." She unglued him and scurried around him to rummage in his backpack—still on said back—and Jude grinned blearily at Anton.

"I'm not awake yet."

"I can tell," Anton said, and offered a tiny smile. Jude sleepy was…stunning. Anton bit his lip, shifting slightly uncomfortably in his uniform, grateful—for perhaps the first time ever—for *not* having a dick for once. Jude cocked his head, and his eyes dropped… thankfully just to Anton's hands.

"Whassat?"

"Another present."

"Mate, you got a stalker."

Emma laughed. "It's probably you being a troll!"

"He wishes," Jude yawned. "No way am I getting up early, to come to *school* early, to give him a present *every Monday*. I fancy him, I'm not proposing marriage to him."

"Aw, shame!"

Anton rolled his eyes and showed him the keyring. "S'kinda nice, though."

"Better'n flowers," Jude agreed. "Or like…a love note written on human skin."

"Ew, Jude!" Emma exclaimed, and hit him.

"Ow! What? Stalkers are creepy! They go nuts and like…murder your squirrels and shit!"

"Squirrels? Where did *squirrels* come from?!"

Anton quietly put the keyring on his house keys and left them in the locker before shutting it and following the others back to their form room. He didn't quite know what he felt about the gifts—on the one hand, it was kind of sweet and he liked having somebody who had a crush on him. On the other hand…well, Jude. He had that whole nice guy thing going on, but how persistently nice could you be when your new boyfriend was accepting gifts from some secret admirer?

On a whim, Anton caught Jude's elbow at the classroom door and pulled him back into the corridor, away from the rest of the class, and blurted out, "D'you mind?" before his brain could quite catch up.

Or Jude could, apparently, because he got a blank look and a, "What?"

"About the presents."

"What, in your locker?"

"Yeah."

"Nah."

Anton blinked. "No?"

"Yeah, nah," Jude repeated, not particularly helpfully. "Not like I can rag on someone for liking you."

"Yeah, but—"

"And anyway, I got there first, di'n't I?" Jude added, with a grin that could only be described as shit-eating. Anton pulled a face and punched him in the arm, feeling his own face flushing pink. "Ow! Jesus, what is it with Mondays and punching me?"

"You're like a super-shit on Mondays."

"You *wound* me," Jude said exaggeratedly.

"Then I would suggest Williams is in the right," a chilly voice interrupted, and then Miss Taylor was shepherding them into the classroom with her folders. "Sit down, both of you. And quiet! This is a school, not the monkey cage at London Zoo!"

"Shame, could fling my faeces at Kalinowski," Walsh called lazily from the back.

"You *know* the word faeces?" Emma asked witheringly, shooting Walsh a filthy look, and Miss Taylor rapped on her desk.

"That's enough!" she barked. "It's already Monday, I don't feel like making my morning any worse with your antics." Out of the corner of his eye, Anton saw Jude rock back on his chair and start mumbling with Larimer behind him. "Today's PSHE topic usually generates a fair amount of discussion, so we're going to launch right into it. Gender identity."

Anton felt the entire world freeze.

Actually, scratch that. It didn't freeze, it *flexed*. The classroom seemed to bend around him, Miss Taylor's voice echoing like she was shouting in a swimming pool. His pulse was suddenly thundering in his ears, deafeningly loud and making the entire room shiver in time with it. The hard 'd' and 't' sounds in the phrase, *gen-der id-en-ti-ty,* repeated themselves in time with his heart, too, getting louder and louder—

"—are individuals whose biological sex does not match their psychological gender—"

He was going to be sick. He needed not to be here—here, where the teacher was droning about the gender spectrum like nobody in the room knew, here where he could feel his face getting hotter and hotter, and her voice was getting further and further away—

"—know a transgender person?"

Anton saw it—*saw* it, the way her eyes flicked so momentarily in his direction—and then, like something out of a horror movie, he saw a single, lonely hand lift into the air, clear across the classroom. A hand belonging to a blazer-covered arm, attached to a shoulder below a long, freckled neck, topped by a stunning face and a crop of brilliantly red hair.

"Anton?" Emma whispered, those big brown eyes suddenly on him. "Are you alright, you look a bit…clammy."

"Kalinowski?"

The world shuddered—

"Emma keeps nicking my jeans, does that make her a tranny?"

—and popped.

"Oi, you fucking twat!"

"Brown! Less of—"

Anton's chest expanded, cold air rushing into his lungs like he'd been drowning, and the world snapped back into place, his vision shivering for a moment as though an elastic band had been released and the classroom had settled back into the right place. Voices rose and returned to normal, laughter and jeers at both Emma and Jude as Emma hefted a geography textbook off her desk and flung it full-force at her cackling stepbrother.

"*Stop it!*" Miss Taylor roared. "Brown, don't throw things or use foul language! Kalinowski, don't you ever use that disgusting term again!"

"What, 'Emma'?"

"You know perfectly well what. Larimer, stop sniggering, it's not funny. *This*," she snapped, slamming a hand down on her desk, "is what I'm talking about with this class! You think everything's a big joke!"

"But it *should* be!"

Jude's voice rang out like a bell, deep and clear, and Anton could only feel his own breathing as he—and the rest of the class—turned to stare.

"It should be just a joke, 'cause anything that's not a huge deal is a joke. Like literally anything, it's only not okay to make jokes if it's like in seriously bad taste, like joking about someone who got murdered last week in front of their kid or something. And if you want being gay or trans or whatever else to be all accepted and stuff, you gotta not let it be a big deal."

Miss Taylor drew herself up, blinking. For a brief moment, the class was quiet.

"But you're making fun of trans people," Isabel said, her actually speaking up in class somehow more shocking than Jude's challenge.

"Yeah, but you're also making it all normal," Jude said, twisting around to look at her. "Like if you give them special, like, immunity from being made fun of, then you're saying you can't make fun of them like you can make fun of normal people. You're saying they ain't normal." His accent was getting thicker, the consonants sharpening and the vowels dragging and beginning to drawl.

"But making fun of them is wrong, too," Isabel said. "You can't make jokes about someone because they're transgender."

"Why not?" Jude asked. "Nobody'd rag on me for making a blonde joke about you. You've all called me shit 'cause I'm ginger."

"Or 'cause you're a Polack."

"Walsh," Miss Taylor snapped, but her voice was softer than usual.

"Or that, yeah. And c'mon, nobody in here can seriously say they ain't laughed at Larimer for the whole puppet-with-arthritis walk thing he has going on—lay off!" Jude yowled as Larimer almost casually picked up a book and slapped him with it. "What I'm saying is, why's that okay but—I dunno, it'd be wrong for Emma to call me a bender now I'm dating another boy?"

The strength of his accent turned 'another' into 'anuvva' and Anton curled his toes at the impassioned speech. Biting his lip, he stared outright, but Jude wouldn't look him in the eye. And Anton was quietly grateful for being able to hide in the midst of a point that he *knew* was aimed at him. Or maybe not quite *him*, but at other people *about* him.

"Because if there was another gay person around, they might find that horrible," Isabel said. "They might feel they're being laughed at and discriminated against because of something they can't help."

"Then they need to man up," Jude said flippantly.

"Kalin—"

"No, really. They don't know the history 'tween me and Ems, an' if they did, they couldn't get pissy about it. 'Cause isn't that what it should be about, not being a dick? Me and Ems, we get each other. We know what we can say and what's actually gonna hurt the other's feelings, and shouldn't that be what it's about? Not some magical 'ooh, we can't make fun of Larimer 'cause he wears skirts on Saturday nights!'? If someone doesn't like what you just said, they should call you on it, and *then* you shut up about it. Not just all the time, just in case. Then you're giving people special treatment, and that's like, going against the point of equal rights and shit."

"That's one point of view," Miss Taylor said, "but—"

"But nothing," Jude insisted bullishly. "That should be it, right? Don't be a dick. Someone don't like what you said, then don't say it, but you gotta take responsibility for saying you don't like it, too. Like, there's a word for a girl I won't ever say in our house, right, 'cause Emma hates it. I'll say it all I want at football, but it makes her mad, so I don't in front of her."

"Pussy," a voice said from the back.

"Thorney, mate, if you want a bit of pussy, I'm still man enough to give it you."

The sobriety dissolved into half-muted sniggering, and Miss Taylor sighed heavily through her nose. "Thorne. Don't call other people that word, please? And Kalinowski, the fewer references you can manage to make to your sex life in a day, the better, thank you. Now—Kalinowski has a good point, certainly, but transgender people can often feel that humour playing off their gender identity is dehumanising and disrespectful—"

Anton tuned her out, fumbling in his bag—hopefully surreptitiously—for his phone. He wasn't stupid. He knew what Jude had been getting at, and who he'd been talking to. He knew he'd started it for Anton, because if he hadn't, the entire lesson would have been Miss Taylor droning on about cisgender and transgender issues, and gender neutral bathrooms, and hormone treatment, and everyone would have ignored the hell out of it. And it wasn't outing him, but it *was* broaching the topic a bit, so…

Thank you :) but dont ever call me a tranny >:(

Jude's phone beeped, and his head dropped.

"Don't even think about answering that, Kalinowski," Miss Taylor warned, barely breaking flow. "As I was saying, jokes at the expense of transgender individuals can create an atmosphere of aggression against them and make other people questioning their gender identity to feel uncomfortable, whether that is your intention or not…"

Jude's head slowly dropped again. A moment later, Anton's phone—because he was smarter than Jude, apparently—lit up in the gloom under the table.

Deal x

THEY DIDN'T DISCUSS it at lunchtime, or on the way home, or at all until Anton invited Jude over once Larimer had tripped over a curb and headed on his own way.

"Sure," Jude said, and tilted his head. "You okay?"

"Yeah?"

"You're quiet."

"Mm."

"Um. I'm sorry about this morning?"

Anton blinked, fumbling with his keys. "What?"

"Well, I guess that's probably why you're quiet…"

"I'm not angry with you," Anton blurted out, and Jude's

shoulders sagged. "Actually—thanks. For getting everyone talking about it without…you know, giving me away."

"That was the idea, yeah."

"And it worked. So thanks," Anton said. Once they were safely inside, front door closed and outside world locked away, he leaned up and kissed Jude on the cheek.

"I'm guessing, though, you don't want me saying nothing about—you know, Natasha, for this presentation?"

"Definitely not," Anton said, maybe a little sharply, and bit his lip. "I don't want to be out, Jude. I know that sounds weird, but I *like* people not knowing, and—"

"And fine," Jude interrupted. "I dunno if it's weird or not, I don't exactly have a billion queer mates and hang out down Soho for fun, but it's your life. Whatever you wanna do, that's fine. I'll make up some outrageous lies and rile up Tayles."

"Like what?"

"Mate, your name is *Anton*. I told you, you're a Russian spy."

"Oh whatever."

"See? A real spy would deny it."

Anton rolled his eyes, detouring into the kitchen for drinks before deciding—seeing Mum and Lily in the garden, with Mum attempting to hang up the washing and Lily determined on pulling it down again—to stay out of the way. "Living room," he said, interrupting Jude's increasingly wild stories with a can in hand and a shove in the chest.

"Bully."

"Oh whatever."

"Tran—"

Anton glared.

"—sgender bully."

"Are you *trying* to get slapped?"

"Maybe, does it turn you on?"

They fell onto the sofa, Jude sprawling in the corner and beckoning until Anton shuffled along to lean back against him, flicking the TV on and relaxing with his head rising and falling in time with Jude's chest, Jude's arm propped along the back of the sofa. It was nice, just calm and without…

Without that anxiety of Jude finding anything out, because he already knew.

"Thanks," he said quietly as he flicked through the channels to find something to watch.

"For what?" Jude asked.

"Being so chilled about this."

"About what?"

"Me."

"Honestly, Anton?"

"Huh?"

"I've been freaking out more about me."

"You?" Anton asked, and looked up. He could nearly see right up Jude's nose from his angle, but didn't bother to correct it.

"Yeah. I mean, you know, I've always been bang into girls, pun totally intended, and then this new kid goes 'uh, I don't think so' when he's told to introduce himself to the class, and *bam*. I know what a crush feels like, and I went and had one like, right away. And I'd never liked a boy before."

Anton blinked, and reached up to clumsily scratch behind Jude's ear. Jude gave him a startled look, but then tilted his head into it and pulled a face as though trying it out.

"Feels weird," he mumbled, seemingly to himself, then blinked again. "Anyway, yeah. I'd never had a crush on a guy before. Not even a 'oh hey, he's pretty fit.' It took me by surprise. But then I hang out with Larimer and Walsh so maybe it's not that surprising."

Anton laughed. "So…it's okay? I mean, you said the other day, you still see me like a boy, so…"

"So I guess maybe I'm bisexual," Jude said. "Point is, I told Emma—about my crush, I haven't told her anything about this—and she pointed out I can't say I'm, like, supportive about gays and stuff if I wig out first time I have a crush on a boy. So I decided to just go for it and work it out as I went, and here we are."

"Well…maybe you're not. I mean, I still have…girly plumbing."

Jude laughed. "Girly-plumbing, that's brilliant. Nah but seriously, I must be a bit bent. Or I might have fancied you if you'd said 'oh hey yeah I'm trans' that day, but you didn't, and I didn't know. I honest-to-god believed you were a boy and always had been, and I still fancied you. Still do. So I must be a bit bent, and I was having to just get my head around that a bit at first."

Anton smiled. "Well," he said, "how about...we figure out how we do this, you being maybe bisexual and me being a boy that's not quite yet finished, and we just work it all out together, yeah?"

"I can—"

"Hey!" The shriek was piercing, and then a lump collided heavily with Anton's chest. He grunted, and the lump crawled over him to occupy what little space remained on Jude's chest instead.

"Lily! Leave the boys alone!" Mum shouted from the kitchen.

"Tasha's sitting on Jude! I wanna sit on Jude, too!"

"Oh my God, that sounds *so* wrong," Jude cackled, and Anton groaned, covering his face in both hands.

"Tasha! Move *over*!"

"You *suck*, Lily!"

Jude just laughed harder, then plonked Lily unceremoniously on the floor and tugged on Anton's shoulders. "C'mon, take up all the space and she'll lose," he advised, then—to Anton's pleased surprise—kissed the top of his head. "We'll work on it. After you stick 'toons on or whatever, she nearly stood on my balls."

"What's balls?"

"Lily!"

Anton stuck the cartoons on, scowled at his cousin, and—actually, felt fine.

Because Jude's arm was around him, and he was maybe bisexual and didn't mind the maybe, and Anton wasn't finished yet but it might not matter, and—

They were gonna work on it.

Chapter 15

JUDE STAYED FOR dinner.

Lily had thrown a tantrum when he'd made noises about going home, then Aunt Kerry had bribed him with her special spag bol. So Jude had caved, because his friends were kind of right, Anton suspected, and he really was a bit of a wuss. Maybe that was behind the whole nice guy thing. He was too soft to be a bastard.

Not that Anton hadn't exploited it after dinner when Aunt Kerry started telling Lily it was bath time. "Come on," he'd said. "This'll be messy. Let's go to my room."

It worked. In more ways than one: it got Jude in his bedroom, *and* it let them close the door behind them to limit the number of places Lily could hide. But then Anton found himself standing in the middle of his bedroom, Jude sitting cross-legged on his bed, and the door closed.

"Er," he said.

Jude laughed. "Alright, don't wig out, I'm not going to jump you the second we're on our own," he said, then smirked. "Maybe."

"Oh, shut up," Anton groused, sliding onto the bed beside him. "We should probably work on our presentation for PSHE.

We've not done anything on it."

"Told you, if you don't want me to tell about Natasha, I'll make something up. Spy."

Anton shoved him in the shoulder; Jude rocked sideways, cackling. "You're such a loon," Anton told him seriously, then leaned over to rummage in his bedside drawer for paper and a pen. "I'm not making it up, though, so you need to tell me some stuff I can say."

"This is dumb, you're like the only new kid we've had in forever."

"Just tell me some labels."

"I don't know," Jude said. He started to fidget with the duvet. "I don't really use any. Why would I?"

"Labels help you express your identity," Anton said, "and convey what you are to other people. And to yourself, sometimes."

Jude stared.

"It's what my psychiatrist says," Anton defended himself, and tapped the pen against Jude's hand. "If we'd never met, how would you tell me who you are?"

"Uh, 'hi I'm Jude'?"

"But what's that?"

"I don't know. I'm…a guy?"

"Okay, so that's part of your identity, you're male."

Jude screwed up his face. "I'm…from London? Urgh, this is stupid. What are yours?"

"Well, the obvious one is that I'm transgender."

"But—look, I get why now you're using it, like right now, but what about in ten, twenty, thirty years when you're all done and you're off in some fancy house with your lawyer husband? Are you still going to use it, or will you just be a man?"

"My lawyer husband?"

"Missing the point, Ant."

"I don't know," Anton said honestly. "I think maybe I'll just call myself male, you know? I like people not knowing. I like people just thinking I've always been male. So maybe I'll drop it, but for now, that label's good. It's better than knowing something's wrong but not what."

"When you were a kid, you mean?"

"Yeah."

"Fair enough," Jude said. "I mean, if it helps. But this project's assuming we all use them or need them, and I don't."

"You said you weren't sure if you were bisexual or not?" Anton probed gently.

"Yeah, but honestly, I'm not sure I really care neither," Jude said. "So I might like guys, too, big deal, right? It's not like I have to get it tattooed on my arm or added to some big government registry or something. I didn't exactly go around saying I was straight all the time either."

Anton was faintly jealous of Jude for it, truth be told. It was easy for Jude, and Anton wished he could have that same ease. He said as much, and Jude winced.

"Shit, sorry, I don't mean—"

"No, it's fine," Anton interrupted. "Maybe I should just present that? That you don't like using labels? You know, make the point that some people don't and that's cool, too."

"Anything to get you to stop talking about school."

Anton rolled his eyes, still making notes. "What d'you want to talk about?"

"Don't really feel like talking at all."

The paper and pen were suddenly slid out of Anton's hands, and then Jude was just *there*, all up in his space so Anton could feel the heat rolling off him. They settled back against the pillows, Jude's weight surprisingly heavy all along Anton's body, and Anton scowled, mock-affronted.

"I was writing."

"Yeah, you *were*."

"I was practically doing homework."

"And thus I am rescuing you from a fate worse than detention. See? I'm practically a hero." Jude's expression was nothing short of smug, and Anton laughed giddily, looping his arms around Jude's neck and drawing him down into a kiss.

It was peaceful. That was Anton's first realisation. It wasn't the same as the hurried fumble in the tube station; it was just…kind of sweet, kind of contented, somewhere in that zone.

Jude was heavy, but he was warm, and it was like having a super cuddly duvet all over you. He had one hand planted on the mattress to support a bit of his weight, and the other had found its way under Anton's T-shirt and was squeezing his waist, about halfway between his hip and the bottom of the binder.

Somehow, Jude's stillness was the most relaxing thing about it all, and Anton found himself drifting a little, lost in the quiet and the sensation of Jude's stubble rasping on his skin. Jude's uniform was scratchy, his tie an annoyance, and Anton eventually broke away to pull at it, tossing the irritating fabric away to the sound of Jude's sniggering.

"Didn't think you hated ties that much."

"I do when they're digging into my chest."

"Does the strip show stop there?"

Anton hesitated, and Jude—still sitting up on his heels astride Anton's thighs having removed his tie—tilted his head.

"I can take my shirt off if you want."

"I won't, though."

"Didn't say you had to."

Anton eyed him. He *did* want. He'd rumpled Jude's hair up, and his trousers weren't exactly hiding anything anymore, but…

"You won't mind?"

"What, being the only one in my pants? Nah. Anyway I'm wearing a vest so you can pretend it's a really shitty binder, if you want."

Anton blinked. "You're wearing a vest?"

"Yeah."

"Really?"

"Er, yeah."

"Why?"

Jude coloured. "The school shirts are shit."

"What's that got to do with anything?"

"They itch."

"Itch what?"

Jude blew upwards into his hair, which was the same colour as his face all of a sudden. "My nipples, alright? I have to wear a vest or I'd be walking around at school all day in some weird turned-on-by-pain thing."

Anton laughed. He didn't *mean* to, it just sort of burst out, and Jude rolled his eyes. "Sorry! Sorry, sorry, that's really bad of me, just—wow, *really?*"

"Yes!"

"Can I—?"

Jude shrugged and in a way that Anton envied, just unbuttoned his shirt like it was nothing. He was wearing a plain white vest underneath, and Anton gently touched his fingers to the hem of it. Cotton, washed and re-washed so many times it had been worn smooth. Jude's skin was hot through the fabric, and Anton paused before deciding to hell with the vest, and pushing his hand up underneath it.

"Pervert," Jude said, then leaned down and caught Anton's mouth with his own again. It was hungrier this time, more deliberate and calculated, and Anton bit Jude's lip for the attack before settling, exploring blindly under that thin vest. Jude was fuzzier than Anton had imagined, and he actually had abs, the lucky fu—

His fingers found one nipple, and had barely grazed it when Jude twitched. A full-body twitch, almost like his hips had gone for it and his brain had intervened, and Anton broke the kiss.

"Seriously?"

"Oh yeah."

He did it again, and watched in fascination as Jude's eyes rolled up in his head and he exhaled shakily. Anton's own breathing caught at the sight of him, and he tugged gently on Jude's hair again to get another kiss, alternating the movement of his hand inside Jude's vest with the exact rhythm of their kisses. They resettled, Jude somehow heavier than before, one of his legs slowly pushing between Anton's like it had at the tube station. His hands started wandering, too, around Anton's waist and hips, and—

It was like a cold shock when Jude's fingers touched the bottom of the binder. They were under his shirt, and Anton had liked the play of them over his stomach, but the moment they touched his binder, it was like a chill.

For a split second, he simply—paused.

Then his brain caught up. This was Jude. Just Jude. Jude who had taken his shirt off without any expectation Anton would do the same, who *knew* now and still hadn't bailed on the whole thing, who'd outright said he still fancied Anton, who'd said in the cinema that day to just push if—

Anton pushed Jude's hand back down. "Not the binder," he mumbled, and Jude simply hummed and kissed him again, his hand returning to stroking at the crook of Anton's hip in a way that was both thrilling and nerve-wracking at the same time. It was dangerously low, and yet heavy and settled the way it had been on that first date in the cinema. Somehow, Anton knew it wasn't moving anywhere else for a little while.

Yet...

Yet, oddly, Anton suddenly didn't know how to feel. He'd literally just opened his legs for Jude. He was on the bottom, so to speak, and—well, they'd be this way round if he were a girl, wouldn't they? Jude had tried to touch his chest like he would a girl, and Anton was—

With another chill, albeit a less powerful one, Anton realised he was damp. Jude was a heavy weight between Anton's legs, and Anton was *wet*—

"Much as I'm enjoying that," Jude mumbled, his voice a shock in the midst of Anton's suddenly creeping thoughts, "unless you actually want a shag in the next five minutes, you might want to stop it."

"Um—wh—?"

"Your hand."

Anton started, realising his hand was still massaging Jude's chest, and a sudden wash of relief hit him so hard it knocked the wind out of him. He laughed breathlessly, and stopped it, removing his hand and winding both into Jude's hair to kiss him soundly again. It was okay. It was all okay. It was just Jude, and if Anton needed a breather, Jude wouldn't be a dick about it. And maybe Jude needed a breather, too. "Okay," he mumbled against Jude's lower lip, "but I'm making a note of that."

"If you attack my nipples at school, I'll fucking kill you."

"No, you'll drag me into the loos and do things to me."

"Me? You're the evil sod touching up my nipples. Fuck, my dick actually *hurts* right now."

Despite the bitchy tone, though, Jude stayed wrapped around him. Still. Relaxed. And okay, Anton *could* feel…well, something near his hip that didn't belong to *him*, and okay, it was probably more than a bit cruel to leave Jude just hanging like that, but…

But Jude also wasn't doing anything about it. And something about that, about the way he was simply whining between kisses that were getting steadily lazier again…

Something sealed over in Anton's chest, the cold receding under the idle warmth of Jude's lax body, and he whispered, "Next time I attack your nipples, you better have a condom."

Chapter 16

WERE U AT???

"I'm guessing by the silly look on your face, it's Jude?" Aunt Kerry commented, and Anton scowled at her. "I'm just saying, you look gormless when he texts you!"

"Shut up, Auntie."

"Meh-meh-meh, shut-up-Auntie."

"How are you a mum?" Anton demanded, and Aunt Kerry laughed as she pulled the car over outside the clinic.

"I'm enjoying what's left before my two turn into bitchy teenagers, too," she proclaimed dramatically, then gave Anton a fond smile. "Need me to come in?"

"No. But thanks."

"Alright, honey. Ring me when you're done and I'll come and pick you up again."

Anton nodded, already sliding out of the car and thumbing out an answer to Jude. *Not coming 2 school 2day, got appt at clinic.*

!??! DAFUQ was the fast—and funny—reply, and Anton snorted into his sleeve before cancelling the call that suddenly came in.

Counselling clinic! he said, just in case any of the other boys were near Jude's phone. *I have it every 3 months its fine :)*

Counselling???

Anton bit his lip. *R u alone?*

Off topic much? But yes. COUNSELLING???

Gender clinic, he said, and added the link to Ellen's website. *To help with my trans stuff.*

It took Jude a while—presumably he was checking out the website, Anton guessed—and he slid the phone away to sign in at reception and head up to Ellen's waiting room. It didn't ping again for another five minutes, and when it did…

Ohhh i c. Sorry told u i'm a dumbass :(can i come ask loads of dumb ?s later?

Jude's frank admission and honesty made the centre of Anton's chest burn hot for a moment, and he smiled stupidly at the phone screen for a minute. *Okay*, he said eventually. He didn't expect the day's session to go badly, after all, and Jude wanting to know how it went was…nice.

"Anton?"

He looked up guiltily, and switched his phone off at the eye-roll that Ellen offered him from the doorway to her consultation room.

"I've never seen you so glued to that phone before," she said, waving him in with a smile. "Having a row-by-text with your dad?"

"No," Anton said. "Um, Jude."

"And who's Jude when he's at home?"

Ellen Freeman was a psychiatrist specialising in gender identity issues. She was about thirty-five or forty, with dark hair and an expressive face prone to talking more than her mouth did. Anton liked her—all the counsellors and psychiatrists he'd gone through to get to Ellen had been all…fluffy, and *talk to the pencil case if it makes you feel better*, and urgh. Ellen was normal, and Anton liked that. It didn't feel like having psychiatry appointments. It felt like having a chat. He always felt better after seeing Ellen, even if they had to talk about bad things, and she liked giving him practical advice, too, like about binders and voice exercises and stuff. It felt like Ellen actually *helped*.

And cared. So Anton said, "He's my new boyfriend," and sat back to feel a bit smug about it.

Ellen nearly dropped her pen. "Excuse me?"

"Jude. He's my new boyfriend."

"A *boyfriend*," Ellen said, and beamed, pushing her glasses up her nose and twisting in her seat to face Anton more fully. "And where did you spirit a boyfriend from, may I ask?"

"He's in my form at the new school," Anton said.

"Well, I was going to focus this session on how your new school is, but now I don't think I'll bother, off you go."

Anton bit his lip in the middle of his grin, and shrugged. "It's, um. Good."

"Full of stray boyfriends, is it?"

"No, just that one."

"Mhmm. So tell me about 'that one.'"

Anton flushed, and turned the phone around in his hands. "He's—" Funny, fit, awesome, amazing, kind, n—"Nice."

"Nice?"

"Yeah. He's really...nice," Anton repeated lamely.

"Let's pretend I don't understand the word nice for a minute, Anton. Tell me more."

"He's ginger?"

"He's nice and he's ginger, alright..."

Anton blew upwards into his hair. "He's just...he found out," he said, deciding to jump straight into the middle. "He was round my house and Lily called me Tasha and then told him everything. And I just...I bailed. I ran up to my room, and Aunt Kerry had to ask Jude to go, and—he turned up the next morning before school, and just...he asked if I'd meant to tell him, and when I said yes, he just went 'well, I'm not mad, then' and we went to this cafe place near Baker Street and talked. And he listened. And he didn't wig out, and he's still my boyfriend."

Ellen's smile was very wide. "Nice," she echoed, and nodded. "Yes, he sounds nice. Does he know other transgender people?"

"No," Anton said. "He's just...you know, nice. His stepsister— I thought she was his girlfriend at first, actually—but his stepsister, Emma, she said to me she might be bisexual and Jude knows about that, and then *he* said to me that he's never had a crush on a guy before but he wasn't like totally freaked about it. And he likes to ask questions, you know, he's like…he's trying to understand, but he's not bothered that he *doesn't* understand. You know?"

"Do you mind that he doesn't understand?"

"No," Anton said honestly. "He doesn't…you know, he doesn't tease me. I can talk about it without feeling like I'm being stupid, or he's judging me for it. So I don't mind that I have to triple-explain stuff, or he puts his foot in it sometimes."

"Like?"

"Like, um…like when I said I was going to get top surgery, he said it was a shame. And for a minute I was like, it's not your fucking place to say if it's a shame or not, but then he said sorry and it was just a straight-guy outburst about boobs and to ignore him."

Ellen nodded. "That's quite a common initial outlook for cisgender people to have on surgery—it must hurt, or it's a bit extreme, or why would you want to do it as you already look pretty, that kind of thing. Did it bother you?"

"A little bit, but then he said sorry and he hasn't said it again, so it's fine. He's usually really considerate," Anton insisted. "He, like, broached the subject of transgender people in PSHE at school without giving away it was me or he actually knew anyone who's trans. And, um, we've made out a bit and he's, you know, he touched my chest and I shoved his hand away because it felt horrible and he didn't say a thing, he just moved his hand and carried on. He didn't insist or want to talk about it, he was just like 'okay' and didn't do it."

"That's really important, you know that, Anton?" Ellen said seriously. "It's absolutely vital that Jude respects your boundaries with physical intimacy—and that's nothing to do with your gender identity, either. You could be cisgender female—or cisgender male—and that would still be *really* important."

"Yeah, I know," Anton said, feeling his face heat up a little bit.

"You don't have to tell me, obviously, but have you gone any further than a bit of making out?"

"No."

"Then I suggest you do discuss the matter," Ellen said. "You need to know what Jude's thinking. Is he experienced with boys?"

"No, I don't think so. He said I'm the first boy he's ever crushed on, and he said he wasn't sure until I told him I'm trans that he was going to be able to get to the sex part with me anyway, 'cause he's only been with girls."

"Then you need to discuss it," Ellen repeated. "He may be thinking of you sexually as a girl, imagining engaging in heterosexual acts with you—and if you're comfortable with that, then fine. But if you want to engage in acts more common to homosexual boys than a heterosexual couple, then you need to discuss that. Jude may not be keen on the idea of having any attention reciprocated."

"You mean anal," Anton said, wrinkling his nose.

"I mean a lot of things," Ellen said, tutting. "Gay sex isn't just anal. At the end of the day, Jude is going to be approaching this as blind as you are, and you need to be very honest and open with each other. He'll have boundaries, too."

Anton fidgeted, biting his lip. "Um...is it...I mean, I could ask my doctor, but...you're here and I reckon you'd know...is it normal that I, um...I got...wet."

"When you and Jude were intimate?"

"Yeah. Like...you know. Down there."

"That's physically perfectly—"

"I know it's *physically* normal, but it was like...I was grossed out and I didn't like it, like how I don't like my chest, but at the same time, I just wanted him to carry on doing what he was doing, and it was really exciting. Is that normal? That it could feel good and a bit gross at the same time?"

Ellen chuckled. "Yes," she said firmly, and Anton relaxed. "Cisgender sex can be just the same way. Most sex acts are a bit gross if you think about them too hard, but as long as you are comfortable, consenting, and enjoying it more than it's disgusting, then it's fine."

"And he was, um, he was hard, and it was...you know, pressing against me, and it felt really nice—over my clothes, we weren't naked or anything..."

"Alright..."

"I just, you know…I kind of wanted him to…touch me. You know. There. Even though I'm still…"

"Anton, all transgender men experience sex in different ways. Just like straight and gay men the world over. Some don't have sex at all because it triggers too much dysphoria, others enjoy sex in a way that would be physically indistinguishable from sex they would have had as a cisgender female, others still engage mostly in homosexual acts. And there is an enormous spectrum of perfectly healthy, normal sexual behaviour between those options. If it doesn't trigger your dysphoria, then don't worry about it."

"But it would be…you know, I'd be the girl. If we'd just carried on, like."

"If you enjoy what Jude does, then encourage him to keep doing it. If you don't enjoy it, tell him to stop. Don't try and analyse what you're doing or feeling to see if it's 'male enough.' Plenty of transmen still have and enjoy vaginal sex on a regular basis, and it doesn't make them any less male, or undo their transition. I have plenty of adult transmen on my patient list who won't have bottom surgery for the very reason that it would change their sex life, and they're perfectly happy with it as it is. It doesn't make them less male to enjoy using what they happen to have. Alright?"

Anton chewed on the corner of his lip, but nodded. "It's just…daunting," he admitted. "I don't know what I'm doing."

"Of course you don't," Ellen said, "but that's something you have in common with millions of cisgender teenagers as well. There's nothing abnormal or worrying in what you've said to me here. You just need to be very open and honest with Jude, and judging by his reaction to your gender identity, it sounds like he will be perfectly receptive to that discussion."

"He will be," Anton said, convinced.

"The rules aren't different for the two of you. You sort out what you both enjoy, and you do it—consensually, safely, and not in public."

"Ellen!"

"Worth saying," she smirked, then clicked her fingers. "One thing you must remember, though, Anton—and a lot of transmen forget this one—you can still get pregnant. Protection. Use it."

Anton grimaced, resisting the urge to cross his legs. "I'm not going to get pregnant, Ellen."

"Engage in vaginal sex without a condom, and you might well do," she said firmly. "So you're starting to be sexually intimate with Jude—what about the wider picture? What do you do together that doesn't involve condoms?"

"Everything?" Anton suggested sarcastically, then shrugged. "You know. Hang out. Go to the cinema sometimes. Play football. We're going ice-skating at the weekend 'cause it's Emma's birthday, so..."

"Your mutual friends are aware, then?"

"That we're dating," Anton said slowly.

"And about your gender identity?"

Anton mutely shook his head. To his relief, Ellen merely made a note and nodded.

"Are they accepting of that relationship?"

"Yeah," Anton said. "Some of the boys tease Jude a bit, but it's not like nasty teasing. And he's really—he doesn't get weird in public or anything, and there's this one kid, Will Thorne, he says stuff sometimes and Jude just gets in his face, like. It's not secret."

"Would you say it would be a different relationship if you were a cisgender male?"

Anton opened his mouth—and paused. Would it be? They'd have done more than a bit of kissing on his bed, he was pretty sure. Jude obviously wanted to, and Anton kind of did, too, so maybe if he wasn't so weird about getting naked and letting Jude see him, touch him properly, then...

"Maybe we'd have...done more. You know, in bed."

This was what he liked about Ellen—she didn't call him on it or challenge him, she simply said, "Anything else?"

Anton frowned, thinking, then slowly shook his head. It wouldn't be, really. Jude would still have suddenly gotten his first crush on a guy, and—oh.

"Actually," Anton said, "maybe it'd be the same. Jude said, you know, when I told him, he said it eased a bit of his worry that he'd get down to the sex bit and it'd be like, a major turn-off for him, another guy's junk. So maybe we'd not be further into that."

Ellen nodded. "My point is, Anton," she said gently, "that it sounds to me like you have a perfectly normal relationship right now. It's going to get harder if you're still together when you start to medically transition, but Jude's ability to accept your social transition is a hugely important first step, and aside from that, it sounds like you've managed to keep a very normal, healthy relationship going right over that bump in the road."

Anton fidgeted with the knee of his jeans, biting his lip. "I'm...I'm still scared I'll get my kit off and he'll realise how weird this all is."

"I think from the sound of it, if he is a little thrown, he'll be open to discussing it," Ellen said gently. "Everyone gets nervous, Anton. I'm sure Jude is nervous, too. You know, if he's interested in learning about your issues like you suggested, he's perfectly welcome to join us for a short session if you would like? I'm no relationship counsellor but I'm sure I can hear out any concerns he might have, or have some suggestions for the both of you together."

It actually sounded like a cool idea, 'cause for all Jude was all eager to learn and stuff, Anton still found himself snapping sometimes, assuming that stupid questions were being asked out of malice instead of just ignorance, and he thought maybe Ellen would be better with that stuff. "I'll ask," he promised, mentally crossing his fingers that Jude would like the idea, too.

"Alright—now, I have the information your mother wanted regarding the legality around your gender when it comes to applications for sixth form or university in a couple of years—but first, I want you to do something in time for our next session, Anton."

"Uh-huh?"

"I want you to sit Jude down somewhere neutral—your living room, or his, but not a bedroom—and I want you to discuss sex. Tell him what we've discussed today, get his views on things, find out his experiences. And very importantly, find out his boundaries."

"His boundaries?"

"Mhmm. Jude's going to have sexual boundaries, too, and I think it's important you realise that. You're not on an uneven playing field when it comes to sex—you're attracted to each other, and there will be things both or one of you doesn't want to do. Jude will have those limits, too. You may have them—or find them—relating to your dysphoria, but everyone has boundaries relating to a myriad of things. Find out some of Jude's. Broach the topic, and have an open, frank discussion with him. Alright?"

Anton nodded slowly, turning it over. Jude would probably come over after school. He'd been all curious and said he wanted to ask dumb questions. So...then?

"Okay."

Chapter 17

JUDE DIDN'T COME over. And he wasn't at school on Friday. Emma had a scathing story about him slipping on ice in the back garden and giving himself an almighty concussion, but Jude—when Anton texted him at break—told a heroic story of rescuing a cat from a shed roof. Given Jude's wide-eyed, slightly terror-laced respect of Max, Anton was inclined to believe Emma.

With Friday lost, Anton dithered all of Saturday morning about whether to invite Jude over, still trying to find his feet with exactly how comfortable he—and Jude, really—was with it all. Jude starting to…well, trying to do stuff, had brought a lot of the anxiety back. And even if Ellen had been really nice and talked loads about it, Anton still wasn't sure…

Well, what he *would* like. And if Jude would like it, too. What if he didn't like doing it *any* way? Or what if he only liked it this one way, and Jude hated that way? And what if—

His phone interrupted his anxiety about eleven, with just a *ur place or mine???* and by eleven thirty, the doorbell was ringing.

"I'll get it!" Anton called to Aunt Kerry, who was doing something she called cooking and he called nuclear warfare in the kitchen. Lo and behold, Jude was on the doorstep, grinning with a fading black eye, and Anton stared. "Holy shit."

"Good, innit?"

"And you expect me to believe you got that from rescuing a cat?"

"Fell out of the tree, didn't I?"

"You said it was a shed roof."

"Must've been the concussion talking."

Anton shook his head. Jude just beamed that big, beautiful smile, and rocked forward on his feet to kiss Anton sharply. His mouth was cold, but soft.

"S'pose you ought to come in, then."

"Please, I'm freezing. Any colder, and *I'll* be the girl."

Anton laughed, the joke not prickling like it once would have done, and shut the door on the chill as Jude shed his layers on the mat. There were not-quite-frozen raindrops in his hair, which Anton brushed out before offering Jude another kiss. He felt…oddly fluttery. Anxious and calm all at once. Like…

His brain twigged. Like he had been when Jude had gotten hard. A bit scared of it, but really excited at the same time.

"So how'd your session with Ellie go?"

"Ellen," Anton corrected. They followed the heat back into the kitchen, and Jude perched on a stool. Molly started circling his feet hopefully. "No, Molly. D'you want a drink?"

"Okay," Jude said, eyeing Molly. "Is that one a nice one?"

"Nicer than Max," Aunt Kerry said cheerfully. Jude narrowed his eyes at Molly, then patted his lap. She leaped up.

"Holy hell, she's heavy."

"They're Maine Coons," Anton said, sliding a can of Pepsi across the kitchen island towards him. "They're like the biggest or second biggest domestic housecat or something."

"I believe it. This is like having your Lily on my lap," Jude said. He experimentally scratched Molly's head and she cuddled right into his chest, purring loudly. "Okay, this one I like."

Anton smiled, pulling up the stool opposite. Aunt Kerry deposited some of her latest biscuits—still warm, and still dubious-looking—on a plate between them.

"So," Jude prompted, "how did Ellen go?"

"Okay," Anton said. "I like Ellen, she's okay. She doesn't think I'm too young to know like some of the other doctors have."

"How many doctors d'you have to see?"

"At the minute, just Ellen. But your GP has to refer you to the mental health people—"

"The mental health lot? Why? They're for crazies."

Anton frowned. "Well...transgenderism's not a...a crazy thing..."

"So why're they sending you to the head doctors? That doesn't make sense."

"Well, no, but...I guess...there's nobody else to see."

"That's stupid," Jude said flatly. "That's like sending Emma to the head doctor 'cause she had a girlfriend that one time."

Anton shrugged awkwardly. "I dunno. That's just where you go. I guess maybe they have to weed out the actually crazy people. But after that...I'm too young to start medical transition, I told you, so I see Ellen as often as I need to, or every three months minimum, and work through any problems and manage my dysphoria and stuff. And then when I'm sixteen, I'll be legal and I might be able to start hormone therapy and stuff."

Although his back was to Aunt Kerry, Anton could feel her eyes on them. Jude simply sat thoughtfully scratching Molly, and eventually said, "So what do you and Ellen talk about?"

"What's going on in my life? Like school and stuff. It's been about school loads lately. And Thursday we talked about you."

"About me?"

"Uh-huh."

"Did you tell her about my sweet moves on the football field?"

Aunt Kerry laughed. So did Anton. "No. She's not into football."

"Urgh, man, find yourself another shrink."

Anton smiled, watching Jude's fingers in Molly's fur absently. "Like...like Ellen's all about me having a normal life, you know. Like...as if I was born a boy, a normal life."

"You're doing pretty good so far."

Anton felt his face heat a little at Jude's easy tone. "Thank you," he said carefully. Ellen kept telling him off for that, too, arguing when people complimented him. "And, you know, Ellen's always saying if I fancied someone and I was cisgender—"

"You were what now?"

"Like you. Gender and sex matching up. That."

"Oh. Oh, right, yeah, sorry."

"S'okay. But Ellen's always saying if I was cisgender and I fancied someone, I'd ask them out. I mean, you know, provided the guy wasn't a huge homophobe or had a crazy knife-wielding girlfriend or something." Jude laughed. "So she was really pleased at…this."

"This?"

"You 'n' me."

"Being…?"

Jude's voice was half-teasing, half-not, and Anton scowled, broke off a bit of a dodgy-looking biscuit, and flicked it at Jude's forehead. "You being my boyfriend," he clarified, and the word thrummed on his tongue.

"Ohh, yeah, that thing."

"Larimer and Walsh are right, sometimes you *are* a stupid wanker," Anton said, but Jude just grinned.

"Wouldn't you like to know?"

Anton rolled his eyes, and opened his mouth to tell Jude about the rest of the session—then stopped. "Er," he said. "D'you wanna go into the living room?"

"Anton," Aunt Kerry said warningly.

"Not for *that*, Jesus!" Anton exploded, heat flooding his face. "I have some stuff from the session I need to talk to Jude about in *private*, that's all."

"No funny business," she said anyway, and Jude grinned this totally unhelpful, lecherous grin.

"Stop it," Anton said, jabbing a finger at his face before taking the Pepsi cans and vanishing into the living room. They *did* have to talk about his session with Ellen, but there was no way Anton was going to talk about sex with Jude in front of Aunt Kerry. Or sex *at all* in front of Aunt Kerry.

It took Jude a little while to follow—and when he did, he was still carrying Molly, all floppy fur draped over both arms. Anton smiled and shut the living room door before unlatching Molly's claws and ignoring her plaintive wail as he detached her from Jude's T-shirt.

"She likes you."

"Yeah, well, I don't like her claws," Jude groused. They dropped onto the sofa, and Molly immediately sat by Jude's feet. "So, I'm guessing as this isn't your room, this isn't about me wanking?"

"Not exactly," Anton admitted. He folded himself into a cross-legged position and started picking at the sofa cushions. "Um, Ellen and I talked about sex."

"Okay?"

"And about how...about how you and me need to talk about it, too," Anton mumbled.

"Fine," Jude said. He twisted to face Anton, one arm propped up against the back of the sofa. "So, what d'you wanna talk about regarding *le fooking*?"

That startled a laugh out of Anton, and Jude grinned again.

"S'better. Don't look so severe all the time."

Anton licked his lips. "Well, it's a serious topic..."

"Yeah, but it's not like...I-have-HIV serious. It's just sex, people have sex all the time."

"Cisgender people."

"Oh come on, you can't tell me trans people never have sex."

"No, but it's...different," Anton said awkwardly. "Like...boundaries are different and stuff, and that's kind of what we need to talk about. Um. Boundaries, and...and how we're gonna do stuff."

Jude tilted his head, and unfolded his arm so it lay flat along the top of the sofa. He wiggled his fingers, and Anton rested his head against them. "Hey," Jude said quietly, "don't look so anxious."

"I feel anxious," Anton returned.

"Yeah, but that's normal," Jude said. "It's not all, you know, clothes off, brace yourself. There's loads of sex stuff."

"But my boundaries are gonna be different to yours."

"Uh, *yeah*, welcome to sex," Jude said flippantly, and snorted. "That's not a trans thing either. My boundaries would be different to yours even if you did have a dick. Like...like okay, if you had a dick, right, and you weren't cut, you might not want me touching you in a certain way because it'd be like…a sensory overload. Whereas I'm circumcised, so the head isn't as sensitive as it would have been otherwise, yeah?"

Anton blinked, and glanced down at Jude's crotch without quite meaning to. "Uh," he said.

"Judaism. Takes stuff outta you. Or off you, as the case may be."

"I thought…I thought you said you were from a Catholic—"

Jude smirked. "I am, I'm fucking with you. I *am* cut, though."

"So why are you, um…?"

"I dunno," Jude said. "Health reasons? I *was* born in a Jewish part of London, it was probably normal back then. My point is, two guys are gonna have different things they like and don't like anyway."

"Mine might be weirder though."

"Might be?"

Anton grimaced. "I don't really know yet."

"You've not had sex before?"

"No."

Jude shrugged. "Okay."

Anton eyed him suspiciously. "Have you?" he asked after a minute.

"Yeah."

"You have?!"

"Uh, yeah?" Jude repeated. "A few times, actually. I told you, I had a girlfriend."

"How old were you? When you, um…"

"Popped my cherry?"

"Jude!"

Jude laughed. "Twelve."

"*Twelve!*"

"Man, you are such a prude. Yes, I was twelve. Her name was Grace, and it was totally graceless. She was two years older than me and she lived around the corner. Might still live around the corner, I don't really know. Anyway she asked me if I liked girls yet, I said I liked girls just fine, and she took off all her clothes."

Anton could feel his jaw hanging open.

"I had sex before I even had a blowjob," Jude said. "And it

was kind of crap actually. Much better with Megan, I knew what to do with it by then."

"Holy shit."

Jude laughed again, and ruffled Anton's hair. "Gonna be different with you anyway, especially if it turns out you don't like it the, uh, traditional straight way."

"Vaginally," Anton said, and wrinkled his nose. The word itself was grim.

"Yeah."

"I don't know."

Jude's hand started to scratch lightly again. "We'll figure it out. No big deal."

Anton could feel a little lump forming in his throat again. "But what if it is a big deal? I mean, what if I can't even let you touch me there without massive dysphoria issues? I couldn't even let you touch my chest the other day, and—"

"And," Jude interrupted softly, "you didn't mind me getting hard. You even liked it when I moved a bit. And—you know, not trying to be arrogant or anything here, but I can read body language, Anton. You were pretty into it, aside from the blip with the chest."

Anton opened his mouth, and shut it again with a click. He had been. He couldn't deny it, nor did he want to.

"Were you turned on?"

"I—yes. Yeah."

"Then we can figure it out," Jude said, shrugging. "I can obviously do stuff that turns you on, I think we've proved that you turn me on—which honestly was my slightly bigger concern, given as how I know what you're packing but I honestly do see you as a guy, Anton, so I wasn't totally sure my dick and my brain were gonna agree with each other on the whole you being attractive thing. I was a bit worried my dick would decide you were too much of a guy for its tastes. So, you know, I'm not worried anymore. So I can't grope your chest, so what. I don't think I'd appreciate you groping mine either."

Anton laughed, but it wobbled dangerously. Jude grimaced, and reached.

"C'mere."

Anton shuffled sideways into the hug. Molly saw her chance and jumped up with a reproachful chirp, draping herself across their legs like a huge, fuzzy blanket.

"It's okay," Jude said, once the hug had settled, squashed as it was under the massive cat. "So you're going to be a bit unpredictable with what I can't do, so what? Would it be easier if I shared some of my boundaries first?"

"Maybe," Anton mumbled.

"Okay, well, if you pull my hair I will seriously cut you up. I *hate* hair-pulling. Like every person I've ever made out with has pulled my hair, and it's nasty as fuck, why does anyone *do* that?"

Anton smiled at the outrage, and reached up to stroke a finger tentatively through Jude's hair. "I think it's the colour," he said, watching the auburn shimmer and seem to bend in the light.

"So? Red isn't the universal sign for 'give me a good yank, it's okay, it doesn't hurt.' It *does* hurt. So yeah, you can touch my hair all you want, but you pull it, I will make with the revenge and you won't need a surgeon to sort out your chest."

Anton laughed properly then, twisting a lock of it around his finger but making sure—*very* sure—not to pull.

"And I'm not that big on having my arse touched either. Just feels a bit weird, kind of like...you're on the wrong side, all the good stuff's at the front, not the back," Jude continued mildly. "Also I don't do sex standing up. Or anything else that involves coming."

"Why?"

"Go weak in the knees when I'm done," Jude said bluntly, and Anton grinned. "What? It's true. Anyway, those are my big ones. Don't fucking pull my hair, and I'd prefer you left my arse alone, too."

Anton bit his lip. "That's still...I mean...mine is going to be about...about me hating how I feel, and..."

"I hate how having my hair pulled feels. I know it's not the same, but it kind of is," Jude pointed out quietly. "Look, at the end of the day, I want to have sex with you. But that's not just, you know, getting my dick inside you. A handjob is sex, you know? If you don't like me touching you, we can try touching over your underwear, or grinding, or loads of other stuff. Megan rode my thigh once and got herself off that way. There's loads of stuff, it doesn't matter if your dysphoria means a bit of it's out-of-bounds. And you never know, it might not. It might be too busy being like a guy and all 'woo, sex!' to notice."

Anton laughed a little shakily. "Is that what your brain does?"

"Yeah. I wouldn't normally just drop my pants in front of you, it's a bit embarrassing really, just whipping it out in front of people like that. But when I know I might get something for it, sure."

Anton took a deep breath. "Okay. Well. I think we…I think we figured out my chest is out-of-bounds. Sex or no sex."

"Okay," Jude said easily. "Honestly? I'll forget the first couple of times. Just shove my hand away, okay? I'm not gonna get pissy if you just push my hand away. And I'm warning you right now, if I sleep with you—and I mean sleep-sleep, not sex-sleep—my hand always tended to end up cupping one of Megan's boobs when I slept with her, so that might happen the odd time."

Anton swallowed. "I'll just…push it away." And hope for the best.

"'Kay," Jude said. "I won't touch them on purpose though, yeah?"

"Yeah."

"If you don't pull my hair on purpose."

Chapter 18

THE MOMENT ANTON got into the car on Saturday morning, he knew it was a trap. Because of the way Mum said, "So…" as he put his seatbelt on.

"Uh…"

"Kerry said something interesting last night after you went to bed."

"Um…"

"She told me you and Jude went off to have some serious discussion about something Ellen said."

Anton flushed. "Oh. Well. Yeah."

"You've told Jude about Ellen?"

"Yeah," Anton said, relieved Aunt Kerry either hadn't heard or hadn't told Mum what exactly they'd been talking about. "He was curious, and Ellen said I ought to talk to him about…about the process and stuff, what I'm doing to transition…"

"Anything in particular?"

Anton swallowed. "Um. Well, you know, healthy relationship stuff. Like things I should expect from him and things I should give him a bit of leeway with, like…like not getting angry at him if he doesn't get something right away, but I still have the right to expect him to respect my boundaries and stuff."

"Boundaries and stuff?" Mum echoed.

Anton flushed and groaned. "Fine! We were talking about sex." Mum made a shrill noise and nearly jerked the car into on-coming traffic. "Mum! Jesus!"

"What on earth did you need to discuss sex for? You're too young for sex!"

"I'm fifteen!"

"That's too young!"

Anton snorted. "Ellen didn't think so."

"You discussed your sex life with Ellen?!"

"Yes," Anton retorted defensively. "She says it's perfectly normal and seeing as how I'm—attracted to guys, she says it's important to experiment safely with someone I trust when I feel ready to. So me and Jude talked about...boundaries. We didn't screw on the sofa while Aunt Kerry was making dinner, God, Mum."

"Anton!"

"Ellen was really positive about it!" Anton argued. "She said a lot of trans people struggle with sex because of their body issues, and she said it was really good that I was open to actually trying stuff out instead of just shoving Jude away because I don't match yet."

"And if you were an adult, I might agree with her, but you're fifteen!"

"So's Jude."

"Oh, that helps."

"What? I'm just saying, it's not like he's thirty or something. Anyway, he told me he was twelve when he did it for—"

"*Twelve*?!" Mum practically shrieked, and Anton grimaced. Thank God the skating rink was only one more roundabout away. She was totally going to kill them both.

"Mum! I've had sex ed! And I talked to Ellen! I'm not to—to get herpes or pregnant or something."

"Anton, honey—"

The moment she pulled into the car park, though, Anton was undoing his seatbelt. "It's not a big deal," he insisted, sliding out. "I'll ring when I want picking up. Or I might go back to Ju—"

"You will not."

"Fine, I'll bring Jude back to ours then," he said defiantly, and shut the door on her spluttering. Okay, so part of it was kind of funny, but...Ellen had *said* it was a good development. She was the expert. And Anton needed good developments, he needed to be normal or they'd not allow him to get hormones and surgery when he was older. If he had, you know, a totally healthy sex life and a boyfriend and everything, that would make him normal. It would make him like any other g—uh, guy that liked guys. And anyway, normal aside, he *wanted* to. Now he knew Jude wasn't going to tell the whole school about him and still liked him, Anton wasn't going to let being fifteen get in the way.

The skating rink was enormous, one that Anton had been to when he was little with his parents and for primary school birthday parties and never since. It wasn't difficult to find the others, though, Emma taunting Larimer for his gracelessness audible from the entrance. Jude, sprawled out on a bench, clocked him first and grinned, then Isabel was demanding his shoe size, Anton was trying to get Emma to take her present instead of hit Larimer, and—

It felt so *nice*. For a split second, Anton felt a lump forming in his throat, then he swallowed it back down, asked Isabel for some size fives, and tensed fractionally when Walsh did a double take at the number.

"Size *five*? Fuck me, you've got girls' feet."

"Trust me, he's doing fine in all the other measurements," Jude drawled lazily, and Anton laughed, cuffing him around the head then stooping to kiss him quickly as a silent thanks. Walsh eyed them both, then slowly turned away.

"What's up with him?"

"Fuck knows, he's being shady as fuck today," Jude said dismissively. "You alright?"

"Yeah. Aunt Kerry heard us and Mum was freaking out in the car about us talking about sex."

"Oh right, yeah, 'cause you're a total fucking virgin."

"Isn't fucking virgin an oxymoron?"

"What's an oxymoron?"

"It's like saying 'clever Jude'," Emma called mockingly, then came to throw her arms around Anton's neck in a hug. "Take him off my hands today?" she wheedled. "He's being a pest."

"I am *not.*"

"It'd be the best birthday present ever."

"*Hey!*"

"I suppose I could do that," Anton said thoughtfully, and Jude kicked him. "Ow!"

"You're supposed to be on *my* side. Bros before hos."

"But you're not my bro, you're my ho."

Emma cackled with laughter, and Jude's affronted scowl was nothing short of ridiculously attractive, so Anton softened.

"I suppose I *could* be on your side occasionally."

A bit, anyway.

"Why the hell do I fancy you?" Jude groused, bending over to start putting his skates on. Anton slid onto the bench beside him to do the same, and knocked their knees lightly together.

"I dunno," he said, "but I'm glad you do."

"Right now, I'm not convinced."

Jude grumbled all the way to the ice, but was mollified by Anton not really being any good at skating and wanting to hang onto him all the time. Larimer, naturally, started falling over the minute he put one blade on the rink, and then it was just a big blurry mess of people crashing into each other, shouting and laughing, and the warm weight of Jude's arm or hand when Anton struck out for an anchor.

"Oh no," Jude said, when Anton tried for both hands. "I am not doing some girly Disney on Ice romantic shit."

"Okay, so hold my hands and pull me around."

"Lazy."

"Do it and I'll kiss you again."

Jude grinned, reaching out his free hand, and then Anton instantly regretted it. Turned out that Jude was only skating slow for his benefit. The minute he had both of Anton's hands, the lazy skate turned into some Olympic medallist racer thing, and Anton just had to hope when they crashed and both died, it would be fast.

But…

Okay, so maybe it was *kind* of fun, too. Jude was flushed with the cold in the rink, his hair was even messier than usual, and when he deposited Anton at the wall at one end of the rink, he deliberately skidded off to crash into Emma and bring them both crashing down with a war-cry. He was being silly, larger-than-life, and beautiful, and Anton wanted to—

So when Jude came back for Anton, presumably for another death-defying lap, Anton kissed him instead.

"Told you," Jude said, pulling back surprisingly fast. "I am not up for that kissing on the ice shit."

"Oh, come *on*..."

"If nothing else, Walsh will totally annihilate us both."

Anton considered that. Walsh was still looking at him funny from the other end of the rink, and he frowned back.

"How about we get him before he gets us?"

"See, *now* we're speaking the same language."

THEY SKATED FOR about an hour and a half before Emma declared it was time for them to buy her a ton of food, and they migrated from the ice to the cafe, most of them sporting bruises, and Isabel with a bloodied sleeve and a big plaster provided by the onsite first aider. But it had been fun...even if Anton was never going skating with Jude again. He was too murderous.

But as they de-booted, Anton glanced uneasily around the crowded venue, and wondered if he couldn't get away with it. He'd presumed they'd go elsewhere for food and he could sneak off for a bit, but if they were staying...

When he bent to put his trainers back on, his bladder groaned under the pressure, and he winced. There was nothing else for it.

"Jude," he whispered as the others handed back their skates. "Hang about a minute?"

Jude glanced at him quizzically, but shrugged and went back to arguing the merits of chips versus curly fries with Larimer until the food pull got too strong and they were being slowly abandoned. Only then did Anton catch at Jude's sleeve and stop him from getting up.

"What?"

"Can you, er…?"

Jude cocked his head when Anton trailed off. "Can I what?"

Anton felt his face flaming red. "I, um…I need to go to the loo."

"They're over there. Want me to wait?"

"No, can you…fuck—can you come? I've not…I've not actually had to go to the men's before."

"What, *ever*?"

Anton shook his head. His cheeks were burning. "I've never had to at school," he mumbled. "I avoid it. In case…you know." He used the stalls, obviously, but people might look under the door and see which way his shoes were. Ellen said it was a bit paranoid and he needed to push himself, but…

He could start today, right?

Right, apparently, as Jude just shrugged. "Okay," he said, and nudged Anton towards the marked doors by the entrance. Anton apologised again, and Jude laughed. "Oh, shut up. It's just the bogs. I can preen while you piss, that's what girls do, isn't it?"

Anton rolled his eyes and hit him before ducking into the toilets ahead of him. There was one guy washing his hands, and Anton hastily shot into one of the stalls and slammed the door. He heard Jude's low laugh, then his Timbaland boots settled across the bottom of the door and it creaked under his weight. Anton…kind of appreciated the silent show of support.

It was one of the annoying things that he argued with Mum and Ellen over. He didn't like having to ration water at school so he didn't have to piss, but…there was just something *about* toilets. The boys' room was for *boys*. If he went in there, and he was found out—hell, if he went in there, he *would* be found out. They'd know, somehow. Anton wasn't *meant* to be in there.

Ellen called it a societal hang-up and said it was no different from ticking 'male' on surveys, or buying clothes from the men's section of shops. Mum said nobody would come into the stalls and see him anyway, and whose business was it of theirs? Aunt Kerry always pointed out that they didn't have a special bathroom for boys in the house so why couldn't he use whichever one he liked in public?

But they weren't the ones *doing* it. It just felt weird, he hated it, and he avoided it whenever possible. It made his skin crawl, and he felt…vulnerable. Exposed. And he hated it.

Except with the dark shadow of Jude's boots across the bottom of the door, he didn't anymore. The way the door creaked when Jude's phone trilled and he shifted to get it out of his pocket, Anton felt kind of…defended. He was just going for a slash, and then they'd rejoin the others. And maybe if he could do that a few times with Jude following him around, he could get over this toilet thing.

"Oi, let me out," he said, rapping on the door with his knuckles after he was done, and Jude groaned.

"Sounds like effort."

"*Move.*"

"Al*right*, jeez." When the door was released, Jude pulled a face at him, and held up his mobile. "Walsh wants us to stop shagging and get over there, Emma's refusing to order any food until we get back."

"Tell him to sod off," Anton said daringly, sticking his hands under the tap, and being quietly grateful that the other guy had gone and they were alone. Jude laughed. "It's not like he's going to waste away. We'll only be a minute."

"One minute? That's a shit shag. I demand at least five."

Anton laughed, drying his hands on some loo roll that Jude handed him. "Not in here, that's minging."

"Well, no, but—"

The kiss came out of nowhere. The sink hit Anton's arse as he was pushed backwards into it, and Jude's hands were tight in his hair, pulling it all out of place and twisting him open to Jude's mouth. Anton fisted his fingers into Jude's T-shirt, clinging dizzily to him and hoping his brain cells would start up again in a minute and he'd be able to proper *experience* it, like, and—

Then Jude was gone, stepping back and grinning, mouth flushed pink and…fucking kissable. Git. Anton scowled.

"Rude," he said.

"What? S'what they think we're doing, I'd hate to disappoint."

"You can't just…snog-and-run like that, it's fucking rude!"

"Ooh, sorr-ee," Jude said mockingly, heading for the door. Anton hit his back then daringly jumped up and landed on him in a demand for a piggy-back. "Fuck!" Jude yelped, but his arms clamped around Anton's knees anyway. "Jesus. Fine. Just this once. Christ, you're heavier than you look. Oi, *Emma*!" he yelled as he heaved them back towards the cafe. "Emma, congrats, Anton is fatter than you are!"

"Oh fuck off, Jude, you fucking wanker!" she bellowed back, and Jude laughed, his back heaving under Anton's chest.

And Anton didn't really mind the mild insult. He was feeling too elated at having broached the men's room, and gotten necked for it, and…

"Thanks," he whispered into Jude's ear before sliding down and letting Emma attack him. He didn't dare say it louder, in case the others asked instead of mocking their hair and red lips, but…

Jude smiled, and Anton knew he'd been understood.

Chapter 19

SOMETHING HAD HAPPENED on Sunday.

Anton had decided to keep the peace at home, and went with Dad on a day out. He'd spent most of the day on his phone, to be honest, tuning out Dad's attempts at talking to him—because he kept saying Natasha, and she didn't exist anymore, so *shut up, Dad*—and getting revenge when he'd found what he was looking for on Amazon and pilfering Dad's credit card to pay for it. He'd been wanting one for ages, for *him*, and if Dad couldn't talk to him then he could bloody well pay for him, right?

But anyway, it meant he hadn't seen Jude, and when he'd texted that night asking if Jude was free Monday evening, he'd had no answer. And Anton hadn't thought that strange...until he got to school, and wasn't attacked by a good-looking ginger guy at his locker. Which had been a near-daily experience since Jude had asked him out, so...

Something was wrong.

Anton headed to his form room (complete with yet *another* locker gift) with more than a little trepidation. Jude didn't do quiet, not where Anton was concerned. And Anton hadn't really seen

Jude in a bad mood...ever. Sure, he sounded off at Will Thorne occasionally, and he got a bit pissy when he did, but it was fleeting stuff. Anton shook himself. Maybe he was overreacting—maybe Jude was just busy, or plotting something sinister with Walsh, or—

Not in at all.

Frowning, Anton sank into his seat, already fumbling in his pocket for his phone. "Where's Jude?" he asked Emma, and she grimaced.

"I'm...not really sure."

"What d'you mean?"

She blew upwards into her hair. "There was a bit of a row last night. Okay, more than a bit. Jude and his dad had a proper screaming match."

Anton blinked. "Jude...has screaming matches?"

"Not often," she admitted. She kept her eyes on her notebook, doodling absently, and Anton felt a twinge of sympathy. For all she bitched and Jude moaned, they were pretty close for steps.

"Are you okay?"

"Me? Yeah, yeah...I'm just a bit worried, you know? He was gone before I got up this morning, and I thought he'd be here, but I haven't seen him..."

Anton glanced over. Larimer was draped awkwardly all over his chair and talking to Isabel, but..."Walsh isn't here either. Maybe they're together—he'll be fine if he's with Walsh, right?"

"Maybe."

"What was the row about?"

Emma grimaced. "Jude's mum. It's always about that."

"Why?"

"Jude's parents had a really shitty marriage," she confided in a whisper. "Like, really toxic. They were both cheating on each other, they'd shout and scream and have these huge arguments all the time, and then they split up after his dad met my mum. And Jude's mum went back to Ireland and took Sean but not Jude, and I think sometimes Jude feels like his dad wanted him to go, too. Like neither of his parents really wanted to keep him. That's why he's so super nice even when dickheads like Thorney are ragging on him, he wants people to like him and stick around."

Anton opened his mouth, probably to insult one or both of Jude's parents for not wanting to keep him because *hello*, who didn't want to keep Jude?—but was stopped when the classroom door opened and Miss Taylor marched in, looking her usual acerbic self. The class settled, conversation dying, and so Anton had no chance to question Emma further or—when Jude did show up, unsurprisingly with Walsh, more surprisingly halfway through registration and without even cracking a smile at Miss Taylor's acidic greeting. He looked…not quite angry or upset, but distinctly sour, like Mum when one of the cats had left half a bird under the sofa and it hadn't been discovered for a few days.

Anton didn't quite dare text him in the middle of Miss Taylor's lecture about lateness, so he waited it out until they were all moved into their PSHE pairings and Jude came to take Emma's seat. When he did, Anton simply slid his fingers into Jude's on the desk and whispered, "Are you okay?"

Jude pulled a face and shrugged. Anton bit his lip.

"Hey, d'you want to come over tonight?" he attempted. "I ordered something from Amazon and it should get here today, and I want your opinion."

"On what?"

"You'll have to come over to find out."

Jude smiled, but it was half-hearted. "Yeah, okay."

"Hey." Anton squeezed his hand tighter. "You'll feel better, promise. It'll make you laugh. Well, one part of it will, you better not laugh at the first part."

Jude exhaled in a huffing sort of noise, and nudged his shoulder against Anton's. "Sorry. I'm just moody. Bad day yesterday."

"D'you want to talk about it?"

"Not really."

"Okay, so let's ignore it and talk about something better."

"Preferably, your assignment," came a sharp interruption, and then Miss Taylor was looming over their table, clipboard perched on her hip. "Come on, where are you two with your presentations?"

"Um, nearly done?" Anton hedged.

"Without any notes."

"We use our memories?"

"This is stupid," Jude interrupted, sitting back and folding his arms in a belligerent fashion. "I don't use any labels, and even if I did, it's nobody's business anyway."

"Then you are perfectly entitled to express that position in a presentation, Kalinowski, but there will *be* a presentation."

"What if I don't want to be presented? I'm not a project."

"The curriculum has been set and you will be marked on these presentations, so—"

"So what, give me an F then."

"It would be Anton's F."

"What, because *I* don't feel like baring my fucking soul—"

"Language!"

"—*he* gets punished? Great education, there. What's the point of this stupid project again? Get us to respect each other or some such shit, right—"

"Kalinowski, *out!*"

"How is telling thirty-five people I'm bent going to make anyone respect me anyway—"

Miss Taylor slammed her clipboard down on the table. The room was entirely silent, everyone staring in open fascination at Jude's outburst.

"Headmaster's office. Now."

Jude stood up, the chair catching on the cheap carpet and falling backwards against the desk behind them. "This is bullshit," he said loudly. "Maybe some people keep things quiet for a reason, yeah? Maybe some people don't *want* the whole universe knowing what they are."

"Now!"

Jude stormed out, not even bothering to pause for his bag, and Miss Taylor straightened slowly, eyeballing the rest of the class. They waited.

"The pupils here, and this group especially," she said quietly, "have too much of a tendency to make inappropriate jokes and remarks without consideration of other people's feelings. You don't show each other enough respect, and the board of governors feels that this project will help break down some of the barriers between you all. *However.* I am not asking you to share things that you don't want to share. What you choose to tell your project partner is of course your choice. But you will *all* present something, and you will *all* be marked on that something. Without exception."

Anton stared at the closed door, knowing suddenly who Jude had really been talking about, and felt—despite the outburst, despite Jude's mood, despite there being something clearly wrong that had shaken Jude's usually upbeat demeanour—warm.

SEEING AS HOW Jude hadn't attacked Anton at his locker in the morning, Anton launched a counter-attack after school, and hugged Jude from behind before even saying hello. It made Jude jump and swear at him, but then that still-absurdly-good-looking face softened.

"I'm sorry about this morning," he said, and Anton shrugged.

"It's okay. You were right, just…a bit not the right way to say it."

Jude smiled wanly. "Yeah, maybe."

"You still feeling shit?"

"Just grumpy. They called my dad. He's going to have a massive go at me when I get home."

"So come to mine first," Anton said, taking Jude's hand and stuffing it in his own jacket pocket. He felt oddly possessive when Jude looked down, he decided, and leaned up to kiss the corner of Jude's mouth. "I still have that thing I want your opinion on."

"What is it?"

"Come over and see. I bought a couple of things off Amazon yesterday when Dad was droning on at me and insisting on…you know."

"Your former spy name?"

Anton rolled his eyes, but smiled at the code. At least moody Jude was still entertainingly crazy. And it was kind of nice to have a way to mention it without anyone overhearing and catching on. "Yeah," he said, tugging on Jude's captured hand to tow him along once the locker was closed. "Anyway, he was being his usual jerk self so I reckoned he could pay for what I wanted on Amazon. So I pinched his credit card. He'll go mad when he finds out what I bought, but I put next-day delivery on, so he can't stop it."

"I'm guessing it's some kind of spy gadget, then?"

"It's…to do with that, yeah."

"To do with it?"

"Well…I bought two things, and one of them is like…only for spies. And the other one is used by, um…non-spies?"

"Civilians. God, I have to get you watching more spy movies."

"Wait, spy movies or spy-spy movies?"

"Wait, what?"

Anton laughed at the bewildered expression on Jude's face, so much better than the frown, and dropped his head to Jude's shoulder briefly as they waited for the traffic lights outside school to change for them.

"Thanks," Jude said quietly.

"For what?"

"Not pushing and just trying to make me feel better."

"Well, you do that for me about my spy stuff."

"That's different." ˙

"Maybe, maybe not. As long as you're okay, though. You're weird upset, I don't like it."

Jude chuckled, and his arm came around Anton's waist to squeeze briefly before they crossed the road and the conversation—very deliberately, Anton suspected, and without a hint of seamlessness to it—turned to the upcoming Spurs match on Saturday. But Anton went with it, criticised Jude's choice of line-up, and let them into the house to the sound of Jude being a little bit more animated and cheerful than he had all day.

Didn't make the hug on the doormat any less surprising, though.

"Hello?" Anton tried, rubbing his hands into Jude's hair before passing them down his neck and locking them tightly around his shoulders. "Jude? You okay?"

The hug contracted for a moment, then Jude let go and was stepping back. He *looked* okay, but Anton frowned, uncertain.

"I just…needed that," Jude said, then toed off his shoes and unzipped his coat. "Come on then, what's this spy thing?"

Anton grinned. He felt terrified and excited all at once: excited that he'd dared to go ahead and buy them, and terrified that Jude wouldn't like them. Or at least, the first one, the *important* one. If Jude didn't like the second one, then Anton would just pass it off as a joke, and it didn't really matter. But the first...

"Okay, so..." Anton seized the parcel on the side table, shaking it lightly to feel the weight inside shift around, and took a deep breath. "I'm going to get changed, and you're going to sit on my bed and wait and keep your eyes closed until I tell you to open them."

"It's clothes?"

"Sort of."

Jude followed Anton upstairs, tried for a bit of wheedling at the bedroom door, but eventually did as he was told and let Anton shut him in the bedroom. Then Anton took his box and retreated to the bathroom, his hands starting to shake. Thank God Aunt Kerry was out. There was no way he could do this with anyone else in the house, not try it on and show Jude and maybe...maybe...

He locked the door, and tore into the box.

And it was perfect. Lying there in pristine plastic wrap, which he tore through even more efficiently than the box, and a neutral colour that would let him wear white pants without it being seen. It wasn't quite the same as his skin tone, but it was close.

It was a packer.

In fact, both objects were packers, but the first one, the one he'd been wanting for a while, that was the standard soft packer. It looked just like a cock and balls, frankly, and was heavy in the palm of his hand. With it, all the forums and Ellen promised, his trousers and briefs would fit right and not give him away by being too empty when he sat down or stretched. With it, he'd look more like a boy. He'd kind of have a dick, even though it wouldn't actually be attached to him and he couldn't feel it or wank with it. But it was a dick, all the same. He'd even be able, *maybe,* to use the same changing rooms as men once he'd had his top surgery and could get rid of the binder.

Anton's palms were sweating slightly as he pulled out the

waistband of his briefs and, looking down as little as he had to, arranged himself. And when he took an experimental step back towards the door, he nearly staggered. Jesus, the way it *moved!* Was this how Jude felt when he walked around? Was this what that whole man-swagger thing was about? Holy shit.

And it felt—amazing. It felt *incredible,* that soft weight in his pants, the gentle press against the very tops of his inner thighs. He'd have to get some, like, medical glue or something, to keep it in place properly, but…for now, his briefs worked just fine, and it felt…it felt…

God, it was even better than the first time he'd looked in the mirror with the binder on under his T-shirt. He felt *male.*

With a surge of confidence, Anton took the other packer out of the pocket and tore the wrapping off that, too. It had been suggested on Amazon when he'd bought the first one, and he'd done it…because of Jude, really. It was a harder material, and could be bent to be erect. It was basically like a strap-on dildo, as far as his research could tell him, and…well, it could be used…to fuck. And maybe Jude wouldn't want Anton to fuck him, in which case Anton was okay with just putting it away and forgetting about it, but maybe…*maybe*…

Anton took a deep breath, put the hard packer back in the box, and…took off his trousers. And then his blazer, his tie, his school shirt…he stripped right down to his briefs and binder, and looked down at the bulge in his pants. God. He was…he was getting there. He was *he.* He was totally, absolutely, irreversibly getting there.

Squaring his shoulders, Anton took the box, opened the bathroom door and crossed back to his room, knocking and saying, "Eyes closed!" before slipping inside. He abandoned the box on the floor and locked the door behind him before turning to face Jude, taking another deep breath, and whispering, "You can look now."

Jude opened his eyes, and—stared.

His gaze was like being caught in the headlights, and a little of Anton's confidence shivered under the intensity of it…until Jude shifted, his feet dropping to the carpet from their former residence on the duvet, and he saw the bulge in Jude's not-exactly-forgiving school trousers.

"What d'you think?" Anton asked.

Jude's answer was to come up off the bed like a predator on the hunt, push Anton back into the locked door, and kiss him. Hard. And open, like he was trying to eat Anton rather than kiss him. Jude was heavy, a pressure all along Anton's front and the wood at his back giving even less room to move, and that tell-tale thigh ended up between Anton's knees again. Anton beamed giddily around the kiss as the packer shifted on Jude's leg, and then he could feel something else being packed pretty well, too.

"You're fucking packing," Jude said hoarsely.

"Uh-huh."

"Is that what it's even called?"

"Uh-huh."

"Like a gun?"

"Yeah."

"Like, is that a gun in your pocket?"

Anton laughed breathlessly, clinging to Jude's shoulders. He was practically straddling Jude's leg, and one of Jude's hands was right at the top of his bare thigh, almost cupping his arse. And Anton wanted more. He didn't want Jude in his uniform anymore, and he didn't want to be at the door. "I can feel more than one gun in this situation."

"Yeah? Well, I'm always armed when you're around."

"That was awful," Anton whispered, biting down hard on Jude's bottom lip as a punishment. "Can we—can we just—"

"Your bed. My turn to strip and show off what I'm packing, yeah?"

"Oh my God, yeah."

Chapter 20

"YOU," MUM SAID, "are too happy this morning."

"That's not allowed?" Anton asked. He was making his lunch, mostly because he didn't trust Mum not to sneak carrot sticks in there lately, and she'd been eyeing him ever since he'd come down from his shower.

"Not before nine. You've got a worse scowl than Lily before nine."

Anton shrugged. He'd been humming and smiling all the previous evening and that morning, and he knew Mum was suspicious, but come on. He wasn't about to say to his *mother*, "Yeah, well, that's because my boyfriend was all over me after seeing me packing in my underwear, so I gave him a hand job before he went down on me." He'd not been fucked *that* stupid.

He *was* still riding the high, though. He'd been terrified of getting a dysphoria attack, or being unable to sleep with Jude without feeling like a girl. And okay, looking back, Jude hadn't so much as touched the binder, never mind his chest, but…well, giving head involved touching other stuff, too, you know?

"I'm just looking forward to today."

"Right."

"I am!"

"Of course," Mum said as the doorbell started ringing. "Oh for God's sake," she muttered.

Anton ignored her, turning up the radio on the kitchen island and starting to hum along. His skin was still buzzing from the previous night. He wanted to ditch school and get under Jude's clothes again. He wanted to feel that rasp of invisible stubble on his cheek, on his neck, on his hip. He'd nearly had to rub one out in the shower that morning, he'd felt so much sheer *want* in his blood. If this was the rest of his relationship with Jude, he was so fucked. Literally and metaphorically. He'd never get anything done again, not like this, and Anton wasn't totally opposed to the idea, really. And if—

"Anton! It's Jude!"

What?! Jude was even harder to get out of bed for school than Anton, by all accounts. What was he doing here? Anton put down the knife and wandered into the hall, blinking in confusion at the figure on the doorstep in heavy jeans and a black coat.

"School's cancelled!" Jude beamed, and Anton stared. Mum was already calling them, by the looks of it.

"School's—?"

"It's on the website and everything. The central heating's fucked, place is sealed shut like an icy tomb. We can't go. Free day off! So come on, get changed, we're going for a quick footie game then round Larimer's once his mum's gone to work."

Mum was still on the phone, and Anton glanced her way uncertainly. It was a bit too good to be true, wasn't it? The day he wanted more than anything just to steal Jude and do it all over again, and school got cancelled? But then she sighed, hung up, and nodded. "Take your phone and keys with you, and text me at lunchtime with what you're going to do for food."

"Okay," Anton said, and grinned at Jude. "Let me just change."

He jogged upstairs, listening to Mum be all mumsy and ask Jude if he wanted anything to drink and 'just put your coat, there, honey'—and then there were socks padding up the stairs, and a shadow in Anton's bedroom doorway.

"I'm changing!" Anton scolded, and Jude laughed, shutting the door with a snap behind him. The kiss he offered was gentle but intent, something filthy and promising behind it, and Anton had to smack his hand away from the opened fly of Anton's school trousers. "Mum's downstairs."

"And we're not." Jude's hand came back, but around that top-of-leg, bottom-of-arse region again. Anton laughed a little breathlessly, kissing Jude sharply before pushing him away.

"Behave!"

"Boring."

"I'm not having my mum catch us, she's already accusing me of being too happy this morning," Anton said. He was trying for sombre, but his mouth was twisting itself up into a huge smile, and Jude laughed, kissing both corners of it in an exaggerated fashion.

"I'm totally taking credit."

Anton looped both arms around Jude's shoulders and kissed him slowly. "You should," he breathed when they parted, foreheads still touching. "I felt so fucking confident when I put that packer in, and then the way you looked at me…"

"Knew you had legs to kill for."

"I never thought anybody would be able to look at me like that. I thought they'd always see this…this mash-up between what I was and what I want to be, and not see…*me*."

"Eh?"

"I never thought anyone would be able to find me sexy when I'm not finished yet," Anton translated softly, and kissed Jude again, so lightly that their lips barely made contact. "I'm not happy with how I feel yet. I need the hormones, I need the surgery. But the way you looked at me…just for a minute, just for a while, I was everything I wanted to be."

Jude's smile was as gentle as his fingers against Anton's back. "Happy to be of service," he said quietly, then grinned. "*More* than happy."

"Might steal you off somewhere private later."

"We're somewhere private right now…"

"*No*," Anton scolded, stepping back. In a fit of bravery, he dropped his trousers and turned his back on Jude to rummage for his jeans. Jude made an appreciative noise and called him a twat, making Anton beam stupidly at his chest of drawers before wriggling into his favourite combat jeans.

"Oh fuck you, that's dirty pool."

"What, they're my favourites."

"They make your admittedly nice arse into something completely bloody ridiculous and you know it. I'm going to have a semi all day."

"Poor you," Anton said mockingly, then grinned, palming his crotch. "So will I, sort of."

"I have to make the joke I was too carried away to make yesterday."

"What?"

"That was your dick in a box."

Anton laughed, caught off-guard by the sudden switch in Jude's tone, and punched him in the shoulder before rummaging up a T-shirt. For a split second, he hesitated, then called himself stupid—after all, he'd been in his binder and nothing else when Jude had gone down on him the previous night, Jude knew the damn thing was there and what it looked like—and tore his school shirt off. Jude whistled obscenely before the T-shirt went on, and Anton scowled at him.

"Stop trying for a shag!"

"Never!"

Jude grabbed him and bundled him out of the bedroom door, managing to bite his ear before they barrelled down the stairs and Anton had to duck away to get his shoes and coat. Mum, standing in the kitchen doorway with a grizzling Rose, raised her eyebrows at him, and Anton grinned at her unashamedly.

Who cared what she thought had been going on upstairs? Who cared that it nearly *had?*

Everything—literally every tiny, little thing—was coming up right.

SOMETHING WASN'T RIGHT.

The group split after football. Emma had cried off the entire day, saying she had to plan her fundraiser. The girls had decided to use their day off to go see some film that none of the boys could be persuaded was worth the price of the ticket. The boys, by contrast, all seemed to want to play some game on Larimer's home entertainment system that involved a lot of random slaughter, and was decried by the girls as 'interactive Game of Thrones for morons.' Anton had to admit he wasn't much of a gamer, but…hey, Jude was going.

But something—namely Walsh—was off.

He kept giving Anton long sideways glances, and distracting Jude whenever Jude would put his arm around Anton. He even made Jude help him raid Larimer's parent's kitchen after Jude wriggled his toes under Anton's thigh on one of the sofas. (Yeah, one of. Larimer's house was obscene.)

Anton felt…twitchy.

Walsh had mocked the size of his feet at Emma's birthday, but he'd not said anything else, and he'd been fine with Anton the previous week. Had Jude told him something? Did he have some weird bro jealousy thing going on now one of his best mates was going off with someone else and getting laid? But if he did, why now? Okay, Anton supposed it could be the getting laid thing, but why would Walsh care about that specifically? Jude had been passing over his friends for Anton for a little while now, before sex was even a possibility. And Anton hadn't done anything stupid like let Walsh overhear him asking Jude to accompany him to the toilets. If anything, he was looking more masculine than ever now he had the packer, and Larimer was teasing Jude even more about being a reformed gayboy after Jude had let slip at the kick-about that getting laid did wonders for your football skills. Even Larimer and Walsh could do that math.

"Is Walsh okay?" he asked Jude under cover of Walsh and Larimer duking it out over some quest or other on the screen.

"Huh? Yeah. Why?"

"Never mind," Anton said quickly as Larimer lost, and Jude laughed, pulling himself up off the sofa.

"I need to piss. You girls want anything while I'm up?"

"The PIN for your phone."

"The meaning of life."

"It's 'don't get your pubes caught in your fly'," Jude deadpanned, wandering off, and Anton suddenly found Walsh eyeballing him again.

"What?" he asked. "Have I got something on my face?"

"No," Walsh said slowly. "You and Jude. How's that going?"

"Er, fine."

"So you fucked yet."

Anton frowned. "Why do you care?"

"Because there's something about you, Williams."

And just like that, Anton felt cold.

"Like what?" he managed, but his chest felt tight and airless. Walsh knew something. He'd guessed or he'd seen or he'd been smarter than Anton gave him credit for, but he knew *something*, and in Anton's experience, *something* didn't last long before it hit on the truth. And when it did—fuck, *fuck*, the way Walsh was just glowering at him, the way he'd said it, oh God—

"Are you fucking Jude around?"

"What? No."

"Thing is, Williams, I don't like people fucking with my friends. You could screw him over. We both know that he's pussy-whipped." The phrase made Anton flinch. "But you do that, I'll fuck you over so hard you won't know what hit you."

Anton licked his lips. "What makes you think I'm going to?"

"I don't know why you're so cagey, but you are. And cagey people, they got shit to hide."

"Sure it's not just you're mad now your best mate's off with someone else?" Anton dared, attempting to deflect it, but Walsh wasn't a girl, and batted it aside like it meant nothing.

"Piss off. This is about you, not me. And when I find out what's going on with you, he'll know. I don't let my friends get fucked over."

Anton jutted out his chin. "My life's my business. What makes you think he doesn't already know?"

Walsh snorted. "Because he runs at the mouth and would have told us."

Something in Anton's chest jumped in victory—because, of course, Jude hadn't. "Maybe he just doesn't want to tell you every little detail about our relationship."

Walsh snarled—and then there were footsteps on the stairs,

and Jude flopped back onto the sofa, burying his toes under Anton's thigh and reaching for his phone on the table. "What's got you wound up?"

"Walsh reckons there's something weird about your boyfriend," Larimer said conversationally.

"Yeah? Like what?"

"Reckons Anton's hiding something."

Jude snorted. "Yeah, there's a couple of things." Anton grimaced. "Seriously, you should see his room. He actually owns Chaucer."

"*What.*"

"I know! Fucking Chaucer! And understands it!"

Walsh narrowed his eyes at Anton, ignoring Jude and Larimer's mocking argument, before slowly twisting back around to face the screen. Anton swallowed, suddenly uneasy and unhappy, suddenly wanting to not be there.

"Hey," he whispered, clenching his thigh to squish Jude's toes. "You wanna go back to mine? Mum'll be putting dinner on soon, and it's homemade cottage pie."

"Score," Jude said, grinning over the top of his phone. "Yeah, okay. Larimer, kick Walsh's arse or you're not cribbing off me in maths anymore."

Walsh turned to stare again, and Anton felt his throat dry up as he fumbled for his shoes and coat. He knew. Or if he didn't, he would soon, and then—what would he do about it? Would he confront Anton, or just tell Jude, or do either one in front of other people? It would get out. Fast. And then…and then…

"You okay?" Jude asked as he closed the front door behind them.

"No."

"What's up?"

"I—Walsh—he knows."

"He knows what?"

"About me. Or if he doesn't, he's about two steps away from guessing, and then what's he going to, he'll tell people, Jude, he'll tell everyone and—!"

"Whoa! Whoa, whoa, hey-hey-hey, c'mere. C'mere…"

The hug came the moment they turned the corner off Larimer's road, and Anton clung to Jude's coat, burying his face in the still-warm fabric and taking a deep, shaking breath. "I'm going to be caught," he breathed, hating the high whine of his voice, and Jude squeezed tightly.

"Calm down."

"I'm going to be fucking caught!"

"And it's not going to be like before," Jude said firmly. "You have me this time around. If it all comes out, then there's nothing we can do about that, but you're not going to be on your own. Alright?"

Anton fisted his hands in the coat, and Jude nudged his jaw against the side of Anton's head.

"What did he say?"

"He said—he said I was being cagey, and he knew there was something off about me, and he commented on my shoe size at the rink, you remember? And he said if I fucked you over, he'd do me over worse, and—"

"Okay. Okay, slow up. Right…this may be my fault."

"*What*?!"

"Hey, whoa! I've not said a single word about your spy stuff, okay?"

Anton swallowed, pushing back a little to look Jude in the eye. "Then how could it be your fault?"

Jude exhaled, a plume of white vapour climbing into the frosty air. "Alright, look, before you told me—well, Lily told me—you were being really…well, weird. One minute it was all happiness I'd asked you out, you were all affectionate and flirty and it was great, and the next minute I was Jack the Ripper and you wouldn't stop in the same room. And I unloaded a little to Walsh about it, said I was confused, I didn't know where I stood or why you were behaving that way…we both reckoned maybe there'd been or there was someone else in the picture, and then…from his perspective, I guess overnight I've gone from being unsure where I stand and whether asking you out was a good idea or not to…hey, yeah, I have a boyfriend and everything is awesome all the time and fuck footie, I'm going out with Anton."

Anton swallowed, trying to push his own fear away and step back from the situation. When Jude put it like that…

"Okay," he whispered. "So...what, he could think I've wrapped you round my little finger and you're just not...telling him when things are bad?"

"Well, you kinda have..."

"Seriously."

"Yeah, maybe. I've got a bit of a track record for letting people walk all over me when I'm dating them, and Walsh is...touchy about people he cares about."

"Touchy?"

Jude nodded. "You keep saying people like me, I'm nice, I'm popular—it's not really *me* that caused that, you know?"

"What d'you mean?"

"Nice guys finish last, I told you. Initially, I had all female friends. I make friends with girls easily—girlfriends even easier—but the other guys were a bit suss. Like, you know, I was probably gay, or I was always flirting with the girl they liked, the other guys didn't like it much. Not until Year Eight, and then Walsh decided I was alright."

Anton cocked his head, frowning. "Walsh? Why? Just out of nowhere?"

"Nah," Jude said. "This guy at football was talking smack about his girlfriend one night—you know, crap weather, only half the team turn up, you kind of piss about and don't train? Anyway, he was calling her a slag and all sorts, and I told him he was bang out of order. Got in a fight, got beaten up, got the kid kicked out of the club. Turns out the girlfriend was Walsh's sister. Word got back to him, he decided I was alright."

"That's...nice."

Jude laughed. "Me all over, innit?"

"Yeah, but...Walsh isn't...you know, nice like you."

"He is," Jude said, "but he's rougher with it. You would be, really."

"Why?" Anton asked curiously, and Jude hesitated.

"It's his thing to say," he said eventually, "but...you know, Walsh is defensive about the people he loves. Hyper-defensive. Hence whaling on Will so bad that time in PE. He's...look, he's just lost someone before, like in a bad way, and he's a bit paranoid about it happening again. So when I stuck up for his sister, he figured I was worth having around. And now…you know, me and Larimer, we're with Walsh. He gets this territory thing going. Like, he'll be a bit of a dick if you call Isabel or Emma a bitch, but he'll go apeshit if you go after me or Larimer. And the other kids learned that, so I'm not the target I should be."

Anton rolled his eyes. "My old school, they'd have crucified you."

"Unless you were in with the dangerous lot, right?"

"Walsh isn't dangerous."

"He is," Jude said significantly, and Anton drew back, surprised. "What…proper…?"

"Proper knife in his jacket, one wrong move away from a young offenders prison or something. He's a nasty guy if you've crossed him."

"He's your best friend."

"Don't make me blind," Jude replied, then grinned. "He's alright now—better now his stepdad's cleared off. But he's dangerous defensive sometimes, hence…well, hence that. He don't care if you or me are benders, he don't care if you've turned up and turned *me,* but he won't take you fucking me around. And I think maybe from his perspective, that's what it might look like is going to happen, given I've gone from not really sure where I stand to 'I am totally committed here.'"

"And what if…what if he does work it out?"

Jude shrugged. "He'll probably come to me first. Honestly, he's not any more clued up than I am and he won't want to just yell it in the middle of the class because then it reflects on me, too, especially if I didn't know. You know, oh hey Jude, how fucking stupid are you that you didn't realise your boyfriend's a chick, that attitude."

Anton closed his eyes, feeling sick.

"Hey," Jude whispered, knocking their foreheads together lightly. "If he does, I will tell him in no uncertain terms to keep it quiet. If he realises I know already, he won't have grounds to be mad at you or think you're fucking with me. I think he might be assuming I know nothing."

"We've had sex," Anton whispered croakily. "How could you

not know?"

"Maybe that's why he's not sure yet."

"Oh God…"

"Hey. *Hey.* It's going to be alright. If he comes to me about anything, I will tell him to keep his conclusions behind his teeth. And he will, okay. He's only wary because he thinks you're screwing with me. If he figures you're not, he'll go back to liking you just fine. And he does, usually. He thinks you're pretty cool most of the time."

"He's a good friend to you," Anton croaked, and Jude hugged him again, rocking them slightly. "I just—I'm sorry, I just…when people found out last time…"

"You were on your own, in a dangerous place, with nobody saying it was okay. Well, I'm saying it's okay. And if I'm on your side, so is Walsh, whether he really wants to be or not. And you know Emma would be on your side, too. Probably Isabel. And Larimer doesn't fucking care about anything anyway, you could be an alien and he'd just ask something weird like how you crap."

Anton laughed shakily, and rubbed at his eyes. "D'you…could you come over? Stay the night?"

Jude frowned. "Is that a good idea? You're a bit shook up…"

"That's why I think I need you to," Anton admitted. "I mean, Mum and Aunt Kerry will argue about whether you're allowed to sleep in my room, and if they say no I'll smuggle you in at two in the morning anyway, but I just…I think I need someone who…looks at me the way you did yesterday. And this morning."

"Don't let Walsh shake your confidence, man. You were fucking hot yesterday and this morning. Seriously, that swagger is like pure sex."

"Come off it…"

"No, seriously. You're good-looking anyway, but when you packed and the way it obviously made you feel, you were fucking stunning. I don't just pounce anyone, you know."

Anton laughed weakly, and looped his arms around Jude's neck to hug the guy tightly again. "Make me feel like that again, then," he mumbled, and Jude's grip tightened.

"I'll try. Depending on who wins the argument about where I sleep, huh?"

Chapter 21

AUNT KERRY WON the argument.

The argument being a fiercely whispered one between Mum and Aunt Kerry in the kitchen—which Jude and Anton, in the living room with the TV on low and throwing toys for Molly, could hear every word of regardless—about whether it was appropriate to allow Jude to sleep in Anton's room. Aunt Kerry voted yes, as they were both boys. Mum voted no, because 'they're hardly just friends, Kerry!'

"Oh please," Jude said quietly, reaching to scratch Molly between the ears. "Like I need to be in your room to molest you."

"I think there has to be an element of me not wanting you to do it if it's molestation," Anton confessed, and Jude grinned.

"Now there's an invite if I ever heard one."

"Maybe."

Judging by the clattering in the airing cupboard and then in Anton's room, though, Kerry had won and was putting out the camp bed.

"Just so we're clear," Jude said conversationally as Molly tired of their laziness and brought back one of her toys like a dog playing fetch, "what do you want out of me staying the night?"

Anton flushed. "Uh."

"I mean, am I staying on the camp bed and it's all hands-off, clothes-on, leaving-a-light-on type stuff, or…?"

Jude trailed off. Anton bit his lip. "I'd…like *some* 'or.'"

"Like?"

"Like…" he glanced towards the open living room door, and leaned closer. "Like you not staying on the camp bed."

"I am *not* sleeping on your floor, man, that's harsh."

Anton laughed, the anxiety popping like a bubble, and shoved Jude in the shoulder. "Arse."

"What, you want my arse? We talked about my arse."

Anton grinned, even as he bit his lip again. "Might want to see it, though. And the rest of you. I didn't get to see much last time."

"You weren't complaining."

"I'm complaining now."

"And your mum is worried about *me*?" Jude asked incredulously. He pointed a finger in Anton's face. "You're a pervert."

Anton attempted to bite him. Unfortunately, Jude had better reflexes than that, and jerked his hand back just in time.

"See?"

"Don't put your hands where I can bite them, then."

"Perv."

Anton tugged on the neck of Jude's T-shirt. "Honestly?"

"Please."

"I don't really know what I want out of you staying over, I'm still feeling…off, but…let's see what happens?"

"Okay, but your mum's gonna get really suspicious if I have to take a cold shower at, like…one in the morning."

Anton rolled his eyes as the credits of the TV show they'd been ignoring rolled, too, and pulled himself up off the sofa. "C'mon, then," he said. "We can watch a movie in my room."

"Sure. 'Watch a movie.'"

Anton towed Jude upstairs by the hand, ignoring his jibe. There was a nervous excitement building in his gut, made worse by the rough skin of Jude's palm against his own. He wanted to touch Jude's chest again, wanted to touch Jude's cock again, but Walsh had rattled him, and he worried that this time, Jude wouldn't be able to touch him back without...without...

"You know, I can *see* you deciding what to do," Jude said conversationally as Anton towed him into the bedroom. The camp bed looked almost innocent, the side table separating it from Anton's bed.

"Haven't decided yet," Anton said, finally letting go and rummaging for a DVD on his desk. "Um...you said you hadn't finished all the Marvel movies yet?"

"Not even halfway."

"Want to ignore one you've already seen, then?"

"Sure."

When Anton turned back from setting up the TV, Jude had closed the door and was sitting cross-legged on Anton's bed, shrugging out of the jumper he'd been wearing all day. The ice outside made the room bright, and combined with the white T-shirt Jude had on under his jumper, it made his red hair look like fire itself.

Anton didn't realise he'd moved—much less that he'd kissed Jude—until his brain vaguely registered the soft rasp of stubble against his thumbs where he held Jude's jaw between his hands. Jude's smile broke the kiss, his nose nudging lightly for a moment against Anton's, then he pulled back and settled against the pillows, grinning.

"C'mon," he said, "let's at least not be total slags and watch the first five minutes, yeah?"

Anton laughed, and allowed Jude to arrange the hug. To his surprise, they ended up tangled together on the pillows with Jude's head burrowed into Anton's neck, his breath warm and washing gently over Anton's shoulder. His arm was solid, slung low over Anton's waist, and Anton traced the fine blond hairs along it, pausing at every freckle he found, and watched Jude's fingers tap out a soft rhythm in time to the music of the opening credits.

Something warm settled in the middle of Anton's chest, and the itch to touch died down. Jude's heavy heat was comforting, and despite the breathing touching the edge of the binder, Anton felt relaxed. The drum of Jude's fingers was nice, and there was something...so *relaxed* about the way Jude had wriggled around Anton, the gentle press of his knee into the side of Anton's leg. Even the squish of Jude's other arm trapped between them was nice, and Anton shifted up to let Jude slide the spare limb under his back.

"Better?"

"For now. It'll go dead later. Ssh, I can barely remember this movie."

They stayed that way for the longest time. Jude seemed to be actually watching the movie—judging by his outraged commentary every time someone did something stupid, which was apparently a lot—but Anton concentrated instead on the heat rising off Jude's arm, and the coarse ginger hairs he was combing through the fingers of his other hand. Jude was a total radiator. His scalp was hot, his neck was hot, his arm was hot—Anton was warming up just lying there with him. Who needed a duvet? Maybe they'd have to split up in the summer when it got too warm to hug Jude anymore—and that would seriously blow, because this was so *nice*…

Anton's dreamy thought processes were interrupted about halfway through the movie, when Jude's phone started ringing in his bag. Anton scowled as Jude…de-hugged? Un-hugged? Moved, anyway, leaning right over Anton to hang off the edge of the bed and rummage in his backpack.

And then Anton stopped scowling, because Jude's weight was heavy and hot across his belly and hips, and his T-shirt had ridden up slightly to show Anton a strip of pale, inviting skin. There was a freckle just below his ribs, and Anton touched a finger to it lightly before stroking a hand up Jude's back. The cotton of Jude's T-shirt was rough on the back of Anton's hand, but the skin under his palm was smooth and inviting, the softness of a light layer of downy hair barely perceptible over the gentle rise of warmth.

Anton ignored Jude's conversation—with his stepmum, by the sound of it—and pushed the hand higher and tugged on Jude's shoulder, coaxing him into lying more along Anton's chest. The angle was easier, and Anton pushed his hand right up between Jude's shoulders and tested out the edges of bone against muscle.

"You're a git," Jude informed Anton as he hung up, and dropped the phone back into the bag. Jude shifted and settled, elbows either side of Anton's face, and grinned down at him. His hips had slid over Anton's, and Anton had the urge to part his knees and hook an ankle over Jude's calf.

"Why?" he asked instead.

"Touching me up when I'm talking to Aunt Lucy."

"Aunt Lucy?"

"Emma's mum."

"Well," Anton said, stroking his hand back down Jude's back. "You had a freckle."

"What were you hoping to do, rub it out?"

"Maybe."

Jude snorted and grinned again, that smile making Anton's stomach twitch, and leaned down. The kiss was gentle, softened by some sleepy, relaxed edge, and Anton hummed contentedly as Jude's weight pressed him down briefly into the mattress before it was lifted again.

"Hey, where're you going?" Anton protested, blearily confused, as Jude climbed off the bed. He caught at Jude's elbow, startled by the sudden change, and Jude laughed.

"Chill, Ant, m'getting changed and into bed. Nearly dozed off on you twice already, I'm not going to be up for much longer."

Anton blinked. "Into—just...um, you know, just take your jeans off and...you can sleep on me if you like. It'll be nice."

Jude paused, hands on the hem of his T-shirt. Suddenly, the humour was gone from that good-looking face, and he looked very sombre. "I don't think that's a good idea, Anton."

Anton blinked, and the warm feeling in his stomach vanished. "What? Why not?"

Jude sighed heavily. "I mean—look, I'd like to. I would. But I don't think it's the best of ideas right now."

"Why not? What d'you mean?"

"I mean...look, you're still rattled. You said so yourself. And you don't even like me putting my hand under your shirt yet," Jude said carefully. He quite abruptly sat down on the camp bed, cross-legged and hooking his elbows around his knees, as though aware he'd been looming. Anton stared, mouth dry, stunned by the sudden severity. "I give off body heat like it's my job, and my hands end up places they shouldn't when I sleep. And if you're going to wear full pyjamas and your binder and everything, you'd boil, and if you don't, I'll freak you out. And I don't want to upset you, especially after this afternoon."

Anton bit his lip, torn. He knew Jude was right. But then…the just…the lying there and watching the movie and just…cuddling, that had been so *nice*…

"What if," he whispered, "I wore my boxers and T-shirt…and you did, too…would that be okay?"

"I have to sleep in just my boxers."

"Okay," Anton said. That didn't bother him—that would be *great*, actually. "That's okay. I'd like that."

Jude tilted his head and frowned. "You can't wear your binder to bed, surely?"

Ah.

That brought Anton's brain to a halt, and he stuttered before taking a deep breath. "No," he whispered.

"Look," Jude said, putting both hands on the edge of the mattress and leaning forward, his eyes large and earnest from that angle. "If you didn't have these body issues—which is *fine*, I don't begrudge them or you for having them—then you wouldn't be able to prise me out of the bed with a crowbar. I *want* to doze off with you. But I also know what I'm like. I cuddle hard when I share the bed, and I won't be awake to know where I can't touch. And if you wear a bunch of layers to ward that off, you'll boil to death."

Anton chewed on his lip. Lose the binder and get to sleep with Jude, but risk being triggered? Especially after Walsh's pointed remarks? Or consign Jude to the camp bed and not get triggered, but also lose the sleepy contentment that had been descending before the phone rang?

"I want you to sleep up here with me," he said finally.

Jude frowned. "You sure?"

"Yeah. I'll wear my T-shirt and boxers. And, um…"

"If my hand goes somewhere it shouldn't, just shove it away," Jude said gently. "I'm not going to get pissy with you if you do. S'your body, s'up to you what I touch."

"Okay," Anton said, a little of the nerves twisting in his chest soothed by Jude's calm expression. "So, um…you mind…"

"I need to go to the toilet anyway," Jude said—probably lying, but Anton didn't call him on it—and he slipped out. Anton nearly exploded out of the bed, ripping his T-shirt off and hastily fumbling to get the binder off, too. They were awkward to put on and remove, and could leave horrible lines and marks sometimes, and he didn't want Jude to see either his breasts or the bruises. He heard the bathroom door close as he got the binder off, and kept his eyes closed as he rummaged in the drawers for a fresh T-shirt to sleep in, something baggier and darker that would hide his shape better.

Anton wasn't big-chested, but they were big enough to be noticeably not a boy's, and he hated them. Their weight shifted when he slept, and each one was a decent handful. If he'd been a real girl, he might have liked them. Jude would probably like them. As it was, he couldn't pull his T-shirt down fast enough, and only opened his eyes once it was in place and they were hidden again.

Then he had to take a deep, steadying breath to push back the skin-crawling nausea.

"It's just Jude," he whispered. "He won't be a dick about it. He'll understand."

It worked, the sick feeling subsiding. He took advantage of Jude being gone to knock back a couple of breath mints from his desk drawer before he heard the bathroom door open again. By the time Jude wandered back into the bedroom, Anton was sitting cross-legged by the pillows, picking at the duvet cover.

And Jude laughed. "Nice shirt."

For a brief moment, Anton's chest seized in horror. Then the part of his brain that wasn't a neurotic mess kicked in, and he flushed hotly.

"Oh, fuck."

"Nah, it's appropriate!" It was Anton's old-and-battered Stonewall shirt. 'Some people are gay, get over it.' Aunt Kerry had bought for him a couple of years ago, and Anton didn't actually like it very much—too confrontational—so had consigned it to his sock drawer as a sleep shirt pretty much immediately. "I like it,"

Jude decided. "Want me to switch DVDs? We can drop off watching another one."

"Okay," Anton said, chewing on the corner of his lip. "You have to sleep shirtless, remember," he added as Jude fumbled with the discs.

"Subtle," Jude teased. The disc clicked in, the DVD menu clicked on—and Jude stripped his shirt off. Just...*effortlessly*. He yanked it up, tore it over his head, and threw it casually at his bag. Anton's flush was entirely different this time, and he hugged his knees to his chest as he stared.

"You look..."

Good. *Very* good. Jude was pretty much what Anton had imagined—and felt. He stared, taking it in like he hadn't paused to do last time. Gingery-blond hair, broad shouldered but wiry build, the edges of muscle becoming obvious but not built up enough to make much difference to his shape...there was a small scar under his left nipple, and he had v-lines leading to his hip bones.

Anton was struck with the weirdest, stupidest urge to lick those v-lines.

"Now *that* is a look I like getting," Jude said, smirking, and Anton pulled a face.

"Oh, shut up."

"No, seriously, my ego is boosted."

"Just...get over here. You promised a hug."

"No I didn't."

"You implied it."

"I implied nothing, *you* were the one who wanted me to sleep here."

Despite his bitching, Jude just kept grinning, and clambered over the mattress to settle back in his previous position, looping both arms around Anton's waist and dragging him down into the duvet and the insane heat that—without the T-shirt—was even more intense. Anton could almost feel it pulsing in time with Jude's heart, and settled on his back again, Jude's nose pressed behind his ear and arm back over his stomach.

"This is comfy," Jude mumbled, and kissed Anton's jaw lightly. "M'gonna sleep in a bit."

"Can I feel you up in the morning?" Anton asked, stroking

Jude's bare arm and feeling torn between red-faced, sick horror that Jude's upper arm was very lightly brushing the edge of his breast, and a thrill of excitement at the sensation of Jude's leg tucking itself between Anton's knees.

"Sure," Jude said, wriggling into a more comfortable position. He linked his hands around Anton's hip, and settled. "Slap me if I get gropey."

"Okay."

"But you can grope me in the morning, f'you want."

Anton smiled, scratching his blunt nails lightly through Jude's hair before resting his head against Jude's forehead and watching the opening scenes on the telly through sleepy, unfocused eyes. The loose feeling of his breasts being unconfined wasn't so disturbing, not with the weight of Jude's arms around his waist. And Jude's legs were warm and surprisingly hairy, his ankles—when Anton rubbed his toes over one of them—bony and oddly nice.

Even if Jude did accidentally grope him, this…this felt like it would be worth it.

Anton felt, even if it was just temporary, better.

Chapter 22

ANTON DIDN'T SEE Jude outside of school again for a few days—apparently Jude had broken one of his stepmum's favourite ornaments and was more grounded than an aeroplane without an engine—and had been toying with the idea of skipping out on Dad's visitation day on Sunday and going to the kick-about to catch up on that lost time. Then on Sunday morning, Jude texted with a *cba with football, 2 cold, want 2 go see a film or sumthing? x* and the decision was made.

"Mum!" Anton yelled, firing off a quick *ok come over? just getting ready x*. "Where's my combat jeans?"

They'd been his favourites before, but now Anton had learned that with the packer, they not only made him feel like ninety-nine percent male and confident about it, but Jude was even more into them, too.

"On the ironing board!" Mum shouted back, then he heard her padding out of the kitchen. "What do you want them for? You know your dad doesn't approve of them!"

"Dad can shove it!" Anton shouted back, rescuing them from the ironing board in the spare room before heading downstairs. He knew his best blue T-shirt was on the drying rack in the utility room. "I'm not going," he told his mother as he passed her in the kitchen. "Jude's just texted asking if I want to go and see a film." And if he was suggesting a film instead of football, it meant the others wouldn't be there, and Anton wanted to avoid Walsh as much as humanly possible.

"Ahh," Mum said, and smiled. She was still in her dressing gown, her hair all pinned up and drying in some fancy style. She was going to a wedding in the afternoon, Anton vaguely remembered, but at that minute she just looked a mix of young and mumsy, what with the combination of her hair and Rose balanced on her hip. "Dad won't be happy."

"Dad's never happy with me," Anton said, shoving the T-shirt on over his head. He ran his fingers through his hair—already damp from the shower—and checked it in the back of a spoon on the drying rack.

"Sweetheart..."

"It's okay, Mum," he said, and squared his shoulders. "Dad's not my problem. If he can't accept it, then...then fuck him. I've got you and Aunt Kerry. And Jude. What do I need Dad for?"

Her face softened, and one hand came up to smooth his hair before he ducked away in time to rescue the artful mussing he'd just administered. "Well," Mum said. "I'm glad to see you're seeing sense about him at last."

Anton shrugged, fiddling with the hem of his T-shirt. "S'like Ellen says," he mumbled. "Not everyone is going to be okay with me, and I have to accept that, but it doesn't mean I have to let it get to me. I have you and Aunt Kerry. Not like I've got no family like some kids."

Mum squeezed his shoulder. Rose cooed, and started to chew on the corner of Mum's dressing gown. "And you have Jude," she reminded him gently. "And you know, you should think about telling your new friends. Jude's one of them. If he's accepted you as you are, then they likely will, too."

Anton fidgeted. "I'm not sure about that," he confessed, biting his lip. There was a lot of ribbing in the Monday lessons when they'd discussed the LGBT community and transgender people, and what with the way Walsh was acting...he just couldn't take the risk.

"Think about it," Mum urged gently. "And don't you worry about your father today if you want to go off with Jude—Jude will be better for you than your dad. I'll get rid of him when he—"

The doorbell rang, and Anton swore.

"Anton!"

"It's Jude, he's too early!" he said, hastily pulling his jeans up and fumbling with the buttons. Shit, had he run round the corner? Had he been standing on his own doormat in his coat and boots when he'd texted?

"I'll stall him, but only for a minute or two," Mum said. Anton bolted into the hall and up the stairs to do his teeth, and slammed into the bathroom just in time to hear her open the door.

"Chris!"

Shit. Anton grimaced, but started to do his teeth anyway. Jude *would* be here soon, and it wasn't like Anton wanted to go and argue with Dad. He'd just...slide around them and leg it. Dad would be too busy arguing with Mum to notice, like always.

"He says he has plans," he heard Mum saying, and he attacked his bottom teeth pretending they were Dad. He could imagine the response to *that.* And it would involve 'she,' too, just to rub salt in the wound. Anton spat, imagining Dad's face in the bottom of the sink, and checked his reflection before heading downstairs. Jude wouldn't be long anyway, even if this time the bell had been Dad. It was only round the corner. And—

"Ah, there you are, Natasha."

His stomach curled up in a tight ball, and—despite his words to Mum earlier—that cold, sick feeling came back. In spite of his binder, in spite of the packer, in spite of his clothes and having gotten the hang of a more masculine walk...it all just dropped away like it meant nothing when Dad said his dead name. Anton hated it, and his father for causing it. No matter how much better he felt since Jude and the new school, no matter how well Ellen or Mum said he was doing, Dad just had this superpower in undoing it all the minute he said Natasha.

"Anton," he ground out between gritted teeth, and sat on the bottom stair to pull on his boots.

"Hop in the car, love," Dad said loudly, deliberately ignoring him. "We've got to nip round to the supermarket quickly, but after that, the day's up to you. How about a trip round Oxford Circus, eh? We've not done that before."

"I hate shopping," Anton said tartly, finishing the laces. "And I'm not coming today. I'm going out."

Dad's lips thinned. "It's Sunday," he said. "Sunday is your day with me—"

"And Monday to Saturday are Mum's days, doesn't mean I spend all of them with her," Anton retorted. "I told you, I'm going out."

"You missed last Sunday, too, and—"

"I have a life."

Dad's gaze snapped up to Mum, and Anton scowled. "For God's sake, Maggie, the courts have granted me—"

"It's nothing to do with Mum!" Anton interrupted loudly. "I've got a date, alright?"

"A *date*," Dad said, like date was another word for leprosy. "You have a *date*?"

Then, to Anton's surprise, he lit up and beamed. Anton hadn't seen his dad smile in years, not since he was a little kid, and it looked strange and out of place on his weathered face. Alien-esque, maybe. It definitely didn't belong, and it was unsettling.

"A date," Dad repeated. "Well, well, well—and where did you find this boy, eh? Or a girl, but—it's a boy, I would imagine, eh? Your mother met him? And when am I going to meet him? Does he go to your school? I hope he's not much older than you, Natasha, I won't have—"

Rose squealed, her happy *I-know-that-face* noise, and a flash of red caught Anton's eye before Dad stepped back, looking around for what had distracted the baby, and Jude came into view, hovering halfway up the drive uncertainly.

"Sorry," he said, glancing between Anton's parents and waving at Rose before his gaze shifted to Anton—and, Anton noted with a spark of smug satisfaction, flickered up and down his legs. "Ready?"

"Yeah, just, um, need to get my wallet—"

"Get a twenty out of my purse, darling," Mum said quietly,

gesturing at her handbag on the phone table. "And make sure you've got your phone. Jude, do you want to come in out of the cold for a minute?"

"Nah, I'm alright, Mrs. Williams. Just snagging Anton and then we'll be off. Movie time!" Jude added cheerfully, and Mum laughed.

Dad, however, had darkened again. He was frowning, and repeated, "Anton?" in Jude's direction.

"Er," Jude said.

"Jude, this is my dad," Anton said tiredly, shoving his jacket on and the filched twenty quid in his jeans pocket. "Dad, this is Jude. My boyfriend," he added pointedly.

Jude paled alarmingly under his shock of red hair; Dad, by contrast, started to go pink. "Boyfriend," he echoed.

"Er," Jude repeated, then coughed. "Um. Nice to meet you, Mr. Williams."

"I can't believe this," Dad snarled. "I thought some bloody progress might have been made at last, but you've got this boy-friend—" He shook a hand at Jude, twisting back to Mum and Anton with fury written in the heavy lines around his eyes and mouth. "—calling her by that name, too? For fuck's—"

"Language, Chris!"

"—sake, Maggie, this is getting ridiculous! Conning the boy into this nonsense! What happens when he finds out, eh? Natasha will be the laughing stock of the school—I presume they've met at school, that is, seeing as how she's refusing to go to any clubs or—"

"I have a name," Jude interrupted.

His voice was suddenly cold, and it made Anton shiver. His face was cold, too, blank and sullen, and it looked like—well, no, it didn't quite look like when he sounded off at Will Thorne, or got arsey with a teacher, because he tended to be angry then. This was…this wasn't angry, this was *furious*, in that horrible frozen way that was more upsetting than scary, and Anton *hated* that expression on Jude's usually amiable face.

"And I'm not thick, and your son's not some kind of cross-dressing liar," Jude continued in that same cold voice.

"That is my daughter, not my son!" Dad blustered. "You've

been carrying on with a girl, whatever you might think, and—"

"I know. I already 'found out', thanks. He told me."

"Do you understand me?" Dad insisted, like Jude hadn't spoken. "Natasha is a girl! She can dress in all the boys' clothes she wants, but she is still female and you are still dating a *girl!*"

"I did notice," Jude said tartly. "I've had my hands in certain places, you know." Dad spluttered and went magenta; Anton blushed furiously, and put both hands over his face. Did Jude realise what that *sounded* like?! "I know what he's got. So what? Still Anton, isn't he? If I was just interested in his bits, there's fitter guys with better pricks than him. Fitter birds, too—no offence, Anton."

And just like that, the embarrassment receded. If not for the icy, aggressive demeanour, Anton could have kissed him.

"This is *absurd*—and Natasha, you are not going anywhere with *this*...*this*...disrespectful, disgusting..." Dad coughed out, bright purple in the face and scowling.

"I'm not the one calling a guy a girl, mate!"

"You can't stop me!" Anton shouted at the same time, flaring up, and Jude snorted, rolling his eyes.

"No offense, but your old man's a twat," he said, and held out a gloved hand in Anton's direction. "C'mon. There's a couple of matinee showings if you fancy it, or we can go hit up HMV first and snag that new Marvel film you were after. Dad gave me lunch money, and I might have pilfered a bit off Emma's mum, too."

Anton caught his hand and squeezed it, neatly sidestepping his dad, who puffed up like a bullfrog and turned on his mother. "Maggie, I'll see you back in court for this—it's *dangerous*, pandering to a mental illness like this, and—"

"Put a sock in it, granddad!" Jude yelled over his shoulder, dragging Anton towards the road. "Time to join the twenty-first century, yeah?"

"Oh my God, he's going to go mental at Mum," Anton whispered as he was hauled around the corner. He wriggled his hand free, and slid it into Jude's elbow instead.

"He's a fucking cunt," Jude said shortly. "Jesus, what a bellend. Does he do that all the time? Show up and shout and call you Natasha?"

"Yeah."

"What, and threaten your mum with the courts?"

"Well," Anton shrugged, "he does it, but they don't really take him seriously, you know. 'Cause of Ellen. She's written letters for the court saying I have, you know, I'm proper transgender and it's not a phase and stuff and how it would be damaging for me to live with my dad, so…it doesn't work, but he shouts about it."

"What a twat," Jude scoffed. "Christ, and I thought my mum was bad."

Anton bit his lip. "You didn't…you never really told me much about your mum."

Jude shrugged. "Not much to tell. Dad had an affair with Emma's mum, my mum found out and went mad, took off with my older brother, but wasn't interested in taking me, too."

Anton dropped his head sideways and bumped it gently against Jude's neck. "Why not?"

"Ran off with this other bloke. Who looks suspiciously like my older brother Sean. Get it?"

Anton cracked a faint smile. "I dunno," he mumbled. "It's better than them splitting up because of you. That's what mine did."

"Nah," Jude said. "Yours split up 'cause your dad's a fucking fuck."

Something sealed over in the middle of Anton's chest, and he dropped his hand again to slide his fingers through Jude's and squeeze. He wanted to say something, let Jude really get what it meant, but his tongue was stuck, and nothing would come out, nothing but—

"Thanks."

Chapter 23

JUDE WAS WAITING at the end of the drive on Tuesday morning, and the first thing he said was, "How's shit with your dad?"

"Er, usual…why?" Anton asked warily, aborting his idea of getting hold of Jude's hand and sharing a pocket on the way to school.

"Only this Chris Williams bloke rang up my dad and had this massive go 'cause I was rude."

Anton blinked, then groaned. "Shit, sorry, Mum must have mentioned your full name at some point to him. Fuck, was your dad angry?"

Jude shrugged. "Not really. Mega confused. Uh, I had to tell him."

Anton's breath caught. "What?"

"Look," Jude said quietly, "your dad was banging on and on about this chick Natasha, but he said enough that Dad worked out I'm supposedly dating Natasha, and then he was all to me 'I thought you were seeing a boy these days?' so—I didn't say it in front of the whole family, and I swore him to secrecy because I know you don't want it out there, but I did tell him. Just, you know, Natasha and Anton, same person, my boyfriend's trans, that's it. Okay?"

Anton unlocked his chest and started to breathe again. "You were…on your own, just the two of you?"

"Yeah, I made sure. In my room, put music on and everything so nobody else could have heard. And then Emma was ribbing me all through dinner about trying to get Dad to like Muse, but whatever."

"And he won't tell?"

"He's a doctor, Anton. He's kind of big on not sharing certain stuff, you know? He won't tell."

Anton nodded, giving in to the original urge and squeezing Jude's hand. "Okay. I think."

"You're not mad at me?"

"I—no. Dad's just…fucking shit up again."

"Well, it didn't work. I got a bit of a bollocking for shouting in the street like a twat, but I get that every week anyway."

Anton laughed feebly.

"And, uh, Walsh was texting me some weird shit last night."

"Oh, *God.*"

"He's—"

"Has he figured it out?"

"Basically…yeah."

Anton stopped dead. They hadn't even reached the end of the road, and he stopped dead in his tracks, staring blankly at Jude. "He'll tell."

"He won't. Not yet, anyway. He hasn't out-and-out asked me about it, that's the point he might sound off, but…he's close."

"*Shit!*"

"Ant, seriously, I can head this off if you just let me say something," Jude said urgently. "If you just let me…hint enough that I know what's going on with you, he'll probably drop it. That's all this is about. He won't really care what you are, what's getting to him is that he thinks *I* don't know, that you're leading me on."

"Shit-shit-shit—"

"Look," Jude said, taking Anton firmly by the shoulders and shaking him slightly. "Let me just text him. Just one text, just a quiet 'I know what you think, and trust me when I say I know who and what Anton is, so drop it, okay.' Just that. I don't have to say anything more than that, and it should work."

"Should," Anton echoed bitterly, and hit out at the hedge. It rustled indignantly. "It's none of his *business*!"

"Hey, I know. And trust me, if you ever tell him, especially how it's upsetting you, he'll be sorry for that. But he's just…defensive."

"He's defective."

Jude laughed, and Anton exhaled shakily.

"Sorry," he mumbled after a minute. "He's your mate, I shouldn't be so mad. It's just…I don't *want* people to know, Jude, that's the point. I want to pass all the time, I don't want people to be guessing everywhere I go."

Jude's hands slid further, until Anton was buried in a hug, and it…kind of helped, but kind of aggravated him, too. Why was this so fucking *easy* for Jude? Why did he not have to prove he was a guy every five minutes? Why would it be okay for Jude to have small feet and not go to the toilet very often at school, but for Anton it was weird and suspicious and earned him funny looks and whispering from Walsh?

"I hate this," he croaked, and Jude tightened his grip.

"You also said you're gonna have hormones and surgery and stuff," he said quietly. "So I'm no pro, but if you're getting dude hormones, you're going to be more guy-like, right?"

"Yeah."

"So, like a second puberty, right?"

"Yeah, I guess."

"So after that, it'll be easier. Nobody'll be making fun of your voice in, like, ten years because it'll sound just like mine and everyone else's. And maybe in ten years you can go shirtless at football and use the men's changing rooms and everything, and nobody will ever know. It's just *this* bit that kind of sucks, and even that's only kind of."

"Why only kind of?"

"'Cause even if the whole school finds out and tries ripping on you for it, you still got me. And you'd totally have Emma, which would be a good shout if everyone found out because she's fucking scary about her equal rights stuff."

Anton laughed a little croakily, and pulled back to rub at his eyes. "She's not that scary."

"Says you. I once said Paki in the house, she nearly beat me to death with the TV remote."

"Well, maybe you deserved that," Anton mumbled, scrubbing at his face and then sighing. "Okay. Okay, let's go."

"It'll be fine," Jude repeated. "They're okay with a gay couple, right?"

"Being trans and being gay are totally different."

"Yeah, but to others—"

"They're still totally different," Anton said bitterly. "I can't even get treatment and I have to see a psychiatrist all the time for when I do get it. If you told your doctor you were gay, you wouldn't be sent to the mental health team. But I'm still seen as sick by even the system that's supposed to help me, and even gay people think I'm a freak, so—"

"You're not a fucking freak, Anton."

"Yeah well, between Walsh and Dad the last few days, I kind of feel like one."

"Yeah? Did you feel like one when I was on my knees in your room?"

Anton paused, then found a real laugh bubbling up from inside his chest. "Oh my God, are you offering to shag me better?"

"Yeah, if you want."

"Maybe later."

"I mean, we still haven't talked about the whole anal versus vaginal thing…"

Anton took a leaf from Emma's book, and thumped Jude in the arm, still sniggering quietly. As Jude tugged him on towards the school, complaining about domestic abuse the whole way, Anton squeezed his hand again one last time before dropping it at the crossing.

"Thanks," he said.

"Anytime. If you don't hit me again, seriously, what is up with your hitting hand…"

❖

JUDE STUCK CLOSE for most of the day, and Anton was grateful for it. Walsh kept making remarks, just little sly comments here and there that had Anton jumpy, and by the time PE rolled around that afternoon, even Jude was starting to get a bit arsey about it. "Just don't start a fight in the changing rooms," Anton had asked before heading to the bathroom to change, and Jude had pulled a face that was a long way from a promise to do as he was told.

Only apparently even that break was enough, because when Anton was changed, he walked right out of the bathroom into Walsh.

"Er."

"Why don't you change with the rest of us."

Anton gritted his teeth. "What's your problem?"

"My problem is there's something funny about you, and my best mate's involved."

"Your best mate knows exactly who and what I am, which is none of *your* business, so why don't you just leave it alone?" Anton seethed. Jude's flippant sex comment that morning had grounded some of his anxiety, and now he was just mad. He wanted to just play football, for Christ's sake! He wanted to just be allowed to go about his day and have a boyfriend and play football and not have people constantly ragging on him for not being *boy* enough. He was binding, he was packing, how much more boyish could he get without hormone treatment anyway?

Walsh, unfortunately, didn't seem to agree. The snarl was something more than a bit feral, and Anton backed up against the door. "My mate's business is my business. You think it's funny, you leading him on like this?"

"What are you talking about?"

"He's not got a fucking clue, has he?"

"About *what.*"

Walsh bared his teeth. "Gotta like dick to be into blokes, *Anton,* and somehow I don't think you've got one."

Every hair on Anton's arms stood up on end. Like a rush of cold water, something flooded his system with cool anger, and before he quite knew what he was doing, he planted his hands in Walsh's chest and shoved.

"Why don't you fuck off with your stupid fucking theories and bullshit to someone who cares!" he bellowed.

A door slammed. "Williams! Walsh!"

Walsh lunged; Mrs. Salter was faster, and slammed them both against either wall of the narrow corridor with a hand firmly in each chest. It pressed down hard on Anton's binder, painful over the already tight compression, but he ground his teeth and refused to let it show. Fuck Walsh, and fuck her, and fuck—

"What the fuck?"

"What you done now, Walsh?"

Voices filtered down the corridor, and Anton pulled away from his teacher, shrugging his shoulders. "Wasn't nothing, miss," he mumbled, glancing down the corridor. He could see a flash of red hair that said Jude was there. "Just a row."

"I won't have catfights in my corridors because two of you have decided you don't like each other," Mrs. Salter snapped. "I don't like any of you, tribe of ingrates the lot of you, but it doesn't mean civility is out of the window. Walsh, ten laps, now. Go! Williams, you can help carry the equipment."

"Fuck that!" Walsh exploded, and Anton beat a hasty retreat to the gawping class. "There's something fucking funny about him and he's not fucking screwing over my mates like this!"

Mrs. Salter exploded; the class, including Anton, wisely scattered to the playing field. His heart was beating a mile a minute, but mostly the other kids didn't seem bothered by what Walsh had said, simply that he'd said it.

"Can't believe he swore at Salter, he's fucking dead now..."

"Reckon we should wear black armbands to next lesson in memory of him?"

"Alas, poor Walsh, we hardly knew ye."

"You what?"

Jude materialised at Anton's elbow as Mrs. Salter appeared in the distance by the gym and started to march out onto the field. "What was that about?"

"Not here."

Jude squinted. "Spy stuff?"

"Yeah, but not here," Anton hissed, and then Mrs. Salter was upon them, lips so thin they had almost disappeared.

"Five laps, all of you. Except you, Williams. Pushing and shoving like a couple of five-year-olds is unacceptable in my lessons—ten laps for you."

Anton groaned but knew better than to argue, simply turning on his heel and setting off. It would keep him out of everyone's way, anyway. He was quietly grateful that nobody seemed too interested in exactly why Walsh had gone off at him, and maybe by the time he'd finished his laps, they'd have forgotten all about it and be too interested in either playing, or avoiding playing.

It was bitterly cold, the winter not letting up in the slightest, and it spurred Anton on to run properly. He scowled at the frozen dirt all the way around the field, slow lap after slow lap, and imagined it to be Walsh's face. For once, feeling angry felt…good. Anton had felt upset and afraid for so long that getting to feel actually just outright angry with Walsh for constantly pushing it was a refreshing change. Like…

It hit him all at once, and he nearly stopped halfway through the last lap.

Like Jude got angry sometimes.

Like Jude had been angry at his dad, and the kids in his last school, and Will Thorne. Like Jude wasn't upset by any of it, because why would he be? It was just idiots sounding off, why should that upset anybody?

Anton clenched his fists, and put the last of his energy into the last half-lap, feeling a surge of aggression and adrenalin. Fuck Walsh. Fuck Dad. Fuck Will Thorne. Fuck everyone and anyone who didn't like it, because *fuck them*, this was Anton and tough shit if they didn't like him being a boy born a girl. He had a fucking boyfriend, and his fucking mum and aunt didn't care, and just because his dick came in a box didn't make it any less real.

So when he skidded back onto the pitch at the end of the lap, he kicked the goalpost, and turned on the waiting huddle of boys.

"We playing or what?"

"More fucking like it, I'm freezing my balls off," Jude complained loudly.

"The state of your genitals is of interest to exactly nobody, Kalinowski!" Mrs. Salter shouted over the wind. It was freezing, and picking up, so Anton bounced from one foot to the other in the goal, waiting for the damp shapes masquerading as classmates to form up properly. His skin itched with energy. He kind of wanted Walsh to have another go, to be honest, because Anton would hit him this time, would just smack him right in the—

The whistle blew.

Apparently, Anton wasn't the only one antsy. Maybe it was the weather, maybe it was the general moody atmosphere, but suddenly even shy Bee was stabbing her cleats into another girl's leg, and Jude's decision to headbutt Jack Stephens for the ball went entirely unremarked by all except the teacher. Even Larimer was going for it, and Anton nearly had his teeth put out by a dodgy save and a foot suspiciously close to his head.

Yet—

He felt *alive,* too. Freezing cold, filthy, and irrepressibly alive. Let anyone try and stop him doing *anything* out here. Let anyone claim he wasn't male enough, that his name wasn't Anton, that he couldn't use the boys' toilets. He'd fucking show them. He was going to go to that football club that Jude had nagged him about, and he was going to get a stand-to-pee packer and use the boys' toilets, and fuck anyone and *everyone* who—

"What the fuck, Williams, are you wearing a bra?!"

Anton picked himself up out of the mud, ball clamped between his gloves, and shouted, "Will you pack it in already, Thorney?"

It had started to rain, and Will Thorne's thin face looked oddly gleeful with his blond hair plastered to it. "I saw it, you're wearing a bra!"

"It's a back brace, you stupid fuc—"

"Williams! Thorne! Break it up!"

"You got a girl in goal! Here, good news, Kalinowski, you're straight after all!"

"Fuck off, Thorney, I know what I had in my hand the other

day, and it weren't no clit!"

"Kalinowski, *language*!" Mrs. Salter bellowed. "Thorne, pack it in! Laps, now!"

"You want to see my tits, is that it?" Anton shouted, suddenly incensed. Fuck Will, too! Who the hell did he think he was?! "You want to see it?!" And without thinking about it, he dropped the ball, dropped the gloves, and ripped off his T-shirt.

The rain was *icy*.

And Thorne's expression was even icier.

"You gonna shut up now, Thorney?" Larimer's idle voice rolled out into the quiet. "Congratulations, now you've seen a back support. My sister's got one just like it."

"Never seen a bra like that," Isabel chimed in scornfully, covered from head to toe in mud, and the girls started sniggering as one. For once, Anton didn't care. He shoved his shirt back on over his head, burning with anger. Would he shut up *now*? Would he finally leave Anton *alone*?

"That's no fucking brace, it's some kind of strapless—"

"For fuck's sake, Thorney, I've had a good grope under there, your boobs are bigger!" Jude shouted, and the uproar kicked off again. Larimer closed it; Jude, suddenly, was at Thorne's front when he had been clear across the pitch only moments ago.

"You calling me a girl, Kalinowski?"

"I'll explain it for the virgin on the field: when you fuck, you tend to get your clothes off!" Jude bellowed.

Mrs. Salter dropped her whistle entirely and started marching in from the sideline. "Thorne, inside, *now*!"

"You calling me a fucking virgin?!"

"I call it as I see it!"

The dull smack of Will's wet fist hitting Jude's jaw was loud.

The crunch of Anton's knuckles against the side of Will's head was louder.

Chapter 24

"SO HOW MUCH trouble are you in?"

Jude laughed. "Don't I get a hello?"

Anton grinned, flopping back onto his bed, phone glued to his ear. Mrs. Salter had gone ballistic, and sent six kids to the head-master for fighting. Parents had been called...especially after Jude had swung another punch Thorne's way outside the head's office.

"Hello. There, happy? Now what's going on?"

"Dad went mental. Aunt Lucy went double-mental. I'm grounded until I'm thirty-five, and Emma smuggled me dessert."

"Yeah?"

"Yeah, she reckons it was justified. For once, I'm not the dumb lout stepbrother she usually thinks I am!"

"Congratulations?"

"Thanks. I'm going to sneak out later, though."

"And go where?"

"Your bed."

Anton put his hand over his mouth to not laugh too loudly. Mum had taken all his electronics away as her punishment, but Aunt Kerry had looked the other way when he'd stolen his phone back. "Yeah?"

"Totally. That was hot as fuck, I nearly had a hard-on in the middle of the game.. I like you angry, you should do angry more."

"Well, Walsh was being a twat, and then Thorne was being a twat…"

"You've totally convinced the rest of the class, Larimer says. The girls were apparently all cooing about how your brace must hurt sometimes when he went to get his stuff from his locker."

"What about Walsh?"

"Haven't heard from him."

"Does…does Larimer's sister really have—?"

"Nah, that was a lie. Between you and me, I think Larimer's figured you out."

Somehow, the little flower of panic didn't open up, and Anton frowned at the ceiling, picking at the absence of it. "Yeah?"

"Yeah, maybe. Tends to keep out of that sort of thing. Smarter than he looks. Just as well. How about you, did your mum go nuts?"

Anton grimaced. "Yeah. She's booked me another appointment with Ellen. Says no part of being a boy means brawling at school."

"Bollocks, it's a rite of passengers."

"Passage?"

"Whatever."

"Jude?"

"Mm?"

"D'you…d'you reckon the others really would be okay if they found out?"

"Thorne'd be a cunt as always. But Walsh and Larimer would be alright. Emma'd love you. Dunno about Isabel but even if she wigged, mate, she's about as dangerous as a kitten, so I wouldn't worry about it."

"I just…I got so angry today with both of them—"

"What, Walsh and Shit-For-Brains?"

"Yeah. I just got angry, and it just hit me out on the field that that's your fault."

Jude sounded genuinely surprised. "My fault?"

"Yeah. You'd get mad at people being shitty to me, but you

didn't get upset, like there was nothing to be upset about. Like anything anyone was saying was just stupid instead of hurtful."

"Well…'cause it's not hurtful to me, really, is it?" Jude said carefully. "It's not about me, it's about them being dumb."

"That's how I felt today."

Jude paused. Anton gripped the phone tightly, just breathing for a minute, and that surge of confidence came over him again. He could do this. He could do anything he wanted, and screw anyone who tried to stand in his way. If he just cleared them out, and only kept the people like Mum and Aunt Kerry and Jude around, then everyone else was just background noise.

"Come over."

"Not yet, I'll get busted."

"So try harder. Come over, and stay late, and we have to try and keep quiet. Come round the back and I'll let you in the kitchen, Mum and Aunt Kerry are watching TV and the girls are in bed, so we have to be really quiet, and—"

"Are you going to rip my clothes off and get really angry and hot again?"

"Yes."

"Ten minutes."

ANTON WOKE UP somewhere around midnight, when Jude's phone lit up silently on the bedside table. "Jude."

"Wha'?"

"Your phone."

Jude grumbled, reaching out. They were tangled impossibly tightly in Anton's bed, the only clothing Anton's T-shirt, and despite the ridiculous heat, the mess, and the fact that trying to stifle laughter when fumbling with a condom and hoping your mum didn't walk in was seriously un-sexy, Anton had never felt more content.

Plus, turned out his dysphoria didn't go totally crazy if Jude put his fingers—or more—in the distinctly feminine regions, so Anton was a bit over content and into actively happy territory.

"S'just Emma," Jude yawned, putting the phone back and re-treating under the duvet. His head planted itself firmly against the side of Anton's neck, and Anton grinned at the ceiling in the dark.

"What'd she say?"

"She's unlocked the back door and if I'm not home by the time Dad gets up for work, she's not covering for me."

"Sounds fair."

"Mm, s'pose…"

"Are you bribing her?"

"She's blackmailing me." Jude's voice was muffled, and Anton peeled the duvet down a bit. "I have to agree to her charity thing."

"Charity thing?"

"You know, getting a bunch of us boys to wax our legs for charity. She's been on about it for ages, surprised she hasn't asked you. Going to do it at school so everyone coughs up cash to watch."

"Leg-waxing?!"

"Yup."

"You're going to let Emma wax your legs, in front of the whole class, just so you won't get in major trouble for this?"

"No, I'm going to let her wax my legs in front of the whole class because she smuggled me out. Getting back in is my problem."

"Why?"

"Sex with you, it's worth a couple of days with sore legs."

"Uh, Jude, have you ever had a full leg waxing?"

"Nope."

"With *your* fur, it's going to be more than a bit sore," Anton said, and scratched his fingers through Jude's head-hair. "Still, that's…sort of sweet."

"Sex will always get my attention."

Anton chuckled, then bit his lip. "Um…I did actually buy *two* packers."

"So?"

"So…one of them is specially designed so you can use it for sex."

"What, it can make you come?"

"No, it would be to make *you* come."

Jude levered himself up, and blinked blearily at Anton in the gloom. From the moon outside, Anton could make out the tufts of Jude's hair sticking up all over the place, and he absently reached out to finger-comb them down. "You want to fuck me?"

"Maybe."

"As in, up the arse?"

"Well…yeah."

Jude made an odd huffing noise. "And you're going to get off how?"

"It, um…presses on me. Externally, you know…"

"Tell you what," Jude said, resettling and pulled the duvet up over both their heads. Anton grinned at the sudden weird cuddle action, and wriggled closer. "Sex with you is just as weird as sex with a girl, I'll say that much."

"Do you want a slap?"

"Depends, does it turn you on?"

Anton laughed quietly, and pressed his nose to the nearest skin he could find. Probably Jude's cheek, by the way it felt raspy with stubble and yet not firm enough to be jaw or neck. "Do you want to try it? It's okay if you don't."

"Right now, no. Too sleepy. In general? Yeah, okay, I'll try it. Can't promise I'll like it, mind, can't say I've given being the catcher much thought, and I'm not big on having my arse groped at the best of times…"

Anton squeezed, discovering he had Jude's neck by the choked noise, and relocated to a better hug position.

"Try is fine," he murmured, and when Jude's hand accidentally found the side of his breasts before sliding around to his back, Anton found that—for once—he didn't much mind.

Chapter 25

THINGS WERE QUIET and awkward at school for the rest of the week. Jude wasn't saying anything about it, but Anton knew he and Walsh had clashed at some point: the tension was enough to cut with a knife. Will Thorne seemed to have been put off by Anton smacking him in the jaw, and Larimer, seemingly unsure of what to do when Jude and Walsh weren't on the best of terms, had surprisingly started to hang out more with Isabel rather than try and deal with it.

Not that Anton blamed him. Jude in a piss was kind of scary.

The weekend was a bit better, though, hiding away in Jude's room and alternating between Anton teaching Jude how to actually make proper use of his Steam account, and messing around in bed, experimenting. (Turned out while Jude quite liked taking it, Anton wasn't too keen on being on top, which was…kind of not what he'd expected, but still okay.)

But on Monday morning, there was a note in his locker.

It was tucked under the now-usual locker gift, and simply had Anton's surname printed on it, folded over to hide the rest of it. "What's that?" Jude asked, then clocked the box. "Are you still getting those?"

"Yeah," Anton said, picking it up. It was big this time, sort of heavy and cube-shaped. Maybe a mug or something. He was beginning to recognise them as more trinket-type gifts lately. "Sorry, I should really—"

"What you sorry for? Free stuff!"

"Free *gifts,* Jude. I shouldn't be taking gifts."

"Why?"

"Well…I've got you. You don't accept gifts from someone else when you have a boyfriend, even I know that."

"Oh, okay."

"You really are too nice…"

Jude laughed. "Just can't say it'd bother me."

Anton frowned. "'It'd.'"

"Eh?"

"You said 'it'd.' Like…it would."

"Yeah, so?"

Anton squinted at him, then it clicked into place. "Oh my Go—Jude! How are you getting these into my locker, I know for a fact you're not at school before me, and we went home together on Friday!"

Jude cackled with mad laughter, and Anton aimed a punch at him. He ducked away, still grinning. "What! You liked them! You said so!"

"You've been sneaking gifts into my locker?!"

"In my defense—"

"You let me think Bee had a crush on me!"

"She *does*," Jude said significantly, and finally stopped moving and let Anton hit him. "Ow! In my defense, if you had even once asked the boys about it, they would have pointed straight at me. I caught Megan the same way."

"Emma knew!"

"Pft, like I'm telling Emma I put gifts in the lockers of people I like, she'd rip me a new one. No, just the boys know. Larimer's been doing it for me."

Anton shook his head, but a smile was pulling itself into place. "You're mad," he accused. "You're—you're—stupid and mad and…"

"And I buy you weekly gifts. Massive boyfriend points right there."

"Well—"

"Thoughtful ones, too. Like the keychain football boots, you really liked those."

"I've been hiding most of them from you so you didn't get the wrong idea!"

"And now you get to show them off!"

"Were you ever going to tell me?"

"Maybe if you got up the guts to tell Bee you're gay, but then you let the whole class know we're dating so I wasn't really sure. I thought maybe if we hit the end of term before you twigged, I'd bring you one in person the first Monday off?"

"Tit," Anton said, but the smile was firmly in place, and...eh, screw school. He caught Jude by the tie and kissed him quickly. "But thank you, I suppose. I'm guessing the note's not a confession?"

"Nothing to do with me."

Anton huffed, not believing him, and reached back into the locker for it. At least it wasn't Jude's handwriting, he suppos—

His breath caught.

"What?"

We know your a girl. Either you tell Jude or we will.

(He means him I won't tell Jude can find that out for himself, Laz.)

Larimer and Walsh.

"Oh my God," Anton said.

"At least it's in your locker, nobody else will have seen it. Larimer. Walsh has better grammar than that...barely."

"And you call me the English nerd," Anton said weakly, and crumpled up the note. "What do I do?"

"What would you do if I called you a girl?"

"Punch you and tell you to watch your gob."

"So do it."

Anton twisted and stared. Jude shrugged, his expression not changing.

"Do it," he repeated. "Drag them out by the ears, tell them you're—" Jude's eyes flicked down the not-quite-empty corridor, "—a spy, and if they call you a girl again they'll get a smack in the face, and do it in front of me. Problem solved, whole class doesn't have to know, and you can make your point about keeping it quiet at the same time."

"That's…not actually a bad idea," Anton admitted quietly. He smoothed out the note between his thumbs. "You think they'd keep it quiet?"

"Yeah. Like I said, they won't really care."

Anton nodded. "Okay."

Jude's eyebrows shot up. "Really?"

"Yeah. I mean, the other day on the field, I was just thinking fuck everyone who wants to get in my way. I guess that includes me."

"You've earned a sex point."

"A what?"

"A sex point. Do something awesome that helps with your spy stuff and makes you see your coolness, and I will give you a sex point. Five points, I will perform a sex act of your choosing."

"You whore," Anton said fondly, and shoved the note back in his locker. "Okay. Come on."

"You gonna get mad?"

"Not yet. Might if Walsh acts like a dick again."

"Well, that's a yes, dick is his permanent setting."

Anton rolled his eyes as they approached the classroom door, then took a deep breath. "You wait here."

"Yessir."

Anton marched in, dumping his bag on his desk and not even bothering to greet Emma before stalking over to Walsh and Larimer, peering at something on Walsh's phone. "You two, a word, outside."

"You what?" Walsh said.

"Now!" Anton snapped, then turned on his heel and marched out again. The whole class was staring, and his heart was in his throat, but it wasn't quite just fear like he'd expected. Some of the previous week's anger had bubbled up, too, and while he was grateful for Jude's lanky presence leaning against the wall outside, he suddenly felt like he didn't *need* it.

"Is this about the note?" Larimer asked the minute the door closed behind them, and Walsh pulled a face.

"Jesus, why do I bother," he muttered, then scowled at Anton.

"You going to come clean, then? Jude, mate, you might wanna sit down."

"Yeah, I think I'm good."

Anton huffed, and folded his arms, hunching in close to Walsh. "Okay, fine, I'm trans."

"You're *what?*"

"Oh come on, you think I do this for fun? I'm trans, you idiot," he hissed as lowly as possible. "That's why I have small feet and I don't like going to the boy's toilets, but I am *not* a girl, do you understand me? If you call me a girl again, I'll hit you."

"And he hits hard," Jude said amiably, and Walsh shot him a look.

"You knew."

"Uh, yeah."

"How long?"

"Long enough," Jude said shortly. "Look, mate, I get it, you're looking out for me. But not cool, yeah? You don't fucking drop sinister hints like that, open your brain. Why the fuck *would* he look like that if he's just a girl like Emma?"

Walsh opened his mouth, and slowly closed it.

"I don't *want* people to know. I am a boy, I want to pass as a boy, and the fewer people know I'm trans then the happier I will be," Anton snapped. "So neither of you say *anything.*"

"Hey, I'm cool with that," Larimer said, holding up his hands. "I said it wasn't our business from the start, it's just…you know, Jude's kinda…dumb."

"Hey!"

"You have a scarred nip because your ex nearly bit it off, and you *still* didn't break up with her," Walsh said shortly, and Anton stared. "You *are* dumb, Jude. But—sorry," he added, and suddenly stuck out a hand to Anton, who shook it in bewilderment. "You're right. Stupid way to go about it, should've just…took you aside and asked. Only I'm not very good at that sensible shit, I just go a bit nuts, and I got it stuck in my head you were out to make a twat out of Jude."

"Yeah, well, I'm not."

"Yeah. Sorry."

Anton shrugged. "Long as you keep quiet and nothing changes, s'okay."

"Nah, that's cool, man. You know, it's not…against you, exactly, it's just he's a fucking retard about when to fucking dump someone, and there was something really off, so…yeah. I mean, you know, if that's all it is and he knows…"

"He is right here, holy Christ."

"Fuck off, period-head."

"Inside the classroom, boys, and Walsh, the less you compare Kalinowski's hair to anything at all, the better!"

Miss Taylor's dry tones interrupted the resolution, and Anton grinned when Larimer nearly walked into the doorframe. Just like that, it seemed, the tension had been popped. Walsh started muttering every name for a ginger kid he could think of, Jude threw something at him before they sat down and earned his first detention, and Anton retreated to his desk, out of the way and feeling…

"What was that?" Emma asked. Anton's phone buzzed in his pocket, and he slid it open as he sat down, rolling his eyes. Honestly, Jude. *Just thought, y dont u have periods????*

Birth control, he sent back flippantly, and shrugged at Emma. "Oh, nothing. It's fine."

Everything was fine.

Epilogue

ON PRESENTATION DAY, Anton expected Jude to meet him from the house.

He didn't.

He expected there to be a fairly quiet classroom, because people would be busy making up their presentations.

It wasn't.

In fact, it was packed out with kids Anton was certain weren't in their year, never mind their class, and he had to fight to get to his desk—at which point, he came across Emma counting money.

"Er," he said. "What's going on?"

There was music coming from somewhere, some pop thing blasting so hard the windows were shaking, and people were yelling and jeering. Over the crowd, he could see Larimer's head stuck up above everyone else's, and a hint of ginger at his shoulder.

"The charity wax!" Emma said brightly, and held out her hand. Anton hastily dug for money. "Larimer's just about finished, I think Isabel's having too much fun showing off Jude's skirt."

"Jude's...what?"

A yelp—a very familiar one, thanks to Anton having discovered Jude was actually ticklish the previous weekend—sounded above the noise, and Anton found himself grinning broadly.

"Is Isabel waxing Jude's legs?" he asked, and handed over a fiver.

"Finally, you get with the program! Yeah, we figured seeing as how I so *nicely* helped him sneak back in after your midnight tryst a few weeks ago, he could wear a skirt instead of shorts while we did it," she said sunnily. "And what better day than presentation day to put Jude in a skirt? Maybe he'll stop making so many cracks about girls now."

"Uh, I doubt it," Anton said, as Jude's indignant yell informed the world that Isabel was an evil harpy bound for hell.

"Yeah, but it's worth a shot. Go see! You're going to be the one putting cream on them later anyway, he's come up bright red and rash-y."

Anton grimaced, elbowing his way through the crowd. Sure enough, when he got close enough to see, Jude's legs were spotted with a fine rash redder than his hair, and—

"Holy shit, Jude, what are you *wearing?*"

A skirt was one thing, but whatever Emma had dressed her stepbrother in was more of an eye-bleeding bright pink belt than any skirt Anton had ever seen.

"Nice, innit?" Jude said. He was sitting on the edge of Larimer's desk, legs propped up on a chair in front of him. His underwear was very visible under the skirt, but thankfully Isabel seemed to be finishing off his bony ankles. His legs looked…kind of weird without their furry covering, actually.

"Not sure it suits."

"Emma says it's doubled takings, so I'm fucked for next year."

"She does this every year?"

"She doesn't *wax* people every year, no, but she does a charity thi—ow! Fucking hell!"

"Nearly done!" Isabel sang, and beamed at Anton. "I told him he should try the girls' uniform, wouldn't he look nice in pleated?"

"Mm, no," Anton said frankly, and Jude rolled his eyes.

"*Thank* you!"

"He looks better naked."

"Oh, *not* helping."

"You didn't ask me to help," Anton said innocently, then grinned. "It's alright, Emma said I can help with the cream later."

"There's creams to make this better?"

"Not totally better. You have to tough it out."

"Yeah, Kalinowski, man up!" someone yelled out of the throng, and then knuckles began beating on the doorframe.

"Alright, everyone, it's nearly nine!" Miss Taylor shouted over the noise, sounding uncharacteristically good-humoured. Isabel beamed, and pulled.

"Fuck!"

"All done, Miss!" she sang. "You can get down now, Jude."

"I hate you," Jude groused, and lurched down off the table like he was drunk. He caught at Anton's arm for a moment, then dropped into his seat with another filthy look thrown Isabel's way. "I hate you!" he repeated loudly.

"Of course you do, Kalinowski. Williams, sit down. I want all of this mess cleared up before first period. Now." She banged down her things. "Presentations. I trust you're all ready?"

A grumble rippled around the room.

"Who wants to go first?"

Another grumble, then Jude groaned and said, "Do we have to stand up?"

"At the front, yes, Kalinowski."

"Best be me then, I reckon."

Anton watched Jude walk gingerly up to the front, and curled his fingers into the top of his folder. They'd agreed last night on the phone what to do—because Anton still wasn't sure. Walsh and Larimer, they'd been totally fine. Part of him thought it would be nice to tell Emma, to have someone to talk to about the wider stuff. But the rest of the class? It would leak out from there, and having a handful of people on his side...was that enough?

"So, uh, yeah, Anton Williams and his labels," Jude said, smoothing out a handwritten note, looking utterly ridiculous in his blazer, shirt, tie, and hot pink miniskirt. Miss Taylor already looked sceptical. "So, uh, Anton is white. I think we all knew that. And he's gay, and I definitely know that..."

The class sniggered. Anton smiled faintly, and Jude glanced up at him. Very slowly, Anton shook his head.

"And he's a guy. And he's totally a Russian spy."

The sniggers got louder; Miss Taylor sighed. "Kalinowski…"

"He could be, he didn't actually say he was English, you know, and his first name is Anton, so yeah, he's blatantly a spy and has super secret spy stuff, hence he just sort of showed up like a random new kid," Jude rambled, then screwed up the note. "He has these mega intense secrets and talks in code, too. If you mention his spy stuff, he hits you—or me, anyway…" Sniggering turned into outright laughter, and Miss Taylor sighed heavily. "Um, that's actually kind of it. 'Cause Anton doesn't have many labels that he uses. And if I just, like, list his labels, you wouldn't actually know any more about him. Like it's not really relevant that he's white, what matters is he's a Spurs fan and he's scary good in goal and he looks awesome naked—"

Anton choked; Miss Taylor smacked the desk.

"Sit down, Kalinowski."

"I'm not finished!"

"Then you can take the assignment seriously."

"I am," Jude said, and took a deep breath. "Thing is, I rang Anton last night and said, what do you want me to say. 'Cause actually it's nobody's business what he is unless he wants them to know. And I know more about him than he's a gay white guy, but all that cool stuff that makes him Anton, that doesn't fit into all the labels. So you could write down all his labels, and you wouldn't know it was him. And like…a million other guys could fit his labels and be nothing like him. So the way I see it, the labels are only the starting point. And all the stuff that's *worth* knowing, that goes way beyond them."

Miss Taylor's 'sit down' was very soft. The class was oddly quiet, before Larimer broke the spell and decided that, given he had a similar problem in the legs and skirt department, he ought to go next.

Slowly, Anton tore a scrap of paper off his notebook, and wrote a note. *Spy stuff is code for I'm trans.*

Then he pushed it towards Emma.

Whose eyes went round. *Srsly?!* she wrote back.

Anton nodded, then added the only clarification he figured she'd need. *My brace is a breast binder.*

Emma crossed it out, looking impatient. *No idiot I get it. Actually I got suspicious when you took your top off in PE cos I've seen binders on the net before. I mean Jude knows and isn't being stupid about it?!*

Anton grinned, trying very hard not to laugh in front of Miss Taylor's watchful eye, and nodded.

FUCK, Emma wrote.

Then she squeezed his elbow and smiled, and Anton turned his attention back to the front.

He would make something up for Jude, some kind of revenge. Maybe even say the waxing and the skirt were his first forays into alternative gender expression. Whatever. It didn't matter, what the others thought, because the others wouldn't know him like Anton did.

They wouldn't know Anton like Jude did, either, and that was good. Great, even. He would just be Anton, *could* just be Anton, without the fear of it going wrong and being caught, without looking over his shoulder all the time and keeping his achievements under lock and key to himself, unable to share them with anyone outside the house.

All that fear was gone, along with Natasha, and he could just be Anton.

The white, gay kid in Year Ten with the slightly mad boyfriend, the ever madder skills in goal, and the super secret spy stuff.

About the Author

MATTHEW J. METZGER is an asexual, transgender author from the wet and windy British Isles. Matthew is a writer of both adult and young adult LGBT fiction, with a love of larger-than-life characters, injecting humour into serious issues, and the uglier, grittier edges of British romance. Matthew currently lives in Bristol, and—when not writing—can usually be found sleeping, working out at the gym, and being owned by his cat.

Find more online at matthewjmetzger.com.

CPSIA information can be obtained
at www.ICGtesting.com
Printed in the USA
LVHW011140230220
647909LV00010B/525